THE OMEGA'S WOLVES

BROKEN ALPHAS BOOK ONE

LEIGH KELSEY

This book was written, produced, and edited in the UK where some spelling, grammar and word usage will vary from US English.

Copyright © Leigh Kelsey 2021

All rights reserved. No part of this publication may be reproduced or transmitted in any form or by any means, electronic or mechanical, without the prior written permission of the author.

This is a work of fiction. Names, characters, places and incidents either are products of the author's imagination or are used fictitiously. Any resemblance to actual events or locales or persons, living or dead, is entirely coincidental.

The right of Leigh Kelsey to be identified as author of this work has been asserted by her in accordance with the Copyright, Designs and Patents Act 1988

www.leighkelsey.co.uk

Want an email when new books release - and four freebies?
Join here by clicking here

Or chat with me in my Facebook group: Leigh Kelsey's Paranormal Den

Cover by EmCat Designs

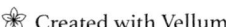 Created with Vellum

BLURB

Worthless. Disposable. Omega.

I've always known my standing in the pack, but I never thought my father would slit my throat as a sacrifice for the wolves' goddess. I should have died, but Luneste refused the blood payment, and instead wrathful moon magic filled my bleeding body.

Fleeing my furious pack, I find safety with four broken, psycho alphas: obsessive Bakkhos, tortured Draven, cruel Wild, and commanding Kaan. But the wolves of my new pack are vicious and unhinged, and even worse enemies hunt them than my father.

Three of my wolves are determined to claim me as their mate, but when Kaan rejects our bond, not even my new magic will save me from the pain.

Broken Alphas is a rejected mates paranormal romance series, with fated mates, four vicious, passionate alphas who badly need love, and a vulnerable omega in desperate need of protection. It also features a pregnancy, and alpha and omega elements, so if you're not a fan of either, this might not be the book for you.

This book is medium burn, with moderate heat, and multiple love interests, and WILL have a HEA in the final book.

THE OMEGA'S WOLVES

LEIGH KELSEY

NOTE

These alphas are broken and twisted, and do some things that could be triggering. Broken Alphas contains violence, obsessive love, dub con, abuse, and past rape mentions (not by any of the guys to the FMC.) Stay safe, and if you need to skip this one to protect your mental health, don't hesitate to do so! If you want wolves without the triggers, try my complete Moonlight Inn series.

Leigh x

1
SACRIFICE

I knew the blood moon was a bad omen. I thought it would bring more dead trees to our packlands, more rot to our farms and food supplies, and more silence where there should have been squalling babies and squeaking pups. But not *this*.

Another scream of defiant rage tore up my throat as the soft skin of my fingertips split and sharp claws slid over blunt, human nails. I sank their vicious points into the wooden wall of our lodge as my dad, the alpha of Grove Pack, and my brothers gripped my legs, my back, and my shoulders, hauling me out of the safe haven of my bedroom and down the hallway of our one-storey home.

The familiar photos and homely comforts of our living area blurred as tears of anger and heartbreak stabbed my eyes, flowing hot down my cheeks. I had to fight, I couldn't stop struggling for one second. If they got me out of the house...

I kicked my legs, but Sander's big hands tightened on my calves until I was as harmless as a flopping fish. He was a damn giant compared to my smaller frame, his strength a brick wall I couldn't hope to smash through. Conn held my middle, but my oldest brother couldn't meet my eyes. He hadn't looked at me once since Dad opened my bedroom door and coaxed me from the corner where I'd sat, nursing a grudge for him locking me in the house for a week.

I'd thought this was a punishment at first, an extension of the grounding our alpha had enforced for me hunting edible berries and plants on Ragnar packlands. I'd returned eight days ago with a bag full of food, but our alpha had taken one look at me and snarled with such brutal dominance that I'd hit the ground face first, gasping and begging for mercy as pain tore through me. I'd risked a war between packs by foraging that food, but what was the point of keeping the peace when our pack was dying one by one? Dad might have been happy to ignore the lush lands that bordered ours, but I wasn't.

"Stop fighting, Nixette," Dad huffed now, as I bucked, trying to throw off Conn's firm grip. "This is for the good of the pack. You want to help the pack survive, don't you?"

"Not like this," I replied, anger warring with terror in my breathless voice. They'd got me halfway across the big living area, and now even upside down and wrestling against their grip, I could see the door beckoning.

No! I'm not dying like this.

Something had broken in my dad three years ago when Mum died. I'd watched his soft smiles harden to stone, his crinkled eyes sharpening and his face unsmiling and stern. And I got it. I *knew* how much it hurt, like a knife shoved so deep inside my chest that I could never get it out. Even years later, I still bumped into that brutal edge and cut myself, and then cried myself to sleep with missing her. But it hadn't changed me like it had changed him. Han Tulay had been a kind family man with a protective streak a mile long, but now ... his focus was honed on the survival of the pack, on making sure no one else wasted away like Mum.

And look what good it had done: we were still dying. We were starving worse now than we'd been even *then*. But he refused to pack up and leave for better woods, and he snarled whenever I suggested making an alliance with our neighbours.

"Luneste will take care of you," he assured me, his voice a rough contrast to his comforting words—the words he used every time we asked how he would fix the dying vegetable patches, or how we'd survive when the last cows and goats died, or why we stayed in these wasted lands when heavy rains flooded our houses.

Luneste will take care of us.

But the lady of the moon had turned her back on us for *years*; why would she pay attention now? Why *should* she?

Sander hefted my feet higher in his huge hands, and I growled between gritted teeth as he carried me out the open door, Conn silent and stoic, and Dad murmuring to the goddess now. Sometimes I thought he cared more about Luneste than he did about his own family.

I definitely knew he loved her more than me, but why had he spared my brothers? Why was it *me* he dragged across the threshold, my claws taking chunks from the door that had always stood between me and danger? Now it stood wide open, allowing the people who should have kept me safe to drag me to certain death.

"Please," I rasped, my growls shaky as the wind hit my skin, brushing along my face like sharp claws. Like a threat. "Please don't do this, Dad."

"Alpha," he corrected, his gaze fixed over my head. He wasn't even watching as I wrenched and bucked against their hold. "You're saving the pack, Nixette. It's an honour—we'll never forget this, and we'll always remember you."

"You're *killing* me," I screamed, struggling harder, gulping down air that tasted of moss and home—of comfort. But there was no comfort to be found in this wood anymore. "*Conn*, please!"

But my brother didn't look at me even as a muscle feathered in his jaw, his hands squeezing my waist. He wouldn't disobey our alpha. Or maybe he couldn't—maybe Dad had used his alpha dominance to get them both to help with this. I held onto that tiny chance that my brothers weren't complicit, that they might stop this.

"You'll be safe with Luneste soon," Dad promised, his fingers digging into my shoulders, making it harder for me to fight. The wind got sharper, slicing through my jeans and vest as the trees opened up, and my breaths shuddered out. We were close to the clearing now, close to where the whole pack would be waiting to watch this—to *bear witness* as our alpha called it.

I wasn't the first sacrifice. The first had been Anelle, the eldest wolf of our pack. She'd gone gently, without fighting, and had thanked our alpha for the honour. I'd thought it was a blessing then, that Luneste would accept her sacrifice and save our dying lands and starving people. By the third sacrifice—Bradley, a healthy thirty-year-old man who'd been part of our pack for as long as I could remember—I saw it for what it was.

The pack who watched saw a man willing to do whatever it took to save his pack. I just saw a man who was out of his depth, twisted by grief, and blinded to what would really save us: asking for help. Hell, even going into the cities and away from the woods could offer some chance at survival.

But that wasn't the way packs worked; we stayed separate. Safe. Obsolete.

"Please," I tried again, lashing out and hooking my claws into the rough bark of the nearest tree, gouging out shards as their hands tightened and hauled me onward. The murmurings of our pack were audible now, a mere fourteen compared to the thirty-six people we used to have. Whether they cared that I was screaming and fighting, I didn't know. I thought I'd be spared because I was the alpha's daughter—I thought I was *safe*. But the alpha wasn't my dad, not anymore, and this monster would kill anyone to save his pack.

But I'd thought I was *part* of the pack. Things had been fraught and tense since Mum died, but I never imagined my dad would sacrifice *me*.

Air rushed past me as they lowered me in a sudden movement, and I cried out as stone met my back hard enough to jostle my bones. It didn't matter if they broke my spine, did it? They were going to kill me anyway. Broken bones would probably just get the job done quicker.

"Please," I tried again, my body shaking as Dale, the man who'd carved my first toy from one of these oaks approached, a rope in his hand.

To tie me up, so I couldn't struggle.

I swung my gaze to my dad, tears stinging my eyes. "*Please*—I'm your daughter, don't you care?"

"Of *course* I care, Nixette," Dad replied, smoothing a strand of pale lilac hair from my face as rope wrapped around my legs, my middle, and my arms. I twisted, but if I couldn't escape their hands, there was no chance of breaking the ropes. My family had bound me, and now they looked down at me with no mercy on their faces.

My pack just watched.

Waited.

This was happening. This fucked up sacrifice was really happening.

And it broke me.

"Do you think Luneste will help?" I demanded, my voice high and screechy. An accusation for all of them to hear, for everyone who watched these murders and did nothing—for my own past self, too. "Do you think our goddess watches you kill people and feels charitable? I think she looks at us and feels shame. And she *should* be ashamed—this is a sham, and killing in her name is fucking disrespectful—"

"*Shut up,* Nixette," Conn hissed, my eldest brother darting forward to cover my mouth with his hand.

I'd never forget it—the second his palm covered my mouth and silenced me. The brother I'd grown up with as a protector, the brother who'd made me laugh and cry and want to thump him for being so annoying like all brothers did to their little sisters. "You'll piss off Luneste if you keep talking like that," he growled, finally meeting my eyes. I expected guilt and loathing there, and found it in spades, but I recoiled at the disappointment, too. As if *I* was the shameful one for fighting for my life, for not accepting this as the fucking *blessing* they told me it was.

Bullshit.

I bucked again, fighting until my last damn breath. I'd never spoken to them like that before, never spoken to *anyone* like that before—swearwords were for inside my head, not rolling off my tongue—but with death near, I stopped caring about my place in the pack, stopped caring that I was lesser and smaller and weak. An omega—a female meant for breeding and fucking, for silence and softness and sweet words.

I hadn't fought it, had accepted my place in the pack. In

the world. My whole life, I'd revelled in the way they protected me, like I was precious, even if it was just to create the next generation of wolves. But it seemed that protection had run out, and even my value as an omega was gone.

"This will change things, Nixette," Dad said gently—or as gently as his new, rough voice ever got. His expression was set in a fierce stare, his grizzled face full of determination. I used to think I looked like him, with the same blue eyes, high cheekbones, and straight nose, but not anymore. I didn't know who this man was. "We were giving Luneste the wrong people before, but you, an omega ... she'll take you, and make the rest of us fertile again. We can have *pups*, Nixette. That's what you're going to do for us. New life —survival."

My lip curled back from my teeth. I was so fucking *sick* of hearing that word—survival. Everything he did was in the name of it, and none of it ever *worked*.

I pried my mouth open and slammed my teeth shut on the meaty part of Conn's palm, gnashing my canines as they grew sharper, the moon's light bathing the clearing and filling me with strength. But it filled everyone else with strength, too, a double-edged sword.

The power of the shift rushed down my spine, making my blood buzz and boil. I could shift and break free of these ropes. I didn't stand a chance of winning them in a fight— my brothers were betas, and my dad was a powerful alpha. But I could *try*. If I limped away bleeding and weak, it was better than them taking my life. If I had my throat ripped out, at least then it would be on *my* terms.

I gnawed my teeth deeper into Conn's palm until he growled and tore his hand away, his blood coating my tongue with an iron tang as I tugged on the knot of my shifting magic.

"Now!"

Light flashed above me, a blade catching Luneste's cold rays. My shift faltered. My body was still covered in skin, not fur, when the knife pushed against my chest, my skin fighting that sharp metal until the very last second—before it sank all the way to the hilt.

2

MOONLIGHT

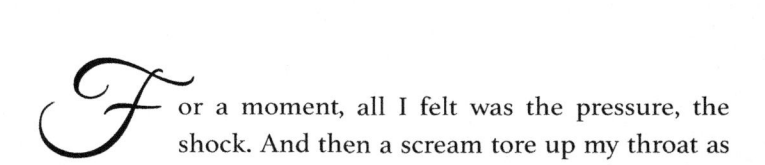

For a moment, all I felt was the pressure, the shock. And then a scream tore up my throat as pain ruptured my middle, sharper and more ruthless than anything I'd experienced before.

My scream was loud enough to send birds rocketing out of the trees in panic, to shake the whole damn world. For a moment, I hoped Luneste heard, and that she came not to accept my sacrifice, but to make my pack pay.

I screamed, defiant and accusatory until the minute my voice cut out and everything went black.

Except there was a light in the darkness, a glowing womanly figure, and my breath hitched.

How could I breathe when I was dead? I *was* dead, wasn't I? My heartless family had murdered me, had buried a knife in my heart because I was disposable, worthless—an omega.

I blinked, and the glowing figure was right in front of me, close enough for me to see her smooth, ageless face, her silver-threaded white hair—the source of the glow—and her mercury-silver eyes crinkled in motherly affection.

"I can't say I'm happy to see you here, Nixette Tulay," she said in a voice like whispers and lullabies.

I jumped as cold fingers framed my face, cool lips pressing to my forehead. What the hell was happening? I was dead. Wasn't I?

But why did I feel *alive*?

"I..."

The woman laughed, a soft murmuring sound full of warmth. "I'm Luneste, dearest. I heard your prayer."

"My ... prayer," I repeated, staring at the woman in front of me. The woman claiming to be my goddess. What the actual *fuck*? "I've gone mad," I breathed. It was the only explanation. I was delusional. Maybe the sacrifice hadn't actually happened, and I'd just fallen asleep in our cabin. Maybe I'd wake up and this whole thing would have been a silly dream. Of course my dad wouldn't kill me. Of course my brothers wouldn't help him.

"Oh, Nixette," the woman—Luneste, apparently—sighed, her eyes lined with silver. "How I wish I could confirm your wishes. But it was real, and you're dead. This is your soul I'm touching."

That was ... actually there weren't words for what that was. I had to be alive—I *felt* alive. Not just a soul. I couldn't be just a soul.

She brushed a tear from my cheeks before I even realised it had fallen, and I swallowed hard, chanting *I'm alive, I'm alive, I'm alive* in my head. "Your body is dead, bleeding onto the rock."

I shook my head, pulling away from her and wrapping shaking arms around my middle, squeezing until it hurt. *I'm alive. That hurt—I'm alive.* "This is just all one big hallucination," I breathed.

The white glow shifted in front of me as I paced away,

and I inhaled sharply at the scene that formed between me and the goddess. Below was the clearing, and my pack still standing, murmuring amongst themselves. And my dad, with the knife still dripping my blood. On the sacrificial stone ... that was me. A red, gaping wound sat in the middle of my chest where the knife had been yanked out, and my eyes stared at the sky, wide and stunned.

And empty. Dead.

I'm ... dead?

I stumbled back, my hands up to ward off the image as if it wasn't now burned into my retinas. "Why are you showing me this?" I rasped, my throat swollen and raw.

"So you can plan your escape, daughter," Luneste replied, her glow expanding to brush my face even across the distance. Cool but affectionate, like a tempestuous cat.

"My..." I turned, staring at the white-haired woman more closely as reality settled in. She was ageless, somewhere between thirty and sixty, with skin smoother than any I'd seen before, and a loose white dress covering her womanly body. "My escape?" I asked, hiding my shaking hands by crossing my arms as I focused on what she'd said —she brought me here to plan *my escape.*

How could I escape when I was dead? None of this made any sense.

"Your words reached me," Luneste explained with a kind smile that turned vicious with retribution. "You didn't pray for me to accept the sacrifice; you wanted me to make your pack pay." She lifted her pale hand, light spilling from her fingers.

"I ... you heard me?" I asked numbly, watching the light fall between her fingers like water, absorbing into the darkness beneath our feet. There was no way this was real, but the scene of the clearing, and my dead body ... it *looked* real.

And the knife had certainly felt real when it pierced my chest. The pain had been as real as anything I'd ever endured before. Deep down, I didn't think it was a nightmarish delusion. *I'm dead?* But *this*—the goddess standing before me, talking to me like I was important to her? I had to be mad. No way was this real.

I was an omega, and not a special one, just a regular omega from a failing pack. Why would our goddess give *me* a vision? I wasn't a hero, wasn't one of the great women of our campfire stories. I was just ... Nixette.

"Cup your hands, daughter," Luneste guided with an encouraging smile, but still with that edge of revenge in her mercury-silver eyes. "What do you have to lose?"

Good question. The answer was ... nothing. If this was a delusion, fine. If it was real ... Luneste was offering revenge on my pack. And after what they'd done, no way would I turn that down. So I cupped my hands and held my breath as Luneste neared, dripping icy moonlight into my hands.

I couldn't stop seeing my own body on the sacrificial stone, left there to chill as they chatted, a gaping wound in my chest.

"I thought you might prefer to take your own revenge," the goddess said, watching every emotion cross my face. "Drink, Nixette, and become more powerful than your father could ever hope to be."

Well, I was never turning *that* down. I'd have to be mad to refuse, so I lifted my hands to my mouth and drank cool liquid moonlight, feeling the icy slide all the way to my belly.

"You've seen where your pack stand; you know where to strike first. None of them can hope to control you with this power flowing through you."

I just stared at Luneste as cold spread through my whole body. Was this real? I was starting to believe it was.

So that made me ... dead?

"Alive," Luneste disagreed gently. "You'll return to your life, your soul intact and your body whole." She smiled, cupping my face again. "When you run, run to these lands. You'll be safe here."

I gasped as an image filled my head: wild forestland left to grow unrestrained, with a single white cottage sat in the middle of overgrown grass beneath a steely sky.

"Find the broken pack and the alpha of alphas; they are your fate."

"I don't know what that means," I replied numbly, reality finally setting in. This was my goddess, the woman I prayed to—here, in front of me, giving me her moonlight to drink, offering me power and justice and ... safety?

"Trust the moon, Nixette. It will guide you true." She smiled deeper, wrinkles forming around her eyes and dimples in her pale cheeks. "You have everything you need: power, purpose, and a path. Now all that's left is to make your pack pay."

Cool lips pressed between my brows, and I sucked in a desperate gasp as pain exploded through my chest, bruises making themselves known up and down my body.

I sat up in a rush, the stone icy beneath me and Luneste's cold rays comforting on my abraded skin as I watched panic spread among my pack. I was back—I was really back. And the hole in my chest was healing, leaving only dried blood crusted on my skin.

The wind was sharp through my ripped shirt as I pushed off the stone slab and stumbled to my feet. My body felt the same as it had before I'd died; I didn't feel undead, or ghostly. I felt like me, only angrier, and stronger.

Alive.

Now all that's left is to make your pack pay.

"Nix," Dad breathed, taking a hesitant step towards me with his hands lifted as if I was a feral wolf. I knew what packs did with ferals, and I had no interest in being caged. "You're back...?"

I smiled, a sharp edged thing I'd always softened before. No more—no more would I hide my full emotions. No more would I stifle my thoughts and silence my voice for this pack.

"Luneste received your sacrifice," I said, breathless with power. Not because I had Luneste's moonlight in my veins, but because I chose to speak—because I refused to murmur and whisper and stay quiet. I raised my voice so everyone could hear, my heart thudding fast at the way they hung back, staring in horror and ... fear. I liked their fear. I was terrified in my final moments; it felt right that they felt the same. "She rejects it. Rejects *you*." I watched their recoil, even my brothers flinching, and my lungs filled with night air. With *relief*.

"The power," Dale, the man who'd tied me up murmured. "Luneste was supposed to give her power to *us*, to the pack."

Dad jolted, staring at me as he realised the truth.

"She was *never* going to give it to you," I replied coldly, and felt it spread throughout me—the icy touch of the moon, that liquid light. "I was right; she's ashamed of you."

Some of the pack jerked back from my vicious words, horror blanching their familiar faces. Faces I now despised. I took a step, cautious with my newly healed body, and watched them scramble back. Good. They would let me go. But my dad stalked forward, and I knew that dangerous gleam in his eyes. He had no intention of letting me run.

"I won't let you kill me again," I hissed, my strength fleeing as I took a step back. I needed to be brave, but all I could see was his face as he drove the knife into me, and all I could feel were bruises being pressed into my waist, my arms, and my ankles as I was dragged out of our home to be killed. "You don't get to hurt me again."

Dad sighed, as if I was being difficult. As if he hadn't *killed* me. If Luneste hadn't heard my prayer, I'd have bled out on the rock behind me. And all he could do was sigh like I was being inconvenient? At least some of the others threw me apologetic, guilty glances, and others fled from my mysterious power. But my dad's reaction made me angry.

"We're not going to kill you, Nixette," he said, a thread of a growl in his voice. To send me to my knees in agony while they grabbed me and threw me back on the stone. *No way in hell.* I grasped the cold power in my belly, ready to use it. "But you have our power, and we need it out of you."

I knew him well enough, even this dark new version of my dad, to predict what he'd say next. *Luneste gave you the power I've been killing people for; I can't let you keep it. I'll excise the magic from your body even if I have to bleed every part of you.*

There was something very wrong with him.

"No," I said, breathy and small as he took a step. But I remembered Luneste's face, remembered the vicious flash in her eyes—that promise of revenge. "No," I repeated firmer, and I stood straighter in front of my treacherous pack, giving a hard tug on the well of cool moonlight inside me until its chill filled my whole body. "She gave it to *me*; it's *mine*."

I hauled hard on that well of ice, praying for help, and light exploded across the clearing around me, bleaching the trees to silver birch, turning tanned faces ivory, and making my dad's eyes pale and monstrous. I watched him jerk towards me, but he flinched back as if it hurt to touch the light.

I didn't hesitate. I sucked in a frantic breath and ran.

Trees and branches rushed past me in a hiss, slicing at my skin as I sped with the wind pushing at my back, as if Luneste had called on reinforcements to help me escape. I ran faster than I knew I could, and pushed myself even faster, breathless and afraid. Every hiss of the wind was my dad reaching for me. Even the familiar dying trees began to feel threatening the further I ran, their branches clamouring to drag me home.

No. Those parklands had stopped being my home the second the knife went in my chest. Tears ran hot down my face, obscuring my vision, but I shoved them off my cheeks and kept running. Escape was the only thought in my mind —escape, and then survive. Everything else could come later.

My lungs started to strain after long minutes, my legs aching and my chest twinging where I'd been stabbed, but I didn't stop racing through the tight, twisting pathways of our woods, past tall trees and low shrubs, all the animals silent as they watched me run for my life.

I didn't know which way to run, didn't know where to find that cottage Luneste had showed me, but I kept running, picking directions at random until I broke out of Tulay packlands. I was in the overgrown in-between place between our lands and Ragnar lands. The road wasn't far from here. Hope caught in my chest. I'd almost done it, almost escaped.

Tears slid down my cheeks again, the pain of their betrayal unbearable.

I twisted off the path, breathing hard through my teeth

and whimpering as footsteps hammered the path behind me. My pack hunting me down. Or maybe just my dad and brothers.

Find the broken pack and the alpha of alphas; they are your fate.

I couldn't stop running until I found them, or until my legs gave out. Whichever happened first. Because if I stopped ... my dad would kill me again, and this time I knew I'd stay dead.

So I ran.

3
FLIGHT

I didn't stop fleeing until my knees buckled and I hit the abrasive tarmac road, miles away from Tulay lands. The pursuit had stopped an hour ago, but if I knew my dad, he'd gone back to get the car. I needed to get off the road, which would make walking even harder, but I tipped my head back to look at the moon, bright white in the dark sky, and I knew I should have been travelling away from the city at the end of the road anyway.

It made no sense how I knew; I just did. Some knowledge placed in me by my goddess, I presumed. I wished she'd placed the location of a little shop or petrol station; I was starving and desperate for a drink. Not that I had anything to pay with.

I had nothing—only the clothes on my back, and they were ragged, dirty, and bloody at this point. Misery threatened to overwhelm me, and a sob clamoured up my throat, but I shoved it back down.

Not until I'd found the broken pack. *Then* I could break, when I was safe.

The cool moonlight in my chest rippled, encouraging me as I hauled myself back to my feet after a few minutes' rest. I needed water, and something to eat, and somewhere warm to shelter when the temperature plummeted in an hour or so.

The soles of my feet stung with every step as I veered off the road, taking cover under the trees and glancing up at the moon every few steps. Luneste had said it would guide me, and I had no other way of finding the broken pack and the alphas of alphas who'd apparently keep me safe. So I followed the moon, walking aimlessly, my teeth beginning to chatter and various parts of my body thumping with insistent pain.

But at least the pain meant I was alive. There was always that.

"This had better be the right way," I huffed to myself, squinting up at the bright disc in the sky, my arms wrapped around my middle, hugging my vest to myself. I needed a coat—or even better, a blanket—but I'd been dragged out of my home in these clothes; they were all I had. "It could be worse," I murmured, dropping my gaze back to the winding path through dark, forested lands. "I could be naked."

It wouldn't have surprised me if Dad and my brothers had stripped their sacrifices, really leant into the whole cult ritual angle. I couldn't believe they'd actually done it, actually *killed* me. Had I meant that little to them? Was I as disposable as a pig being sent to slaughter?

My teeth chattered harder, my feet bleeding, raw pain slashing through my soles and up my ankles with every step. I was far enough from the road now that I couldn't hear the rumble of car engines, but my paranoia still tricked me into thinking I could hear the car coming for me.

They'd killed me—actually killed me. They'd stabbed me through the heart. As if that would have fixed the blight and infertility plaguing Pack Tulay. Anger warmed me the more I thought about it, and I walked on, branches cracking under my feet, the chatter of insects and the low hooting of owls silenced as I drew nearer, and then resuming when I'd passed—the creatures sensing a greater predator. But I wasn't a deadly alpha, with a terrifying growl and violent instincts. I wasn't even a beta with regular wolf strength. I was an omega, good only for fucking and breeding. I shifted with every full moon, but even a pup's dominant growl sent me to my belly on the ground, my whole body shivering. Omegas were bred for submission, for obedience. Not for fighting or strength.

And yet Luneste had given *me* her cold moonlight magic. Not my pack, not the alpha. Me.

I wished I knew what she'd seen when she looked at me. My anger began to crack like ice bearing weight, fractures spreading until I was shaking and cold again.

Another glance at the moon, and I adjusted my course slightly, panting as I crested a slight incline. My arms caving at the exertion, I dug my fingers into the rough bark of the tree beside me and hauled my shaking legs up to the top. Was my family still chasing me? How close were they? I strained my ears—my hearing was one of the few wolf traits I had in spades—but all I heard was the rustle of leaves, the low chitter of living things, and my own ragged breathing.

It wouldn't take an alpha to find me though; my feet were bleeding so badly that I was leaving a trail of blood drops behind me, and no doubt my silver-lilac hairs laid their own trail with the amount of times I'd run my hands through it. But I couldn't hear them *yet*, couldn't smell their deep, earthy scents on the wind.

But there was ... something.

I gripped the tree harder, giving myself a little push to begin the descent on the other side of the hill. The moon pointed this way, and the cool burn of power in my chest agreed, so I dragged myself by my fingernails up another steep incline and flopped onto my belly at the top. A dangerous position for anyone, but especially for a hunted omega.

I rolled over and scooted up, pressing my back to a strong, healthy tree—I'd almost forgotten what they smelled like—and scanned my surroundings with paranoid eyes. The tall trunks could have hidden a slim figure, and the hush of the wind through leaves could have masked the low sounds of breathing. But I still didn't smell the familiar scents of my pack, so I gave myself a hard shake and dragged my hands down my face.

"You're fine," I whispered, pressing my palms to my eyes. "Luneste helped you escape. They're not going to catch you. You won't die again."

But another scent hit my senses and—strength and energy filled my veins like sparkling bubbles. That was ... unexpected.

I jumped to my feet, my wide eyes searching for the source of the scent—like copper and coffee beans. I didn't call out *hello*, because I wasn't an idiot in a horror film, but I did scuff my feet across the dried leaves, letting the crunch alert them that someone was nearby.

Near-silent footsteps answered, and I inhaled in a panicked rush as a giant stepped out of the darkness. I retreated until my back slammed into the tree trunk. The man was enormous, far above six feet, and his shadow stretched even bigger on the floor. I couldn't see his face, but I could *feel* his intensity, and I knew I was his prey. I'd escaped my pack only to be killed by this alpha. And there was no doubt that he was an alpha—he *exuded* dominance and strength, and my bones ached with the need to drop to my knees and show submission.

But I was free of my pack. I had Luneste's power. I could be strong, too, if I chose.

"Stay back," I warned him, reaching for the icy brush of moonlight inside myself.

The giant wasn't deterred; he prowled forward like a shadow given form, and my breath went short and fast. All I could see of him was pale skin, a dark ponytail, and broad shoulders, but the threatening aura coming off him was enough to make me shrink away as if he was monstrous.

"I'm warning you," I hissed, throwing up my hand and releasing—nothing. My moonlight stayed inside me, lapping like a cool ocean against my ribs, content and calm.

The alpha only laughed, a sound like rumbling thunder, and I shuddered, distracted long enough for him to rush forward and grab my hips, throwing me over his shoulder.

"Let me down!" I shrieked, hammering at his muscular back. It was like punching a solid iron door; useless. But that didn't stop me hitting him, or kicking his similarly toned stomach as panic made me shake like a tree in a storm. "I swear, I'll kill you. You'll wish you'd never met me," I threatened weakly, fear making my breath short.

He didn't laugh this time; the giant remained quiet, his whole body tensed against my relentless attacks. The forest moved in a blur of darkness and moonlight as he crested the incline I'd been aiming for—and my breath caught in my throat at the clearing that spread out beneath it. Grass had been left to grow wild around the wreckage of cars—and a black one that looked in much better condition—and sitting like a hulking gargoyle behind the cars was the white cottage Luneste had shown me.

I'd made it.

But the alpha who'd grabbed me seemed more villain than saviour.

What if the goddess was wrong? What if I wasn't safe here, but in even more danger than I'd been at home?

4

ALPHAS

"What are you going to do to me?" I breathed, all the fight going out of me at the sight of that cottage—the gleaming promised land I'd been longing for turned into a dark, twisted paradise.

"I'm taking you to my alpha," the man holding me replied, his voice surprisingly smooth, not like broken glass and gravel like I'd been expecting. More like honey.

"Your alpha," I repeated in a whisper, a chill moving over my body, raising goosebumps from head to toe. "The alpha of alphas."

I was suddenly airborne, sliding down his hard front onto my feet in the wild grass. My stomach pitched when I overbalanced, but big, surprisingly timid hands caught my shoulders, whipping away as soon as I was steady. "Where did you hear that?" he demanded, his smooth, honey voice still a shock.

I peered into the alpha's face, the full moon bright enough for me to make out his features. The alpha's long hair was tied back, not as pitch black as I'd first thought but more a rich brown, and his face was cut from marble, all angles and harshness. He might have been handsome if his brows weren't cut hard over narrowed blue eyes, a scowl etching foreboding lines into his face. I backed up a step at that glare, at the threat in his eyes, at the sheer height of him dwarfing me. He could snap me in half with little effort, and my breathing spiralled out of control.

I reached for the well of moonlight inside me, but it had been useless before, and part of me dreaded it abandoning me again. It was all I had left. What would I do if I couldn't use Luneste's gift to defend myself? She'd promised I'd be *safe* here.

But there was no mistaking the menace in this hulking, glaring alpha.

"You wouldn't believe me even if I told you," I finally replied, eyeing the forest beyond the clearing and wondering if I could run fast enough to escape him.

As if he knew what I planned, the alpha reached out as if to grab me, and I jumped out of the way—towards the cottage's door, as if he'd planned my response and herded me exactly where he wanted me.

He gestured in a clear command—*in*—and I shook, backing up until my back hit the heavy wood. I couldn't willingly walk into a house with a threatening alpha. I knew what would happen, and no way would I ever come out of that place again. Not whole, at least.

I threw my hands up again, tugging hard on the pool of my new power, but no blinding moonlight erupted from me. Nothing happened at all. Oh goddess, the power really was gone.

I had to run; it was the only option I had. The only thing that might save me. But where would I be safe if not here, where Luneste had promised I'd be protected? Nowhere. Not with my dad and brothers out there, hunting me. I just wanted to be *safe*, and this ruined hope hurt like a stab wound in my chest.

And I knew exactly how one of those felt.

I tensed all my muscles, biting the inside of my lip at the pain in my raw feet, but the door ripped away behind me before I could take even one step, and I tumbled into solid strength and huge, constrictive arms.

"What's this, Draven?" asked a deep voice like thunder. "I thought you'd bring us back a deer, not a—" The man who'd trapped me in his arms dipped his head, a nose brushing my neck as he took a deep breath. "An omega."

I shook hard, paralysed by terror, waiting for the growl that would make agony detonate in every cell in my body.

"She trespassed," the giant—Draven—replied.

His pleasant voice shocked me out of my paralysis, and I bucked hard against the arms locked around me, even if a part of me went still and quiet at how it felt to be held. When was the last time I'd had arms around me? Even to restrain me? I couldn't quell the deep, primal reaction that made me tremble for an altogether different reaction than fear.

"Hmm," the alpha holding me replied, because he was absolutely an alpha, too. No beta was ever this big. "A lost omega trespassing on our property."

"*What?*" a new, sharper voice demanded, followed by urgent sounds of movement from within the cottage. "An omega? What the hell?"

I fought harder, kicking the legs behind me to no reaction. There were three of them, and I was dead. For real this time. No way would they let me leave, and if all the horror stories I'd heard were true, they'd use me until I was dead and then put me out with the rubbish. Not every pack were as kind to omegas as my pack had been. Until they'd decided to sacrifice me, at least.

"Easy," the alpha holding me murmured, his voice as deep as death. "There's no need to be scared."

"Like hell there isn't," I hissed, and threw my head back, my skull colliding with a nose hard enough to earn me a satisfying crunch. Even if pain blasted through my head and made me whimper, it felt good to defend myself.

It was still better than the nerve-shredding agony of an alpha's growl.

But the huge alpha wasn't deterred or even hurt; he made a disapproving sound, deep like a storm rolling in. "Careful, you'll only hurt yourself."

I threw my head back again, but he evaded me easily this time, pulling me over the threshold and into the cottage. My stomach dropped, my whole body shaking hard despite the relief of heat and shelter from the wind. They were going to kill me. But before they did, what they did would hurt.

A lot.

"She's petrified," a new voice remarked, cool and unfeeling. "She probably thinks we're going to rape her."

The alpha holding me growled so fiercely that my omega instincts kicked in at the worst time, and I went weak in his arms, my head lolling against his chest and my face red hot. Primal responses moved through my body, my eyes dilating and breathing speeding up. A whine rattled the back of my throat, and slick pooling between my legs—an omega's base reaction to an alpha growl.

This growl of protective fury might have been worse than a growl of command. I wasn't in excruciating pain, but the feeling of my body betraying me was horrific.

I knew the second they smelled my response; the alpha

went still behind me, and another alpha snarled so ferociously that I shrank back, squeezing my eyes shut against the hungry stare of the first.

"She's *mine*," the third, urgent alpha said desperately. I trembled, still caught in my reaction to the unfamiliar growl, as an alpha's hands pawed at my shoulders and arms, pulling me out of the brawny alpha's hold.

"Bakkhos, be fucking careful," the deep-voiced alpha rumbled as I was pulled like a ragdoll against a wiry body. I couldn't catch my breath as arms wound around my waist, frantic lips pressing kisses down my cheek, up my temple, and across my hair. "She's a person, not a toy."

I flinched as the door shut, trapping me with *four* alphas —one menacing, one huge with a powerful growl, one desperately touching me, and one emotionless.

I was never getting out of this cottage. Luneste had lied to me. I wouldn't be safe here; I'd be abused and killed.

This cottage wasn't my sanctuary. It was my coffin.

5

MANIA

"Leave the fucking door open," the chaotic alpha holding me snarled—while somehow still obsessively kissing different parts of me, his arms like a cage around my back, pressing me to his front. I screwed my eyes shut, every part of my body shaking. I didn't dare look at him. If he was anything like Draven, who'd first grabbed me, he'd be utterly terrifying.

"There are six windows open," the huge alpha replied calmly. "You're not trapped, see?"

The crazed alpha made a low sound against my head, pressing a rough kiss to my hair and making me shake harder. "Fine," he conceded. I sensed his attention shift back to me and tensed as his fingers ran through my long hair, every stroke fast and manic. "What's your name, Sunshine?"

I refused to tell them anything. If I was going to die, I'd die defiant.

"Let me go," I hissed instead, battling through the overwhelming urge to submit to them. All of them. But especially the biggest alpha—the second one.

"But you're ours now, Sunshine," the crazed alpha

replied, seriously enough that I knew he was completely insane. "You walked onto our property."

Not by coincidence. Luneste had sent me here. But maybe I was to be her sacrifice after all.

"An omega just for us," he went on, nuzzling my throat with his nose. Silky hair brushed my neck, and I shivered—and then realised exactly how vulnerable I was.

My eyes flew open as danger struck me like lightning. He could rip out my throat. Or worse—force a mate bond with a bite. I'd be chained to him for the rest of my life, however short that life may be.

"Let her go, Bakkhos," Draven, the giant, growled. "You're scaring her."

"I'm not," Bakkhos huffed, clutching me closer and not seeming to notice that I shook against his wiry body. "Am I, Sunshine?"

I dared to glance up, and paled at the dangerous gleam in the blond man's mossy green eyes. There was nothing but intensity in his carved features, but his grin was almost too big for his tattooed face to contain.

Oh, goddess. He was completely unhinged.

Alphas and madness didn't mix well. And it always ended up with someone dead. Any tiny glint of hope I'd had left, any chance of getting out of this alive, shrivelled up and died. I had nothing to lose by admitting the truth. "Yes. You are scaring me."

Bakkhos let go of me so fast I lost my balance, but another alpha caught me—the fourth, uncaring one—like I was a toy they were fighting over, eager to play with.

"Wild," Draven warned in a low growl. I didn't know why he was trying to protect me when *he* was the one who'd grabbed me and brought me here. Or why there was an alpha called Wild. It seemed like a dangerous omen.

I looked up into smiling, gold eyes, and my breathing hitched at the mischievous smirk on this alpha's tanned face. He didn't have Bakkhos' manic gleam, but there was something in his expression, something in the way he held himself, that made a primal part of me go deadly still in the hope he'd overlook me.

Shocking red hair swept back from his sharp-planed face as he bent closer to me, lips tugging into a deeper smirk. "Haven't you heard the rumours in the nearby village, Lilac?"

"That's not my name," I replied weakly, shrinking away from this deadly red-haired alpha. He didn't hold me like Bakkhos had, didn't cover me in kisses. I didn't know which was worse.

"There are dangerous, broken alphas roaming these woods," Wild continued, his voice shockingly cool and compassionless compared to the smirk on his face. "The locals are afraid they'll be caught and slaughtered." He ducked forward, and I went completely still as his tongue dragged up my throat. "They've forbidden their daughters to wander around here, lest we steal them."

My heart beat quicker, danger hammering at my chest until I couldn't breathe. "I'm sorry I trespassed," I squeaked out. "I'll just … leave."

"Wild," Draven warned again, low and rumbling. The sound sent shivers through me as I tried to back away from Wild.

But he trapped me with rough hands on my shoulders, straightening to his full height to give me a wicked, sociopath's grin. "Leave?" he asked, puzzled. "But we were just about to have dinner, and I think you'd be a *delicious* addition."

I whimpered.

Oh, goddess.

"That's enough," the biggest alpha snapped. "Wild, let her go. Omega, take a breath, we're not going to eat you."

"*Well...*," Bakkhos laughed, bright and sparkling, his smile cutting creases into his ink-covered face. "Not like *that*, maybe."

"Bakkhos, *shut the fuck up*," the big alpha growled, deep and breathtakingly dominant.

I hit the floor on my knees so hard that pain cracked up my thighs, gasping for breath as that sound vibrated through me, resonant and deep. I was powerless as my body heated and slick soaked into the rug under me, sliding down my thighs until they were slippery, until my jeans stuck to my legs.

I'd never ... never heard a growl as strong as that before.

"I gave you an order, Wild, give her fucking space."

Wild snorted, full of derision as he strolled a few paces away, lazy and careless. "I was only playing with her, calm down, alpha."

Alpha ... the alpha of alphas. I should probably have figured that out by now.

"You scared the shit out of her," Draven snarled, and the floorboards creaked as he took a threatening step.

I curled over myself, kneeling and gasping for air, wishing I could disappear.

The floor thudded as the biggest alpha knelt before me, and my chest hitched as I got a good look at him. His head was shaved, somehow making his brown eyes more stark, and a thick beard covered the lower half of his face, blood trickling into it from where my head had smashed into him. He was the biggest man I'd ever seen, bigger even than he'd felt pressed against my back, and my breathing froze.

"Breathe," he reminded me, his dark brown eyes sharp

as he watched me closely, blocking out the rest of the room with truly enormous shoulders. No human could ever be that big, no ordinary wolf—he was purebred, deadly alpha. His hands were as big as my head, his arms covered in black ink of moons, knives, and thorns that only made him look more threatening. I could see at least half a dozen scars on his hands, face, and arms, and I only shook harder at that evidence of his battles and survival. He was used to fighting—used to winning.

I didn't stand a chance, and I knew it.

I was so scared of him that I did as he commanded and dragged in a breath, and then another, and another until I was breathing faintly, shivering at the low purr he praised me with. Another alpha trait, and one I'd never experienced before. It hit me so strongly that my eyes rolled back. Relaxation and safety wrapped around me, loosening tension from every muscle until I slumped into waiting arms.

I knew it was a natural alpha trait, but it felt like manipulation, and my stomach twisted even as I expelled a sigh of relief. The alpha of alphas' huge arms settled around my back, his chin resting atop my head.

"That's better, hmm?"

I didn't reply. It was better and so much worse. He'd stripped all my fight and defiance in one simple purr. He'd made me compliant to whatever this broken pack planned to do to me.

"I'm going to pick you up now, and settle you on the couch," he said, low and calm but still deep like thunder crashing. I felt that voice in my belly, fluttering and tightening. More slick gushed from my pussy, far out of my control. My body begged for him, for my first ever alpha, even as I screamed inside at the idea.

"Fuck," Bakkhos choked out, and I lifted my head to see

the crazed alpha fist his dirty blonde hair, pulling hard as he stared at me with tight green eyes. The sight of his need hit me like a bucket of cold water, and I scrambled up, throwing out my hand to keep them all away from me—and gasping as a beam of silver light formed in my palm.

"Whoa," Wild breathed, staring at me with awed golden eyes. The smirk actually fell off his face until he didn't look so much like a bastard. "What power is that, Lilac?"

"Nothing I've seen before," Draven mumbled, watching me from a spot by the window.

I hadn't even noticed my surroundings, but now I stared at the sofa and two armchairs arranged around a flat-screen TV and fireplace, the bare floorboards beneath our feet covered in a thick navy rug, not a carpet as if first suspected. Like the alpha of alphas had said, all the windows were thrown open to let in cool night air, filling the room with an outdoors, woodsy scent that just *barely* cut through the heavy fog of alpha dominance and thick scents.

Those scents did things to me, made me hot and shuddery, feverish with need, but I fought it hard.

"Stay away from me," I warned them, backing away from the alpha of alphas, and keeping an eye on Wild, who seemed the most unpredictable of the pack. "I'll kill you."

Wild snorted, throwing himself into an armchair as if he couldn't care less. But his eyes never left me, a predatory gleam in his gaze.

As if by threatening them, I'd become more interesting to him.

I swung my hand as Bakkhos moved. He practically salivated as he stared at me, his chest moving fast beneath his tight shirt and a hand buried in his shoulder-length hair. "I mean it," I growled, but breathlessly. How could I win against four alphas? Especially one Luneste had called the alpha of alphas.

But the futility wouldn't stop me fighting.

"I don't doubt it, Sunshine," Bakkhos replied, grinning big and crazy as I met his sparkling moss eyes. Not wary of my moonlight at all.

"You must have known the danger of wandering into alpha lands," the biggest alpha said—calm, as if I'd become calm in direct response to his tone. I didn't.

I backed up a few steps, but gasped when I saw that Draven had slid in front of the door, his massively tall frame blocking the only exit. The windows were too damn small for me to climb out of.

Which left ... what? *Run*, my instincts bleated. *Hide*.

Yes. I could find somewhere to hide, and then run out the front door when their backs were turned. And maybe there'd be a back way out of this cottage; I could hope.

"You must have known any alpha you came across would keep you," the alpha of alphas went on, his dark eyes watchful, lacking Bakkhos's mad gleam and Wild's sharp-edged disinterest. "Didn't your people warn you?"

"I..." I shook my head, refusing to let him distract me. I backed up another few steps, this time towards the corridor beyond this big living room. "I'm not from around here."

That was putting it lightly. Luneste knew how far I'd run today.

Wild snorted, shaking his red head. "What idiot enters another pack's lands without knowing the area?"

I inched another few paces, fully aware the biggest alpha knew what I was doing. The fact that he let me ... it didn't bode well for a back door. I held my hand in front of me, cold silver light trickling from my fingers in a warning. But it didn't blind them like it had my pack, didn't send them running from me.

This was not going to end well.

"Someone without other options," the alpha of alphas answered. He stroked his dark beard as he watched me, those foreboding black eyes measuring, assessing.

I shook my head, the presence of so many alphas making my bones quake. I might as well tell the truth. What did I have to lose? "I was sent here. My ... my pack sacrificed me to Luneste," I said, and knew it sounded mad when I added, "but she sent me back. She sent me here, to you."

The alpha of alphas blinked. Clearly that wasn't what he'd been expecting.

Wild snorted. "Well, crazy omega cunt's still omega cunt," he said to his pack members, indolent and smirking.

I went ramrod straight at those words—well, just one. Good men didn't use the word cunt, did they? Fear and rage poured through me, and moonlight flared brighter, purer, in my hand until they winced, backing away. "Don't even *think* about touching me," I warned, my voice deeper than it had ever been before. Hairs stood on end all down my arms, and my hands tingled as power flooded me.

"Sunshine," Bakkhos pleaded—whined, I was tempted to call it. "You're an omega—we're alphas. We have what you need."

I swallowed, backing up further even as more slick rolled down my thighs, darkening my jeans. Cock, he meant—alpha cock, and the knot at the base of their dicks that swelled to lock them inside an omega's pussy, that apparently drove omegas mad with desire because it felt so good. But I wasn't in heat. I was fine, I was safe—I didn't need what he offered. "You don't get to rut me," I tried to growl, but it came out weak and scared.

They would. It would take the *tiniest* effort for them to overpower me.

Bakkhos gave me a wounded look, like I'd broken his heart, and his tattooed face sank into solemn lines. He took a step towards me, an inked hand lifted, but I spun and fled deeper into the house, spooked by the movement.

My breath came short and scratchy as I bolted past the couch and into the corridor I'd spied from across the room. My frantic footsteps echoed like gunshots as I bolted across the room, rattling the photo frames on the hallway wall as I raced past closed doors towards a staircase. I needed to get as far away as possible. The thick scents of alphas were everywhere, cloying in my lungs, making my pussy throb in preparation for something that was *not* about to happen. I could hardly think for the need squeezing me in a vise.

"Wait!" a soft, honey-rich voice called behind me. Draven. He might have been the quietest of the alphas, but he was intimidating and powerful and no way was I letting him do whatever he wanted to me. "What's that mark on your wrist?"

My breath caught in fear, but I didn't stop running, swinging around the newel post and thundering up the stairs—and wincing as the alpha scents grew even thicker. A shudder ran through me, and I swore I felt their physical caresses across my shoulders and down my back, compelling me to relax, to let them give me what I ached for so badly.

At the top of the steps were three doors in a cream and grey corridor; I aimed for the first one since it hung ajar, and whimpered at the concentration of scent on the untidy bed —an alpha of wilderness and embers slept here.

On unsteady legs, goosebumps sweeping up my body and making my nipples hard and sensitive, I stumbled past the bed and slumped in relief at the sight of an en-suite bathroom.

Not questioning my luck—and praying for a lock—I barrelled into the door, the wood cold against my burning skin, and closed it hastily behind myself with trembling hands. A sob slipped free as I spied the deadbolt, my salvation. I wasted no time, gripping it with both hands and ramming it on until the door was locked.

Until I was safe.

For now.

The chill of the bathroom met my heated skin and made chills cover my body, but it filled my lungs like relief, and I took my first full breath in long minutes.

The wood was thin enough that four alphas could definitely smash it down, and the lock wouldn't hold against wolf strength, but it afforded me a scrap of comfort—enough for me to close the toilet lid and sink onto it, dragging my hands down my face.

Luneste had been wrong, or had purposefully lied. I wasn't safe here. The alphas only wanted me for what was between my legs, and with the way I'd responded to the alpha of alphas' growl, there was no doubt they'd get it. The only thing I could hope for at this point was that they didn't use me so brutally that my last moments were spent with a torturing growl in my ears and a cock ruining my insides.

6

BAKKHOS

"I swear to the goddess, Wild, *back off*," Bakkhos growled in the room beyond my tentative safe haven.

I shook, listening to them growl and tussle, my breath hitching every time they came close to the bathroom, waiting for the door to burst in.

"What makes you think you've got first dibs on that pussy?" Wild drawled, coarse and empty of any feeling. "Just because you're already obsessed with her scent—"

A fierce growl answered him, loud enough to make me whimper and press my hands to my mouth as I cowered on the closed lid of the toilet. "No one will force her," Bakkhos snarled, sounding completely feral. "No one."

"As if Kaan would even let us," Wild scoffed.

I sat up, listening intently. Kaan had to be the alpha of alphas. The name fit him—his wild brutality, the intensity in his dark eyes, and the way he'd wrapped his arms around me so I couldn't escape. Kaan. I shuddered hard.

"Get out," Bakkhos seethed, sounding one false move away from ripping out Wild's throat. "You'll scare her."

"*You* scare her, psychopath," Wild laughed cruelly. "If you think you've got a calming bedside manner, boy do I have news for you."

"At least I don't call her by the c word," Bakkhos snarled back.

He had a point.

I strained my ears at the sound of a struggle, and then a thud. The bedroom door slammed shut without another word or laugh from Wild. "Don't worry, Sunshine, he's gone now."

Wild was right; Bakkhos really did think he was calming. He was crazy, but I already knew that much.

I jumped as a weight slid down the bathroom door on the other side; I could picture him sitting with his back to the door, a knee propped up. Already, his image was burned into my brain: his tall, rangy body, his tight T-shirt, the black ink that covered his face like erratic pixels, the crude flowers, trees, and sunbeams messily scrawled on his arms, chest, and neck like a child's crayon drawings. Mostly, I couldn't forget his manic eyes, and the way he'd tracked my every movement. As if, like Wild had said, he really was obsessing over me.

"My name is Bakkhos Emmanuel," he said, quieter but still clearly smiling—I could hear it in his voice. Something brushed the door, making me jump, and I wondered if he'd leant his head back against it. "It means riotous. Bakkhos, I mean."

I frowned, wrapping my arms around my waist. Why wasn't he breaking down the door and grabbing me? Why was he just ... talking?

"I'd tell you more about me," he went on, "but my past is tragic and boring, so I'll skip all those parts. Why don't you tell me about yourself, Sunshine?"

I pressed my lips together, curling my hands into fists in my lap, and said nothing.

"That's alright," he murmured, sounding ... less manic. I frowned deeper. "I wouldn't trust us, either, if I'd just been grabbed. But you can't fight nature, my Sunshine, and neither can we. Alphas are drawn to omegas, and vice versa. Your nature calls to us."

"That's bullshit," I muttered, but apparently his wolf hearing picked up my response because he huffed a laugh. Louder, I snapped, "Just because I'm an omega doesn't give you the right to kidnap me and force me to be your ... your sex slave!"

Nevermind that I'd come here voluntarily.

"Sunshine," Bakkhos replied, a laugh in his voice. "You're an omega—I'm an alpha. We're all slaves to sex."

"That's not what I meant," I said coldly, staring at the back of the door, "and you know it."

"We won't force you," he replied after a while, his laughter gone. "Some alphas would, but we won't."

"I don't believe you," I whispered, my heart racing at the nerve of talking back to him. I'd avoided defiance all my life, had settled into my role as the omega of the pack without complaint, but all that had broken when I'd been dragged out of my home and thrown onto the sacrificial slab. I wouldn't be quiet again; I wouldn't stop fighting.

Even if fighting was useless against four alphas.

"You'll see," Bakkhos replied, his head shifting against the door. "You'll see when we don't mate you against your will. You'll trust us then."

I laughed, a low and bitter sound. "I highly doubt it." Highly doubted they *wouldn't* mate me against my will. "And just because you can growl me into obeying, that doesn't mean I consent."

Bakkhos whined. That was the only way I could describe it. It was a sound I'd never heard from an alpha before, only from betas and omegas. Not that I'd ever met another omega. A knot twisted in my stomach. "You don't want my growl," he breathed, and his voice was so pitiful, I felt sick, another instinctive omega response I assumed. Or maybe plain old sympathy. "You don't want me."

I dragged a hand down my face, annoyed at myself for being moved by his whine. He was a stranger—why should I care if I hurt his feelings? And why was the instinct to purr choking off my air?

"Why am I surprised?" he murmured, and I wondered if his low words were even meant for me. "Why *should* I be surprised? Dad didn't want me, the pack didn't want me. Why would my mate?"

I shot to my feet at that word, my breath catching. Mate. His *mate*? My hands started shaking. Mate bonds were legendary, and so rare that only one in a hundred wolves ever felt one. The bond was soul deep; it twined two or more wolves together for the rest of their lives. According to the stories, the bond was powerful and beautiful, all the best parts of love amplified—support, understanding, care, and respect. Mates would kill for each other, and journey to the ends of the earth if the other was lost. It had always seemed more like a fairy story than a real thing; none in my pack had a mate.

The idea that *I* had ... it was laughable. And yet Luneste's warm voice came to me, unbidden.

Find the broken pack and the alpha of alphas; they are your fate

My fate. My fated mates...?

I shook my head, rolling my eyes at myself. I was being

an idiot. Bakkhos was insane; believing anything he said would only make me as crazy as him.

"I can hear you," he said, shifting against the other side of the door. "Moving. Breathing. Won't you come closer, Sunshine?"

"No," I replied flatly, tiptoeing to the sink and staring at myself in the mirror above it. I should have looked awful, shadows sunk beneath my eyes, my lips bloodless, my eyes bloodshot. I looked ... healthy. As if Luneste had worked her magic on my health, too. I was still too skinny thanks to my pack's dwindling food supply, but my face was far from sallow, my dark blue eyes bright, and my lips were flush with colour.

"I can ... I can tell you about my past if that'd help you trust me?" he offered, and then dissolved into jagged laughter. It was painful to hear. "No, that'd never work. No one wants to hear about a boy in a cage."

I jolted, taking a step towards the door before I could stop myself, the scent of wilderness and embers stronger here—Bakkhos's scent. I'd locked myself in *his* bathroom, then. Was that why he'd thrown Wild out, or because he was ... obsessed with me?

I couldn't stop myself asking, "A cage?"

There were some things that cut through my own terror, and pushed aside my self-preservation, and hearing of a boy in a cage was one of them.

"I ... you want to hear the story, Sunshine?" he asked, something tight in his laughless voice.

I should have said no, should have told him to leave me alone, but something compelled me to say, "Yes."

"Okay." I listened intently to the movement on the other side of the door, trying to picture what he was doing. Tentatively, I stepped closer to the door, only a few paces between me and Bakkhos now. He could tear down the door and be upon me in seconds, but why bother with promises? Why try to reassure me that they wouldn't force me? He gained nothing from it; whether I submitted by choice or not, the end result was the same for him. "Okay," he said again, as if psyching himself up.

"I was born feral," he started in a low voice. "As you probably guessed," he added with a laugh that rose in volume and grew out of control.

"Bakkhos," I interrupted, wrapping my arms around myself at the sound of pure madness echoing in his laugh. There was something wrong with him, but Luneste had called them the broken alphas, so I didn't know why I was surprised.

"Oh," he rasped, his laughter sputtering out. "Yes, you want my story. My twisted, fucked up story." He chuckled again, but stayed in control this time, and my stomach churned. What was I supposed to do with ... all of this? The alphas, their intensity, their scents, their madness? Luneste, help me. "Well, it started when I was born, I suppose," he said with a deep sigh. "I was a normal baby according to most people. Red-faced and bawling all the time, but nothing ... odd. But when I was five, I shifted and went crazy. I don't remember it, I was too young, but I bit anyone who tried to grab me, tore out the throat of another pup, and I..."

I stared at the door in horror. I'd heard of ferals, of course I had, but to be so young ... I'd never even known that was possible. My heart started to twist with sympathy. No wonder he'd gone mad; to have been feral all this time, from such a young age couldn't have been easy.

"My mum, she ... she tried to pick me up."

"No," I breathed, my own grief rising to strike like a snake bite, sudden and agonising. "Bakkhos..."

"She died of blood loss. They didn't tell me that until a while later, but the cage came first—that I do remember."

"The cage," I repeated, cold moving through my middle. "How old were you when..."

"Oh, it happened that day," he replied easily, as if it wasn't one of his most traumatic memories. "I blacked out for all of the first bits, but I remember waking up and not being able to get out, shouting for my mum and dad, and then just crying when all the grownups came to jab sticks into my body. No clothes, obviously. I'd just shifted back, so I was naked." He paused. "The sticks hurt. They cut me everywhere."

I pressed my hand to my mouth, able to clearly picture a tiny Bakkhos caged, abused by his pack. "They should have protected you," I said quietly—barely a whisper. "You were theirs. You were pack."

Bakkhos was quiet for so long that I wondered if he'd left, or maybe he'd gone to get reinforcements to break down the door. I couldn't get the picture of a caged child out of my head, couldn't stop the horror spreading like ice water through my blood, igniting the urge to purr again, even stronger. "I was all wrong," he replied finally, quietly. "Feral —a monster."

"You were *five*," I argued harshly.

His whole body jolted against the door, like he'd flinched, and guilt curdled my stomach. Slowly, carefully, I took the last few steps to the door and slid down the inside of it until I knelt with my knees to my chest.

"You were five," I said, softer. "And a baby. You were innocent. It wasn't your fault you were feral—wolves can't help that. But they can be taught how to control it."

"I know," he replied quietly. "Kaan taught me."

"Your pack should have done that." I shook my head, a

newfound appreciation for my own pack softening the parts that still hurt like crazy. They'd sacrificed me, but at least I'd been fully grown. At least I'd had a childhood—and a good one at that. "Bakkhos?" I asked when he'd said nothing for a long time.

"No one ... no one's ever said that before," he replied, his voice tight.

"Well, it's true." I took a deep breath before voicing the hurt. "And you're not the only one who's been hurt by your family. It's not the same, but my dad and my brothers, they —they sacrificed me to Luneste."

I'd told them that downstairs, but clearly it had a different impact now. Bakkhos inhaled sharply, and then growled so ferociously that my eyes rolled back in my head and I slumped against the door, gasping for breath. Shivers moved up and down my body like a physical touch, and my pussy clenched, slick sticking my jeans to my thighs.

"I'll slaughter them for trying to kill you," he snarled, so fierce that it wasn't hard to believe he was a feral wolf.

"They didn't try," I argued, a sharp pain clawing through my chest at the memory of being pinned to the rock, light flashing on my dad's knife. "They killed me."

The snarl cut off so suddenly, I jumped at the silence. "What?" he asked, sounding as raw now as he had when he told me about the cage.

"My dad stabbed me in the heart," I told him, the words like barbs scraping up my throat. I tasted blood, and realised I'd bitten the end of my tongue. "I died."

"But... I don't understand, Sunshine. Are you a ghost?"

"Luneste brought me back," I explained, prodding my lip with my bleeding tongue to test how badly I'd bitten it. "She refused the sacrifice and gave me power." It sounded crazy saying it out loud, but if anyone would understand crazy, it was Bakkhos. "The silver light—that's her moonlight."

"So you're not a ghost?" he clarified.

"No," I replied, a hitch in my breath. It took a moment to realise I'd laughed, softly and raspy, but it was there all the same. "I'm still a wolf, still alive."

My heart beat and I breathed, at least. But I wasn't sure what to call myself since I'd died and come back. The only word that really fit was miracle.

"Good," he murmured, far from his laughing self. "I can't hug a ghost, and I need to hug you, my Sunshine."

I shook my head, not stupid enough to fall for that. "I'm not coming out of the bathroom, Bakkhos."

"My sister was sacrificed, too," he replied, as if I hadn't spoken. "I never even met her, but I know her name. Ellia. She was sixteen when my pack gave her to the goddess; they thought it would fix the contaminated water in our lake."

I swallowed hard. So my dad wasn't the only one who'd done it. I'd never heard of it happening, but was this common practise then?

"I got the sense Luneste doesn't want sacrifices," I said quietly, twisting my hands in my lap. "She didn't want me to die."

"I wish Ellia hadn't," Bakkhos said, and then without prompting, "What's the mark Draven was talking about?"

I glanced down at the crescent moon and single star on my wrist, my strange birthmark, several shades paler than the rest of my arm. "It's just a birthmark," I replied. "It's nothing."

Bakkhos was quiet—no laughing, no horrific stories.

"Why?" I pressed. Why was it important to them?

"We have the same mark," Bakkhos replied, a smile in

his voice again. "All of us. We figured it might be a mate mark."

There was that word again—mate. It clanged through my soul like a bell, and my hairs stood on end. "And you think I'm your mate?"

"You're mine," Bakkhos said in the urgent, frantic tone I'd first heard him speak. "You're my mate, Sunshine, I know you are. I want to be close to you, closer than I've ever been to anyone. I need—I *need*, Sunshine."

I shuddered as a chill rose all along my body. Something deep inside me ached at his need, desperate to answer it. Maybe not because I was an omega and he was an alpha, but because ... we were mates? A girl could hope anyway. A bristly alpha male sworn to keep me safe, to protect me from anyone who'd try to do me harm—my dad and brothers, for example. Yeah, it would be nice to have a mate right now.

Even if I wasn't sure about all the other stuff that came with it. The rutting, the knotting, the nesting, the biting. I'd never done any of that. With anyone. And it seemed a daunting, terrifying thing to do and have done to me.

"I swear on the moon and goddess I won't hurt you if you open the door," Bakkhos vowed, utterly solemn. "I know how it feels to be hurt by your family; I know how lonely you must feel. I won't make that worse by hurting you. Promise."

I sighed, running my hands down my face. I knew he meant it, could hear the obsessive sincerity in his voice. "You're dangerous," I said, but tentatively. He'd been through so much already; I didn't want to hurt him like his family had. Even if I wasn't his mate, Bakkhos thought I was, and my rejection would sting. "And I can't predict what you'll do."

"You don't feel safe with me," he realised.

My heart twisted at how broken he sounded, and my muscles were already tensed, ready to stand. I forced them to relax, curling my hands into tight fists. "I don't feel safe with anyone," I confessed. "My dad killed me, and my brothers helped while my pack watched and did *nothing*. They knew it was pointless, knew my death wouldn't stop the farmland dying and the infertility in our wolves. They didn't want to admit it to themselves, but they knew. I *trusted* them." My voice broke and I curled my shoulders, bowing over the cruel pain in my chest.

"Sunshine, I *can't*," Bakkhos choked out.

I jumped hard, not breathing at all when the door handle smashed and the wood swung away from behind me.

7
CLAIMING

My stomach crashed, and my heart leapt into my throat, and—Bakkhos dropped to the floor behind me, wrapping his whole self around me. I sagged against his solid weight, melting into his warmth, and the sobs I'd been holding back all day shattered through my chest and up my throat.

"It's alright," he murmured, stroking my hair down my back. "It's okay now, you're safe."

I thought Bakkhos would have savaged me, would have thrown me on the bed and stabbed his cock into me, but he ... he just held me. I broke and sobbed and shook, and he held me through it all, stroking my hair, murmuring that I was safe now, he had me.

By the time I was hollow and empty, my tears dry, I was twisted around, my fingers clutching his shirt so hard it wrinkled, and Bakkhos had both arms wrapped around me as he nuzzled my shoulder.

"Why do you have so many tattoos?" I asked, scratchy and raw.

"Hmm?" Bakkhos lifted his head, black hair flopping

into his face as he gave me a bright smile, so big it filled his entire face and wrinkled the ink on his cheeks, jaw, and forehead. The only place that wasn't inked was his eyelids. It must have hurt, all those needles stabbing into delicate skin.

"This was my first," he said, and lifted his left arm from my back, pointing out a jagged line. A branch, I realised, spotting a lone leaf on the end of it. "I did it when I got out of the cage, so I'd never forget it. They're..." He glanced at his arm, struggling, and my heart clenched to see such a manic, exuberant man subdued. "They're all things I could see from my cage."

I peered closer at his arm, instinct screaming at me to touch him, and this time I didn't ignore it, tracing the knobbled branch to a messy scrawl of a bird, and then a cluster of delicate flowers. His skin was surprisingly soft, and as hot as a fire.

"Buttercups," he said, watching me. "They grew all over the field around my cage."

I almost didn't want to ask, but I had to. "When did you get out?"

"Six years ago," he replied, fixated on the place where I touched him. He was barely breathing.

"How old were you?" I pressed.

"Twenty-three," he answered absently, his mossy eyes glowing with intensity. "That feels *so good*, Sunshine. I need to be touched all the time, especially after being alone and starved of it for so long. My pack knows, and they're good to me, but only Wild can—"

He cut off so suddenly that I peered up at him, frowning at the way he censored himself. "Wild's an asshole," I muttered, startling him into bright, loud laughter.

"He is," Bakkhos agreed, his smile straining even bigger. I jumped as his hands trailed down my sides, feverish and hot. But *fuck*, the touch felt nice. "But Wild's loyal, and he has his own past. Don't judge him too harshly."

I huffed, glaring at the sink basin as if it had offended me. "A past doesn't give him the right to talk about me like that."

Bakkhos made my heart jump by taking my face in his inked hands, meeting my gaze with fervent affection. "I'll gut every single one of your pack for what they did to you, and if they're in wolf form, I'll skin them alive, too." I recoiled, horrified. "But I won't hurt Wild. He's been good to me."

Bakkhos didn't react to my aghast stare; he just smiled, and laid a feathersoft kiss on the bridge of my nose. "Like I'll be good to *you*," he added with a full, beautiful purr.

I groaned quietly as the sound worked through me, as relaxing as a hot bath and every bit as good as a deep massage. He purred louder, the sound rich with promise and protection, and my breath hitched, my body pressing against his instinctively. The sensation of him holding me was too good to resist, and I sighed, settling there, his purr vibrating through his chest to mine until all my worries and fears scattered.

"I didn't get lost," I murmured, my lids heavy over my eyes as I snuggled into him, his scent like a blanket wrapped around me. "When Draven found me, I wasn't lost. I was looking for you all, like Luneste told me to. I just didn't think you'd be so ... dangerous." That seemed like the kindest word for them.

"Draven's scary," Bakkhos replied, stroking my hair down my back and making my eyes roll back. "But he's just quiet. He's not like me, not volatile. You'll be safe with him."

"But not with Wild and Kaan?" I asked, my hazy fog interrupted by a burst of alarm.

"Shh," Bakkhos calmed me. "Nothing will happen to you, my beautiful Sunshine. I know the others are going to love you just as good as I will, you don't have to be scared of them. Kaan's just big and growly, and he's used to getting his way and giving us orders. Wild is ... Wild. Don't believe anything he says; almost everything out of his mouth is a lie, but you'll be safe with him. I know he said the R word like it was nothing before, but it's not nothing to him. He'd never hurt you like that."

I shuddered, even the hint of rape making me cold. But some of my fears were set at ease. I believed every frantic, passionate word out of Bakkhos's mouth. If that made me crazy, so be it. "What happens if I disobey Kaan?"

Bakkhos shook his head, soft dark hair brushing my cheek. "Don't. Everything he does is to keep the pack safe. Now you're with us, pack includes you."

I froze in his arms, my heart tripling speed in my chest. "Do you mean that?" I asked, barely breathing. My old pack had killed me. To have a new one ... I hadn't realised how badly I needed it, hadn't realised that was what had sent me racing across the country following the moon, to this broken pack.

A wolf was nothing without a pack, and I didn't want to be alone.

"Of course I mean it," Bakkhos replied, pulling away to give me a manic stare, the smile on his face strangely gentle even if his eyes were feral. "You're ours now, our mate. That means you're protected." He closed the distance, and my heart leapt as I braced for a kiss, but he just nuzzled his nose against mine.

My heart thudded in my chest as I watched him draw back, a soft purr in his throat. My hand rose of its own accord, tangling in the ends of his hair and bringing his face back to mine. I'd expected the four alphas to claim me in the most brutal ways, but as my lips slanted over Bakkhos's, it was me doing the claiming. Me claiming *him*.

The low, throaty groan he let out had me arching into him, my pussy wet as the sound dissolved into a low, rumbling growl. Bakkhos kissed with every bit as much frantic energy as he spoke, his lips never once leaving mine even as he nipped and sucked and thrust his tongue. Goosebumps rolled down my arms as his fingers dove into my hair and he kissed harder. The feeling of his growl trembling along my tongue had slick pouring from me, and I clawed at his shirt to get him closer, climbing onto his lap as I lost my mind.

And why should I care about losing my mind, after what I'd been through? I'd *died*—kissing a stranger was nothing compared to that.

"Nixette," I gasped against his lips, my eyes rolling back as his kisses trailed down my chin to my throat, burning hot against my skin. "My name is Nixette. Nix."

"Nix," he echoed against my throat, making me shake hard as his tongue brushed the claiming spot, where a wolf would bite another to proclaim to the rest of the pack that they were theirs. "My Nix, my Sunshine."

He sucked my pulse into his mouth, and I swore I turned liquid, melting against him. "Bakkhos," I gasped, digging my fingernails into his scalp and shuddering at the fierce snarl he let out.

"I need to taste you," he breathed, almost a whine. "Goddess, Nix, your scent is driving me crazy. I've been fighting my instinct to touch you since I first smelled your need."

I shook my head, wanting to defend myself. It was a primal reaction to an alpha growl, I couldn't help it, but this time it wasn't quite true. I *wanted* Bakkhos. Not just because he was an alpha who called to the omega in me—because he'd felt the same pain I had, because he was hurting and damaged like me.

Bakkhos went still, staring at me. "You don't want me."

"What?" I breathed.

"It's okay, Sunshine," he murmured, squeezing my shoulder as he tried to pull away. I wrapped my arms around him and stubbornly held on, not sure where he'd got that impression from. "I wouldn't want me, either."

"Bakkhos," I murmured, not letting go.

Oh, I'd shaken my head.

"I ... I was embarrassed by my slick, not saying I don't want you. I do. I didn't expect to, but ... I do."

I pulled back only enough to meet his mossy eyes, and watched the sharpest edge of his hurt soften.

"Don't be embarrassed, Sunshine. You smell beautiful."

I groaned, ducking my head.

"Better than the finest wine. Not that I like wine; I like beer. Better than the best beer, then. And sweeter than any chocolate I've ever eaten." He paused, a low moan rattling his throat. "I need to eat you, my Sunshine. I need to taste you. Please. *Please.*"

I swallowed hard at his need, my own flaring in response. "What about the others? Won't they get angry, and challenge your claim on me?"

Bakkhos frowned, his tattooed face crinkled. "No. You're ours—all of ours. Oh, I need to show you something."

He squeezed my waist and everything inside me went still as he picked me up and moved me off him as if I weighed nothing, the show of strength making every atom in my body sit up and pay attention to him. My clit throbbed, and I watched intently as he scrambled for his jeans button, unfastening them and shimmying the denim down his legs.

My mouth filled with saliva, and I leaned forward for his cock, completely mindless with an omega's need—but he didn't remove his boxers, and instead widened his legs, pointing to a spot on his inner thigh. I was too hot with need, shaking and whining in my throat, to see what he pointed out at first.

His laugh, low and smug, did not help matters. "Here, Sunshine, look."

I peered at the patch of hair on his leg, not seeing until he traced the shape with his finger. "Oh," I breathed, my heart thudding. There it was, a shade paler than his skin: a crescent moon and a tiny dot of a star. "You're ... we're really..."

"Mates," he finished with a beaming grin.

I tentatively reached out a finger, tracing it myself. It was real—the mate bond. His skin was feverishly hot under my touch, hairs tickling my fingers, and I lost my damn mind when his cock jerked against his boxers. My whine was so loud they probably heard it downstairs.

"I know, Sunshine," Bakkhos murmured, catching my face in both his hands and pressing a lingering kiss to my lips. My hand flattened to his hard length before I could stop myself, squeezing him through the fabric and panting at the low growl Bakkhos let out. "*Fuck*, I know. I need you, too. But not on the bathroom floor."

He kissed the bridge of my nose.

"Bed," I said, my skin crying out in relief wherever he touched me: my hips, my waist, my stomach, and back down to squeeze my hips, lifting me onto his lap. I wrapped my arms around his neck, yelping in surprise as he stood suddenly, not even panting at my weight, the alpha in him on clear display: strong and dominant, caring and protective.

His lips met my neck as he walked me backwards through the door, setting my whole body ablaze. "I'll get you nesting materials as soon as possible," he promised, laying kisses on my throat. "As many different fabrics as you could ever dream of."

My heart skipped at the promise of him providing for me, an alpha's first duty and greatest joy—and an omega's too, to provide for their alpha in return. I'd known there were good alphas in the world, but to find one ... rare. So damn rare.

"I've never made a nest before," I admitted. I'd never been in a relationship long enough to, never actually had sex before. I bit my lip, wondering if telling Bakkhos I was a virgin would make him more desperate to be inside me, or if he'd call the whole thing to a halt. The need burning through my body refused to let him stop now, so I kept that fact to myself.

"I've never been inside one," Bakkhos replied, a high flush on his tattooed cheeks as he laid me down on his messy bed. It smelled so intensely of him—embers of fire—that a body-wide shudder gripped me, my toes curling at the combination of that delicious scent and the alpha who laid his body on top of me, pressing me into the twisted sheets.

"Never?" I gasped, trying to remember how to speak.

He shook his head.

"But you must ... being out here with three other alphas, you must have a lot of women around." I tried to hide how unsettled that thought made me, and hoped he thought my legs locking around his was due to need and not possessiveness.

Bakkhos shook his head, his nose in the dip of my collarbone. His tongue traced sparks across my sensitive skin. "No, never. And I..."

He was hesitant enough that I tugged on his hair until he lifted up, his eyes so big and nervous. "What?" I murmured, running my fingers over the black marks scrolling down his forehead to his cheeks and chin.

"You know I was in the cage until I was twenty-three," he said tentatively, his gaze fixed on the swell of my breasts and not my face. "And then Kaan and Wild found me, and made me pack. Well, I ... there hasn't been anyone, and I've been waiting for my mate, if the goddess ever blessed a mad, broken alpha with a perfect mate, and I haven't..."

Surprise was a rocket in my chest. "You haven't slept with anyone? Ever?"

He shook his head. "Not with a woman," he clarified. "There was a time I thought I might, but look at me." He waved a careless hand at his face. "I'm not appealing, my madness is clear for everyone to see."

I couldn't believe it, shock making me dumb. "I *am* looking at you," I said when I recovered, holding his gaze. "And I don't find you unappealing. The opposite, actually. I think you're very attractive," I admitted, forcing myself to be brave and not glance away. "I was scared at first, but that's because I was surrounded by four alphas. Now ... I like looking at you, Bakkhos. I like these." I brushed his black markings again. "I think you're very appealing."

The look in Bakkhos's eyes was brittle and sick with hope. "You're very appealing to me, too, Sunshine." His grin was sudden, like a flash of sunlight through rain clouds. "I guess Luneste didn't think I was too mad for a mate after all. She gave me you."

He ducked to kiss my nose, grinning like a fool. I caught his mouth in a kiss, this one slower and aching with emotion. When he drew away to nuzzle my throat, I breathed, "I've never been with anyone. It'll be a first for both of us."

Bakkhos's smile was the brightest I'd ever seen, his eyes brimming with affection and awe. How had I ever thought he was dangerous? The tattoos, the manic energy ... yes, he was volatile. But one look into his eyes, and he was as excitable and fragile as a puppy, as every bit as quick to love as one.

"Can I claim you, my Sunshine?" he asked, so serious, but still looking at me like I'd roped the moon for him.

I nodded, unable to keep from smiling. "You can claim me, Bakkhos. Can I claim *you?*"

Bakkhos's green eyes flared, his hips bucking against mine, pressing me into the mattress. "Always, Nixette. Always."

Swallowing at the importance of the moment, at the emotion shining in his eyes, I reached for the hem of my shirt and pulled it over my head. I expected a snarl or growl, but Bakkhos had gone quiet, and my face warmed, shyness infecting me as he framed my waist with his heated hands. I shuddered when his palms scorched a trail higher, cupping my boobs through my cotton bra.

"My mate is so beautiful," he breathed, and I gasped as his hot mouth pressed to my chest, right over my breast bone, and then travelled lower as his fingers attempted to get my bra off.

"There's a knack," I said with a soft laugh, reaching for the catch. "It's a pain, I know. Try wearing one everyday."

Bakkhos laughed brightly, and between us we managed to send my bra flying across his messy room. The groan that shook my throat as his mouth closed around my nipple was loud and obscene, and I flushed with embarrassment even as the emotion floated away at how good it felt. And when he started to purr, my eyes rolled back, and stayed that way for seconds.

"Bakkhos," I whined.

He answered only by switching breasts, circling with his tongue before sucking the swollen tip into his mouth and groaning in satisfaction. If he was content to drive me wild, I'd have to take my own revenge. His jeans were somewhere in the bathroom, so only thin cotton stood between my questing fingers and his cock. Downstairs, I heard growling and shouts, but they were so far away as I closed my hand around Bakkhos's hard shaft, practically whispers compared to my mate's ferocious growl.

Need pooled between my legs and I writhed against him, scrambling frantically for my pants and shoving them down to my ankles along with my underwear, and rolling my hips so his hardness brushed my clit.

Bakkhos went silent with a gasp, but my own moan filled the silence, wanton and bold.

"Sunshine," he breathed. "Holy fuck."

He cradled the back of my head and lifted my face for a blistering kiss that made me writhe faster against his cock. "Chase your pleasure, my Nixie," he panted against my cheek. "Make yourself come all over my cock, drench me in your cum."

His words set fire to my body, and my hips moved faster, my breaths breaking as orgasm coiled tight in my lower belly. "Goddess," I choked out, wrapping my hand around the back of his neck and clinging to him. "*Bakkhos.*"

As if he knew exactly what I needed, he tore his shirt over his head and pressed his whole weight down into me, skin to skin, his arms around me. Every part of him taut with need, he thrust against my pussy, the head of his cock sliding over my clit again and again.

My mouth opened on a wordless cry, and release exploded through me, making my back arch. My clit pulsed against his slick-drenched cock with every thrust he made over my sensitive nerves.

"Fuck," he rasped, stealing a messy kiss from my slack lips as I panted and stared, thoroughly dazed in the aftermath of my pleasure. "Fuck, Sunshine, I need you now."

I managed to nod, blinking at the ceiling above my head as Bakkhos gently removed my jeans from my ankles and slid his hands up my calves to my thighs, settling between them—and growling at the sheer amount of slick I'd produced. I was an omega; I couldn't help it, but I was still embarrassed by the volume of my need. At least until he ducked his head and dragged his tongue through my pussy, making deep sounds of pleasure as he lapped up my wetness. "I never thought I'd be lucky enough to be here," he breathed, licking his lips.

"Between my legs?" I asked, laughing softly.

"Licking the delicious pussy of my treasured omega mate."

I swallowed, not sure why my eyes began stinging.

"I think you're the goddess herself," Bakkhos said, gazing up at me. "That's the only explanation. You're too beautiful, too kind."

I flushed, rolling my eyes. "Says the man who's only met one woman."

He kissed my inner thigh. "I've met plenty of women—cruel women, callous women. None as good-hearted as you."

That compliment hit me harder than being called beautiful, and my smile was big enough to make my face hurt.

Here with Bakkhos, I could pretend the last twenty-four hours hadn't happened. My family hadn't attacked me, my dad hadn't killed me. I was just an omega, cherished by her alpha mate.

"Oh, Sunshine," Bakkhos murmured, sliding up my body and wrapping himself around me, kissing—oh, kissing the tears off my cheeks. I hadn't realised I was crying. "Everything's going to be okay now. We'll make sure of it."

Everything might feel better if he stopped subtly reminding me of the rest of his pack. I didn't want to think about the other alphas; not cruel Wild or intimidating Draven or powerful Kaan. Only *him*.

I reached between us and grasped his hard cock, drinking down Bakkhos's throaty groan. Nerves twisted up my stomach, but this felt right, my first time being here with him. I only hesitated a moment before I brought the tip of his cock to my entrance, catching my breath at my body's immediate response—to produce more slick.

Bakkhos pressed his face to my neck, gasping down my scent as I lifted my hips, taking him inside. I bit my lip at the stretch, surprised by the pressure of his girth against my inner walls.

"Holy fuck, Sunshine," he choked out, and my muscles squeezed. His hips made slow, rolling movements, and my heart warmed at my manic, desperate mate taking care not to hurt me as he slowly, gradually, filled me up. "Alright, Nixie?"

I nodded, my face warm and my body strange, so full. I liked the name, especially on his tongue, and sought his mouth with an edge of desperation, kissing him deep and urgently until his hips rested flush against mine and my eyes were wide.

"How does that feel?" Bakkhos asked, rough and gravelly. His moss green eyes were fixed on my face, heavy lidded and sensual, and his hands stroked up and down my body like he couldn't stop touching me. Every glide and caress had tingles moving through me, the rasp of his palms over my nipples making me moan. The steady path of his fingers past my stomach to my pussy made me tense in anticipation. The first sweep of his fingers over my clit had me shuddering, relaxing around his thick cock.

"Full," I managed to choke out, a smile impossible to resist when Bakkhos laughed, laying kisses all along my throat. His silken blond hair made more shivers sweep across me as it brushed my chest. Downstairs had gone silent.

"Painful?" Bakkhos asked, swirling his tongue over my throat now.

I could barely think with his tongue doing that, so close to the claiming spot, and my pussy throbbed around him. "Not much," I replied, staring at the ceiling with wide eyes, panting. "Can you ... can you move now? Please?"

Bakkhos replied with an alpha growl, a sound that resonated through the deepest parts of me, and his hot mouth frantically kissed from my throat down my collarbones to my chest, where he sucked a nipple into his mouth and did wicked things with his tongue. Without a vocal answer, his hips began to move in slow, rolling movements that made my face slacken in shock.

Oh, that was ... that sensation... "Yes," I groaned, clutching his back, his hair, anything to encourage him to continue.

My mate's answering growl brushed over me like a sweeping caress. I shuddered, so sensitive as he thrust deeper, withdrawing all the way before sinking in and making my hands frantically scrabble at his back. I hadn't expected to feel pleasure from my first time, but my climax was already rushing up on me, making me tighten around him. Because he was my mate, or because of how worked up all four alphas made me earlier?

"Nix," Bakkhos choked out, making my stomach squirm in the best of ways when he snarled a deep, desperate sound. He dragged his lips from my breast to my throat, his hips rolling faster, deeper, loud slapping sounds accompanying each thrust. "Oh, goddess, please—I need to bite you."

I nodded hard and fast, so many hormones and endorphins flying around my body, making me feel *incredible*. My instincts were a hundred percent on board with his plea, and it was suddenly everything I needed: to be bitten, to be knotted, to be *his*.

"Knot," I choked out, my pussy squeezing, already trying to milk a knot that wasn't inside me. I knew the stretch would be insane, knew it would be uncomfortable at first, but a deep, primal urge gripped me and would not let go.

"But your first time—" Bakkhos rasped, trembling hard above me, his tongue lapping at my throat now.

"Knot," I snarled, the demand coming from deep inside my chest.

Bakkhos swore and his hips jerked, thrusting deeper until every part of him was hugged by my sensitive walls, as if he was powerless to resist his omega's demand. I whined, writhing on him. He was so deep and *much* thicker now, and I was so full I could barely stand it. But that primitive, instinctive part of me purred—and so did I, a low rumbling sound that shook my chest as sweetly as any promise.

"Oh, *fuck*," Bakkhos choked out, his knot submerged—and swelling behind my pelvic bone, tying us together. Locking his cock deep inside me.

I writhed, squeezing fistfuls of his dark hair, pulling at

the sheets under me as the knot got bigger and even bigger, too much for me to take. Intent on driving me mad, it pressed on every sensitive nerve and blissful spot inside me until I couldn't think. Bakkhos choked on a sound halfway between a growl and a purr and wrapped both arms around me as his cock emptied inside me, sensitising already frazzled nerves until my toes curled and sensations fired erratically inside me.

I panted, tightening around his knot, right on the edge of pleasure and pain—but Bakkhos's fingers circled perfectly on my clit and I crashed off the edge into bone-melting pleasure.

My eyes rolled back, my body arched under him, and I came so hard I saw fireworks behind my closed eyes. My pussy squeezed his knot, milking more from my mate.

Drawing rough, whimpering groans from him. I arched my neck pointedly, and Bakkhos cursed, sinking his teeth into the claiming spot before I could even finish coming on his cock. The scream that tore from my throat was like no sound I'd ever made before, and though I'd had many orgasms before, this was ... there was nothing I could compare it to. Not even an electrical storm or a bomb's detonation or the ocean's fury could do it justice.

His knot pulsed inside me, dragging out my orgasm just when I thought it had ended, and making the sweep of his tongue over the bite even more sensitive. "You're incredible," he rasped, nuzzling my throat.

When I prised my eyelids apart to look at Bakkhos, he looked drugged and dazed, colour high on his inked cheeks and his eyes glassy. Keeping both arms wrapped around us, he rolled over, taking me with him so I was splayed on his chest, the knot keeping us together and dragging a gasp from my lips as it brushed an electric spot inside me.

I didn't have the words to reply to him; I just laid my head on his shoulder and breathed him in, still gasping.

"Sorry I didn't last longer, my Sunshine," he murmured, running his fingers through my hair, comfort striking so deep inside me that I went limp.

I shook my head, sighing against his neck. "No," I breathed. "Mine." It didn't make much sense, but it was the only reply I had.

Bakkhos laughed softly, brushing hair back from my scalp and making my toes curl. "Yours," he agreed, arching his neck to entice me. "Do you want to bite—"

I sank my teeth, sharp at the mere suggestion of marking him, into the thin skin of his throat, and groaned as the nectar of his blood coated my tongue. Any other blood would taste repellant except my mate's. I followed every crimson trickle with my tongue until his quick healing kicked in and sealed the two punctures. I was satisfied to see the two white scars on his throat that marked him as mated. "Mine," I growled again, the words coming from deep in my chest.

"Yours, my Sunshine," he agreed, scattering kisses across my shoulder.

It took a long, long time before I remembered how to think, and longer still until I could properly speak. Everything in my body felt *so good*, the orgasm—well, orgasms— wringing out every bit of tension and fear until I was as relaxed as I'd ever been. His touches and closeness filled an emptiness I hadn't even realised lived at the heart of my soul. I felt ... home.

"Luneste was right," I said, and found my voice scratchy.

Bakkhos's arms tightened reflexively around me, his knot still swollen and full inside me. It would be another twenty minutes until his alpha biology told him his seed had been effective. Not that I could actually get pregnant—female wolves needed to be in heat for that, and I was *far* from being in season. I thought. I'd never actually been in season before, had never responded enough to the males around me for my body's natural response to kick in. There were ways to force an omega into season, but thankfully my pack had never done that to me, however monstrous they'd been in sacrificing me to Luneste.

"Hmm?" Bakkhos replied, stroking long, exploratory touches down my side. "About what, Sunshine?"

"I *am* meant to be here. You are my fate."

His grin was big enough to crinkle every tattoo on his face, his happiness bursting through my chest like an explosion of light. I could *feel* how happy he was, and how pleasure had reduced him to boneless satisfaction. Oh, no—and how mischief wound through his happiness as he stroked my body.

"Your fate," he repeated, liking the sound of it if his emotions were anything to go by. In a strange flash, I heard soft, breathless words inside my head. *I don't know what I did to deserve you, my beautiful Sunshine, but I'll never stop thanking the Goddess for it.*

My heart melted. Was that ... were those his thoughts?

Bakkhos kissed my neck, right over the bite mark, and I swooned. "Do you know what else is your fate, my beautiful Sunshine?"

"What?" I smiled.

"To come all over my knot again." His lips crushed mine in another kiss, his fingers wandering to my pussy. "And again." I jolted, like lightning had struck me as he stroked my clit, still so sensitive. "And again."

"Goddess help me," I breathed.

Bakkhos just laughed.

8
NEVER

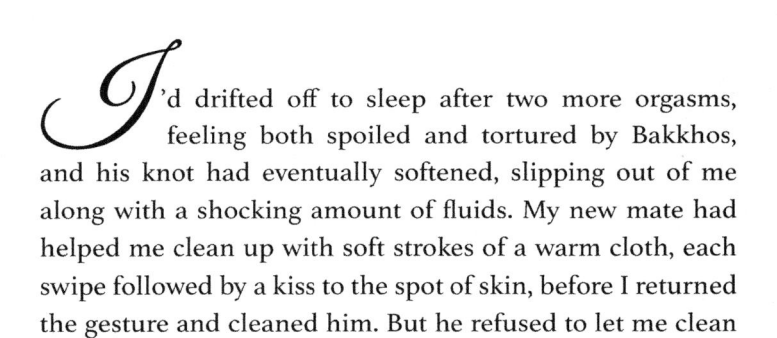

I'd drifted off to sleep after two more orgasms, feeling both spoiled and tortured by Bakkhos, and his knot had eventually softened, slipping out of me along with a shocking amount of fluids. My new mate had helped me clean up with soft strokes of a warm cloth, each swipe followed by a kiss to the spot of skin, before I returned the gesture and cleaned him. But he refused to let me clean his cock, snarling that he *needed* my scent on him, needed to feel my slick on his cock. I'd relented after a while, only because of the frantic edge to his expression.

The door opening woke me some time later, and my heart shot into my throat as a huge shadow filled the doorway. I reached for Bakkhos, about to shake him awake when Kaan's thunder-deep voice murmured, "It's alright, let him sleep. I thought you'd need something to eat and drink after —" He cut off, shook his head, and set a tray on the bedside table.

I clutched the covers to my chest, covering myself as Kaan took several steps back, as if he knew exactly how afraid I was. But everything I knew of cruel, dominant alphas didn't include them providing food and drink for their omega toy. I glanced from the tray to the huge alpha of alphas as he took a seat against the wall, folding his massive body up on the floor beside the door and resting his arms on his knees as he met my gaze.

"You brought me food," I whispered eventually, scanning his rough, bearded face by the light of the moon. He was harsh-looking, carved from brutal stone, but his dark eyes were steady and patient, a strange contrast to his sheer *size*.

"And antiseptic cream for your feet. I saw them bleeding earlier."

"Why?" Why was he doing this?

Kaan shrugged mammoth shoulders, and I half expected his tight blue T-shirt to rip. "I'm the alpha of this pack." He held my gaze. "Making sure you've got all the things you need is my job."

I nodded slowly. This, at least, I understood, and trusted was true. "What do you want from me?"

Kaan blew out a hard breath, scrubbing a hand down his beard. Moonlight caught the vines and thorns inked on his hands—intricate art unlike the scratchy drawings of Bakkhos's tattoos. "That's a hard question to answer. I'm an alpha first and foremost, so I want the best for my pack, and we ... we could use an omega around us. Someone to temper our harshness."

"And what if I don't want to? Will you let me go?" I reached slowly for the plate on the tray and brought the sandwich closer to myself, sitting up carefully so I didn't wake Bakkhos who slept with his arm thrown over me.

"Omega's are rare," Kaan said calmly, his massive body still and only his eyes moving as he tracked my wary movements. "I'm not sure we'd ever find another again."

"So I'm just a thing to you," I muttered, bitter even

though it was the reality of omegas everywhere. We were just things to be found, kept, and possessed.

"You'd have a roof over your head, and food always on your plate, and a pack to run with when you shift. We'd treat you well; I won't let any of these bastards hurt you, no matter how fucked in the head they are. You'd be hard pressed to find a better offer."

I scowled, focusing on the sandwich he'd made for me instead of his harsh face. He was right, and I hated it. I wanted more than being owned. I wanted ... freedom. Happiness. My own life. "I won't be owned," I hissed, but I bit into the sandwich, my eyes sliding shut as smoky cheese and fresh tomatoes burst across my taste buds. It wasn't the fanciest meal ever made, but compared to the crap my pack had been farming lately, it was heaven on a plate.

"You're no more owned than you own Bakkhos," Kaan replied, and I found him looking at the puncture scars on my throat. My mate bite.

Oddly protective of the bite, I covered it with my hand, finishing off half the sandwich and trying not to groan at how good it tasted.

"Whatever you think life will be like with this pack, *my* pack, you have it wrong," Kaan went on in a quiet rumble. He dragged his hand down his beard, and sighed. "My mum was an omega; I'm not about to hurt anyone who's like her."

I paused, watching him. Believing him. "You might not see it as hurt. I ... I have dreams, goals, things I want to be. I won't be chained to a bed like a slave for the rest of my life." Nevermind that I hadn't decided what those dreams and goals were yet, had never allowed myself to dwell on them.

His answering snarl had Bakkhos inching closer, his arm heavy across my lap. I shuddered, shrinking away from Kaan. "We'd *never* do that," he hissed ferociously.

He reined himself in with effort, his hands forming fists. "But you don't know that, so I'll try not to be insulted."

This was him trying? I blinked, watching him scratch his shaved head, clearly agitated.

"I won't deny that I never planned to let you go, but mistreating you was never part of the equation. I *always* planned to make sure you're cared for, and happy with your position in the pack. To make sure you have everything you need, so you'd never even *think* of leaving."

I didn't reply to that, contemplating everything he'd said as I ate the rest of my sandwich.

"So tell me, Omega, what do you need?"

I knew he was watching me, his eyes burning the side of my face as I set aside the plate and reached for the glass, sipping orange juice as my stomach suddenly decided it didn't want a sandwich after being empty all day.

What did I need?

"To not feel ... stifled," I replied quietly. "To not be controlled." I met his dark eyes and said, "I want to be my own person, and to ... to decide what I do, and when I do it."

I'd never had that luxury, but since we were putting offers on the table, I'd try my luck.

"Sweetheart," Kaan sighed, raking a hand over his skull. "Those are basic rights, not luxuries. That's all you want?"

My face hot, I glanced away and nodded. Embarrassment splashed among the cheese and bread in my stomach.

"Then you'll have it, all of it. And anything else you realise you need later." He pushed off the floor, stretching out his back after being scrunched on the floor. My eyes snagged on the silvery mark on his bicep—the crescent moon and star—and my breath caught.

There was the proof: he was my mate, too.

"No," Kaan replied, as if I'd said it out loud. His features shuttered, his calm, patient eyes now turbulent. "I'll be your alpha, but not your mate. Never your mate."

I recoiled as if he'd physically struck me, pain carving a hole in my chest, as brutal as the knife that had killed me.

Kaan took the tray from the bedside table and left before I'd recovered from the crippling pain. And I realised he hadn't even asked my name.

9

CORRUPTED

I woke up warm and comforted, with a sweet scent tickling my senses. A smile curved my lips when I remembered the night before with Bakkhos, his tenderness, his madness, his kisses, and his bite. I flinched away from thoughts of Kaan's rejection, wrapping myself in the heat of Bakkhos's affection instead.

I let out a sleepy groan as he pushed my thighs apart, scraping his teeth along my sensitive inner thigh. Goosebumps covered my skin where his cool hands held my legs wider, and I caught my breath as his teeth travelled closer to my pussy, changing to a sinuous tongue before his mouth reached my clit, rolling expertly over my bundle of nerves until it was swollen and aching.

He feasted on me until I was gasping, grabbing fistfuls of the sheets on either side of me, heat and tension binding into a tight cord in my lower belly. It was too late to fight the devastating force of my orgasm when I realised the sweet scent in my nose wasn't Bakkhos's wilderness and embers, but decadent honey.

I threw my eyes open just in time to watch Wild grin

against my dripping pussy, his golden eyes swimming with mischief and satisfaction. I couldn't fight the climax, not as he wrapped his lips around my clit and sucked, sending me hard and fast over the edge with a luxurious roll of his tongue on frazzled nerves.

I pressed my lips thin to trap my cry, refusing to give him the satisfaction even as my thighs trembled beneath his hands, my hips bucking off the bed when his tongue speared my entrance, swirling and deep.

"Goddess—" I choked, sick and disgusted with both him and myself, wishing I could stop my muscles clamping down around his tongue, wishing my body didn't go limp with relief and satisfaction.

"Get away from me," I hissed the second I stopped twitching, shoving his head away from me and trying to move back. But Wild tightened his hands on my thighs and laughed, a canine tooth poking free. "What are you doing?"

"I think that's quite obvious," he replied, as emotionless as the night before—completely and utterly empty. "I wanted to taste you."

So similar to Bakkhos's need the night before, but so different. Wild seemed ... entitled. Confident and heartless. No matter how Bakkhos defended him, I didn't feel safe with this alpha.

I kicked at his leather-clad shoulders, but that didn't dislodge his hold on me. It only made him smile deeper, sharper. He licked a broad stripe from my pussy—dripping with my own satisfaction—to my clit—aching and sensitive to touch. Completely undeterred by my struggles.

"I'm not just a—a *cunt*," I spat, reaching for my moonlight power and hoping it would burn him from the inside out. He deserved it. I shut out thoughts that reminded me this was how alphas were, this was accepted, encouraged even—alphas were dominant and brutal, they took whatever they wanted and never let it go. Never took no for an answer.

But some alphas were good and kind and took care of their partners. Wild had no excuse for being a heinous bastard.

He laughed. "And yet you *have* a cunt." He ducked forward and sucked my clit, dragging a sharp cry from my throat, and I forgot to fry him with my magic. "And a delicious one, too."

"Stop," I choked out, ignoring my own breathless whines for more. I couldn't help it, couldn't stop them clawing up my throat.

His mouth left my oversensitized clit and I exhaled hard in relief. But he crawled up my body to brush a lock of sweaty hair from my face, his tan leather jacket brushing cool shivers over my bare skin.

"Stop, Lilac?" Wild ducked his head to press a tender kiss to my cheek, and when he drew back there was so much feeling in his eyes that I caught my breath. It brought his angular face to life, made him human—*real*. He reminded me suddenly of Bakkhos, in that moment when his mania had peeled back to show the raw, shaky man beneath. "I wish I *could* stop, but I'm drawn to you. This mate mark here is impossible to resist." He ran shiver-inducing fingertips over my wrist where my crescent moon and star stood pale against my skin. "I need to be closer, I *need* you. You're my goddess-chosen mate, my beautiful other half."

I shuddered, frozen in shock as he kissed a trail up my throat to my ear. "*Or* are those all lies?" he asked with a cruel laugh.

"What?" I jerked in shock, getting whiplash as his tone changed *completely*.

"Maybe," he mused, scraping teeth down my throat—the opposite side to Bakkhos's bite, "I just want to ruin something so pure and pretty until you're as corrupted and messy as me. Or maybe that's a lie, too," he laughed, and I realised he was even madder than Bakkhos. But far, far crueler. If Bakkhos was a blunt weapon, Wild was a game of Russian Roulette.

"Stop," I growled pathetically, pushing at his shoulders, unable to gain purchase on his jacket. "Wild, fuck off."

"Or," he went on, pushing sharp teeth against my throat. A threat—the threat of a claiming mark. My omega went wild, and I wished I could say it was in outrage. But the wolf in me was *desperate* for those teeth to sink into my throat, convinced Wild was our mate, convinced the sun shone out of his malicious backside. "Maybe I'm just looking for any bit of sweetness in my pathetic existence, anything to drown out the nightmares of how I was broken."

I shook my head, dislodging his pained, raw voice. Lies—all of them fucking lies. "Get off me," I snarled, and successfully dislodged him this time. But his hand stroked my body, a claiming, proprietary touch as he looked at me with threats and cruelty cutting lines into his sculpted face.

"Next time I won't stop at tasting your pretty cunt," he said, so flat that I wondered how I'd ever fallen for his lies. "I'll take you here." Before I could squirm away, his middle finger was pushing inside my pussy, curling up until my mouth fell open and so much slick flooded from me that his hand was covered. My face burned with anger, and I kicked my feet out until they connected with his balls. But Wild didn't even react, as if he hadn't felt the pain.

"And here," he went on, sliding a wet finger to my asshole, circling the tight ring until I jumped up and shot across the room, dragging the sheets with me, feeling hot and shaky and desperate for touch—and dirty and used at the same time.

"I'll teach you to like it," he added, his sharp-planed face both empty and menacing. But as I stared, shaking, Wild jerked back, and something like horror wiped the emptiness from his face. His eyes flew wide, stricken.

He fled Bakkhos's bedroom before he could play through his final lie, whatever that charade was supposed to be.

Trembling, I crossed the carpet on weak legs and curled up in the bathroom with my back to the door, keeping it shut in lieu of the broken lock.

I didn't know what to make of anything that had just happened, but I knew all of Kaan's promises of safety were for nothing, and even Bakkhos's vow of protection was empty.

As long as Wild lived in this cottage, I'd never be safe. But if I left, my dad and brothers would find me.

I was trapped between a rock and a hard place.

10

CLEAN

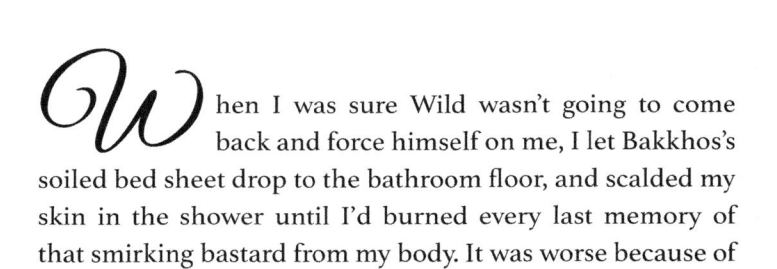

When I was sure Wild wasn't going to come back and force himself on me, I let Bakkhos's soiled bed sheet drop to the bathroom floor, and scalded my skin in the shower until I'd burned every last memory of that smirking bastard from my body. It was worse because of how readily my body responded to him, and how my wolf arched toward him, greedy for more.

When I was as clean as I was ever going to get, I towel-dried my hair, surprised at how well stocked Bakkhos's bathroom was. I couldn't picture my manic mate making sure he had enough towels and face cloths; Kaan, on the other hand, I could. He might have been the alpha of alphas, might have stabbed me in the mating bond, but I believed him when he said he wanted to take care of his pack. But then, I'd believed Wild until he laughed and tormented me.

I didn't have any clothes except the dirty, sweat-stained jeans, shirt, and jacket I'd run away from my pack in, so I rummaged through the pile of clothes on the chair in front of Bakkhos's window—his wardrobe?—and dressed in a pair of black sweatpants and the smallest top I could find: a grey T-shirt in the softest cotton I'd ever felt. I wished Bakkhos was here with me, but my stomach growled, hunger making itself painfully clear, and I dared to tiptoe out into the hall.

I knew I was welcome, at least, thanks to Kaan's visit last night, so I wasn't afraid they'd kick me out for wandering where I wasn't supposed to. Still, I had every reason to worry about the opposite—these broken alphas never letting me go.

The bottom stair creaked beneath my bare feet, and I held my breath, but no one came rushing towards me, so I crept down the short hallway. Running along it last night, I could have sworn the hall was endless, but there were only four doors—one into a man's bedroom, Kaan's if the scent of pine trees and whiskey was anything to go by. Everything was neat; every piece of clothing, every book, and every photo had its place. I closed the door softly, hoping I hadn't left a scent to tell him I'd been snooping as I looked in the next room—Wild's, and strangely empty of everything but a bed and chest of drawers. I left it quickly, his scent making me nauseated.

The next door opened onto a small storage room full of bags of vegetables and hunks of meat hanging from hooks to dry. I pilfered an apple and ate it quickly, in case I couldn't find anything else to eat in the kitchen. I had blurry memories of an open kitchen doorway as I sped past last night, a table and chairs cast in shadows.

Now, the room was bright with sunlight coming through the big window at the far end, and the chrome worktops to my right shone as if recently polished. The well-loved kitchen table in the middle of the room was piled with newspapers and bottles of spirits in various states of emptiness. I was relieved this space didn't smell of alpha, or any of their individual scents; instead a thick lemon scent hung over the room, clearing my lungs of Wild's sickly sweet honey.

I stepped into the room, intent on the fridge beside the cupboards, but I startled. "Oh," I breathed, spotting Draven's massively tall figure at the sink, washing his hands. He was dressed head to toe in black, his dark hair tied at his nape, strands of rich chestnut revealed in the daylight where last night it had looked pure black. "Sorry, I didn't know there was someone in here."

I waited for his reply—but there wasn't one. I frowned, tiptoeing around the table towards the fridge, slanting a look at the giant alpha from the corner of my eye. From this angle, I could see the profile of his ivory face, every line of his features tense and pained, and his deep blue eyes staring straight forward as he washed his hands.

"Draven," I gasped when I caught a glimpse of his hands: red and raw and bleeding. "Draven, *stop*."

Alarm gave me confidence, and I rushed over, catching his wrists to pull his hands out of the water. "You're bleeding!"

Draven startled as if out of a trance, and he sucked down a ragged breath, his sapphire eyes holding mine in shock. "You're touching me," he rasped.

I jumped at his honeyed voice, letting go of him.

"No, it's—I don't ... mind it." A furrow formed between his thick brows. "I usually do."

I still let go of him and stepped back, unable to drag my gaze from his hands for long. They wept blood, as if he'd been scrubbing for long, long minutes. "You should treat your hands," I said, responding automatically to the injury, and searching the various cupboards and drawers around us. "It'll get infected."

"It usually heals in a few minutes," he replied, watching my every move. "I'll be fine."

My heart jolted at one word in that sentence—usually. How many times did he wash his hands until he bled? I glanced away, hiding the way my heart broke for him, knowing pity would make him feel worse. One of the things I'd been good at in my pack had been helping our healer tend to injured and sick wolves. I knew exactly how to treat sores like this, and when I finally uncovered a green first aid kit under the sink, it was second nature to take careful hold of his wrists and dab off the blood with a wet cloth, smearing antibacterial salve on them before wrapping them in bandage. It was second nature, too, to not wound his pride by staring at him with aching sympathy, even if I wanted to.

"This is ... unnecessary," he protested quietly. Everything he did was quiet, reserved. But there was no forgetting that he'd grabbed me from the forest, thrown me over his shoulder, and hauled me here to hand over to his alpha like I was a shiny coin he'd found and called dibs on.

I let go of him the second the bandage was secure, flexing my hands as they tingled, the memory of his fingers against mine seared into my skin.

"You should be careful," I said, putting space between us, breathless at his proximity even as I yelled at myself that he was dangerous, scary, and had essentially kidnapped me. Even if he'd brought me to the place I was destined to be, he'd still grabbed me. "You'll hurt yourself permanently if you keep doing that." I jerked my chin at the sink, still trickling water.

As if noticing it, too, Draven twisted the tap until the water shut off, his fingers lingering, white knuckled on the metal. "I know," he replied finally, quiet and low.

I bit my lip, taking more steps away. "Can I ... can I get something to eat from the fridge? Since I'm living here now..."

Draven jerked his head in a nod, his dark ponytail brushing his shoulder as he glanced out the window, seeming to feel as awkward as I now did. I gladly opened the fridge, using the door as a shield. As I perused shelves of beer, cold meats, and cheese, I heard his question from the night before loud and clear.

What's that mark on your wrist?

Bakkhos had said they all shared the same mark—my mark. Which meant this silent, watchful giant was my mate, too. I bit my lip, painfully aware that he still loomed on the other side of the kitchen, watching me.

"Can I have this?" I asked, shy as I grabbed a bowl of potato salad. I didn't know who'd made it, or if the guys had plans for it, but my stomach growled at the scent of mayonnaise and herbs.

Draven nodded, turning his bandaged hands over and over.

I debated taking the tub of salad and fleeing, but I needed a fork, so I withstood his heavy stare and opened random drawers, my shoulder blades itching at Draven's attention. I planned to leave when I finally found the cutlery; I don't know what made me hold out my arm and say, "You asked me what this mark is. It's my birthmark."

Draven's deep blue eyes fixed to the spot, a wrinkle between his black brows as he nodded. "I knew it looked the same," he said, quietly like everything else he said.

"The same...?"

Draven's shoulders tensed, his whole body tightening in clear discomfort, and I backed up a step, knowing exactly how that felt, but before I could give him even more space, he grabbed the hem of his black shirt and pulled it over his head. "The same as this," he replied at barely a whisper, and laid a hand on his chest where a crescent moon and star three times the size of mine sat right over his heart.

I caught my breath, staring at my mark on his pale skin, and his chest heaved with fast breaths as the moment dragged out. I didn't know what to say, what to do with his obvious discomfort, so I just nodded and said, "It *is* the same."

He sucked in a breath, catching my gaze and about to say something when the front door thudded open. I jumped, reacting with instinctive fear and scrambling across the room to put my back to the wall.

"It's Bakkhos and Kaan," Draven reassured, seeing far too much.

I could feel the vicious point of the knife going into my chest, the bruises forming on my body as my dad and brothers held me still.

Draven frowned deeply, a furrow between his brows, but he just flicked the kettle on as Bakkhos and Kaan came noisily into the cottage. I watched the giant as he put coffee —a *lot* of coffee—in a mug more accurately described as a tankard. He didn't seem worried; I tried to tell my fear that, but it wasn't listening.

"Sunshine!" Bakkhos said with a massive grin when he spotted me, oblivious to my anxiety as he rushed around the kitchen table, shirtless with sweat shining on his ink-covered chest. I bristled, pressing my back into the wall, but when his arms came around me, all my fear fell away as safety wrapped me up.

It was deep and primitive, and logically it didn't make much sense. But Bakkhos was unbalanced and protective; I didn't know how well he could fight, but I knew he'd be unpredictable and crazed, and right now that equalled safety. I rested my head on his shoulder, and didn't even care that it was slick with sweat; that just made his scent fill all my senses with more reassurance.

"Good morning, my mate," Bakkhos said brightly, his green eyes glowing. He pressed a deep kiss to my mouth and turned to Draven. "Make me a cup as well, will you?"

Draven grunted. I couldn't tell if it was a yes or no.

"Um," I said, clinging to Bakkhos. "Could I have one too, please?"

"Yes," Draven replied quietly, getting two more mugs down from a shelf.

"What's with the bandages?" Bakkhos asked, spotting them as Draven began spooning coffee into mugs.

Draven's eyes slid to me, the expression on his face guilty, and then flitted back to the mugs.

"What did you do?" Bakkhos growled, his violence coming on suddenly and without warning. He pressed me behind him as he spun, a vicious snarl tearing up his throat and his whole body as tense as an iron rod.

"Bakkhos," I complained, pushing at his back. But he was immovable. He didn't stop growling.

Draven just stood there and accepted Bakkhos's threats, and my stomach sank at his submission. He should have been defending himself; he'd done nothing wrong.

Well, if he wouldn't defend himself, I would.

"Enough Bakkhos," I said, and wrapped his hair around my fingers, giving a sharp tug. "His hands were hurt and I bandaged them. That's all. And you were the one who said you're all my mates; why are you so mad that I touched him?"

Because I knew that was the crux of the matter. I'd had my hands on Draven, and Bakkhos's wolf was furious.

Bakkhos's snarl quietened, but his wiry body didn't stop shaking, and his teeth were still bared.

"It's not him you should be mad at anyway," I muttered. "It's Wild."

Bakkhos's growl cut off, leaving deadly silence in the kitchen.

It was Draven who took a furious step across the kitchen and asked, "What did he do?"

I swallowed, looking at the floor, my stomach suddenly spinning with sickness. I shouldn't have said that.

"Sunshine," Bakkhos murmured, gentling as he gave me his full attention, messily inked hands framing my face. "It's alright, Nixie, you can tell us."

"Nixie," Draven said, so softly I almost missed it.

My breath hitched, but I admitted, "I woke up and he was touching me. Licking me. I-I thought he was you." I met Bakkhos's manic green eyes and watched murder form there. "He was ... cruel."

"Did he hurt you," Bakkhos demanded gutturally, too flat to be a question.

I gnawed my bottom lip. "No, not really. But I told him to stop. He didn't."

Bakkhos took a sharp breath and pulled me to his chest again, his fingers tangling in my hair as he comforted me. I sank against him, sour that he hadn't been here when I'd needed him but relieved to have him now. I jolted as a mug slammed onto the counter, and I looked up in time to catch Draven's dark ponytail slashing the air as he stalked out of the room.

"Oh no," I breathed, my stomach crashing. "Bakkhos, I think Draven's going to do something stupid."

"Let him," Bakkhos growled, holding me tighter and

making me slump against him, safety crashing over me like a wave. "Wild deserves everything he gets."

But I thought of Draven's quiet intensity, how he saw everything, how in control he was—and the darkness I sensed in his soul.

And I thought he might kill Wild.

11

VIOLENCE

I pushed at Bakkhos's sweaty chest until he let me slip from his hold. My bare feet slapped the laminate floor as I raced out of the kitchen towards the living room, where I could already hear the dull thwacks of fists meeting flesh. No snarls, no growls—only impact, and a low rolling laugh. *Wild's* laugh.

My blood went cold, my skin icy as I skidded into the front room and saw Draven beating the shit out of Wild as the redheaded alpha curled up on the floor, his face split by a gleeful grin. There was something badly wrong with him, I realised. Not just broken—irreparable.

"Draven, *stop*," I breathed, faltering as I came close enough to see the look on his face. It was pure, frozen rage, his eyes glacial. Fear tripped down my spine, but my focus narrowed to the blood on Wild's lip and instinct propelled me forward. "Draven!"

I caught his arm before it could smack into Wild again, but he just used his feet instead, kicking *hard*, and Wild laughed, not even curling around his ribs to protect them.

"*Enough*," I snapped, a growl entering my voice. I

couldn't help it—an omega fury was rushing up on me at the sight of Wild's blood. My instincts either didn't know or didn't care that I hated him.

"Draven, man, stop," Bakkhos said, approaching behind us. But even he couldn't break the cold rage Draven had sunk into, and I inhaled sharply at the violent sound of something breaking in Wild's body.

"*Draven*," a thunderous voice roared, so full of an alpha growl that I stumbled back, breathing fast. A body-wide shudder made my knees weak, and I dropped to the floor before I knew what was happening, my cheek pressed to the rug and my ass presented in the air.

I gasped for air, curling my fingers into the fibers of the rug as the growl moved over my skin like a shiver. I needed his body on top of mine, needed his weight pressing me into the floor, needed him inside me, and I told him all of that in a whine.

"Sunshine," Bakkhos murmured, kneeling beside me and brushing hair from my face so he could see me.

"You—go cool the fuck off. And you—I don't know what you did, but you probably deserved it. Go clean up, " Kaan commanded, so deep that my toes curled and I gasped again. I didn't know who he spoke to, or if they listened. The only thing I cared about was that the growl came closer, the smell of whiskey, sweat, and alpha filling my senses and making my eyes roll back. Fuck, if I came into estrous now ... wait, why was that a bad thing? If I was in heat, this alpha, *my* alpha, would knot me. That was suddenly everything I wanted, and more important than breathing.

"Look at me, Omega," he rumbled, and I shivered hard, lifting my head off the floor. I jolted at the simmering satisfaction in his brown eyes, and flushed at the knowledge he was pleased that I'd presented myself.

But it wasn't a smile splitting his face; instead a frown turned down the edges of his mouth and twitched his dark beard. "Remember what I told you?" His eyes turned kind—and sad. I recoiled. "You can have Bakkhos, or any of the others, but not me."

"Kaan," Bakkhos snarled, shoving in front of me to get in his alpha's face. "What the *fuck?*"

"I mean it," Kaan replied, getting to his feet. His growl had softened, clearing the haze of need and instincts from my body, and now I was just cold. "I'll be her alpha, but not her mate. I don't want any of that."

My stomach cramped, but I pushed to my feet and looked anywhere but at Kaan, refused to let my hurt show. "It's fine, Bakkhos," I said, glad when my voice came out neutral. I made myself meet Kaan's gaze, swallowing the lump in my throat at the apology written across his face. "Really, it's fine," I insisted. "I'm just glad you seem like a good alpha. My last one—wasn't." There was no better way to put it.

Kaan's expression softened further, and he scrubbed a hand down his beard.

"So I'm glad to have you as my alpha," I finished, biting my lip.

Kaan gestured towards the sofa in the middle of the room, just behind the new bloodstain on the rug.

"Is Wild—alright?" I asked hesitantly, half of me hoping he was, the rest hoping he was suffering.

"He'll be fine," Kaan muttered. "Though I'd love to know what set Draven off, he's never like that."

"I did," I replied quietly, taking a seat and sighing as the soft leather swallowed me up. Kaan's gaze shot to me, surprised, as he slumped into one of the arm chairs while Bakkhos cuddled up to me on the sofa. "Wild touched me when I told him not to," I explained. "I felt ... uncomfortable."

That was putting it lightly. I'd felt sick. But also so good. And I hated him for making me feel both at the same time.

Kaan's brown eyes flashed, wrath carving lines in his face. "Where did he touch you?"

I sighed, crossing my arms over my chest.

"Tell him," Bakkhos snarled, pressing the full length of his body against my side and growling. I touched him absently, stroking his arm as it wrapped around me, the urge to comfort coming naturally.

I darted a glance at Kaan, who nodded encouragingly. With a rough sigh, I spat it out, "I woke up and he was licking my pussy. I tried to push him away, but he wouldn't let go, and he was ... cruel. He deserved to get hit, but what Draven did was too far."

"I'll talk to him," Kaan offered, a muscle fluttering in his jaw.

"You said I'd be safe." I hadn't meant to accuse him, but he'd *promised* me. "I didn't feel safe."

The second the words were out, I tensed, braced for an explosion of anger.

If I'd spoken to my dad that way, he'd have roared and forced submission until I stuttered an apology and begged for forgiveness. But Kaan just ran his hand over his head and broke our stare. Ashamed—guilty. "You're right, I did say that. And Wild hurting you is on me." He met my gaze, apology clear in his eyes. "We've been away from an omega for so long, we've forgotten how to behave, but that's no excuse. I'll make sure he asks permission next time."

"There won't be a next time," I muttered. "I'll cut his dick off if he tries to touch me again."

I froze, and my hand flew to my mouth as if I could reel

the words back in. But Kaan just laughed, appreciation in his gaze, and Bakkhos rumbled a purr as he snuggled closer.

Even when Kaan stopped laughing, the smile stayed on his face, and his eyes never left me. I tried not to let my stab of hurt at his rejection show, but it was hard when he looked at me like that. "I can't keep calling you Omega; what's your name, sweetheart?"

"Nixette," I replied, and felt a million miles from last night. I trusted *him* with this, with my name, even if I didn't trust Wild as far as I could throw him. "Nix."

Deep creases formed around Kaan's eyes as he smiled. "Welcome to the pack, Nix. I look forward to you castrating Wild."

Now it was my turn to be startled into laughter. It felt good—laughing, releasing all the wound up tension in my chest.

"I'll make love to you in his blood," Bakkhos murmured, as if that was a sweet, romantic thing to promise. I shot him an alarmed look and opened my mouth, but a loud ring tone cut me off, and Kaan huffed, sliding his phone out of his jeans pocket.

"Kaan," he answered, all low and growly.

My toes curled; I folded my legs under me on the couch and prayed neither of them had noticed.

Chills moved down my arms as his expression shifted, darker with every anxious second until his brows sat low over his eyes, his mouth pressed thin behind his beard. "I see," he said tightly. "Thanks for letting us know, Jon. I'll keep you updated."

"What?" Bakkhos demanded the second Kaan lowered his phone. His stress was infectious through the bond, and my hands started to shake.

"Magnolia pack have been spotted ten miles from here,

trying to cross Jon's packlands," Kaan replied, low and ominous.

"Why?" Bakkhos snarled, jumping off the couch to pace, his inked hands curled into fists. "What the fuck are they doing this close?"

"They're coming for me," a low voice replied, and I startled, leaning over the sofa back to see Draven slink across the room, his dark head ducked and his expression miserable. "I told you they would."

"They won't get any closer," Kaan promised, dark thunder in his voice. He shoved out of the chair and stalked over to Draven, clasping the taller man's shoulders. "And if they do, we'll tear them apart."

I nodded. I didn't know who Magnolia pack were, but they clearly threatened Draven, and the burgeoning embers of an omega fury flickered in my belly at the threat to my mate.

"Who are they?" I asked quietly, watching Draven flinch out of Kaan's embrace.

His dark blue eyes met mine, and I inhaled sharply at the depths of pain swirling in them. "My old pack," he rasped. "They want to be the only wolf pack, the master pack, and they eliminate any competition that stands in their way. They kill wolves." He paused, and dropped his gaze to the floor. "I was their assassin."

12

CORNERED

"What?" I breathed, standing from the sofa to stare at him. I'd thought Draven was terrifying when I first saw him in the shadows of the forest—as tall as a giant, with broad shoulders and a glaring face. But those brief minutes in the kitchen had changed my opinion. He was definitely tall and physically intimidating, but he was timid and quiet.

And ... he killed wolves.

"How many?" I asked, so focused on him that I barely saw how Bakkhos and Kaan reacted. Bakkhos hadn't exploded with rage and surprise, though, so he must have already known. The news was just for me.

Draven shrugged, his gaze pinned to the floor. "I don't know," he said quietly. "I'm sorry."

"They made him," Kaan interjected, his voice low and gentle. "They made you, Draven, you don't have to take full responsibility." The alpha of alphas held my gaze, challenging—or warning me to be careful with Draven. I swallowed.

Draven shrugged, flexing his hands at his sides. He

hadn't taken off the bandages, I noticed. That was good. "It doesn't change any of what I did. It doesn't make me less of a murderer."

Bakkhos threw his hands up, taking a step closer until Draven's eyes flashed with panic and he growled ferociously. I caught my breath at the savage sound, stumbling a step closer, my pussy dripping as the growl worked through my body at the worst possible moment.

"She made you do those things, man," Bakkhos said, undeterred. "You're being too hard on yourself. What choice did you have?"

Draven shook his head, such pain cut into his face that I'd walked around the sofa and was three feet away from him before I'd even blinked.

"Nix," Kaan warned softly.

"Who made you?" I asked, pitching my voice low and not taking my eyes off Draven for even a second. "But if it's too hard to talk about, you don't have to," I added quickly.

His dark head shot up, confusion cutting through the pain. "Why are you so considerate of my comfort?" he demanded, suspicious.

"Because she's your mate, you big lug," Bakkhos huffed, shaking his blond head.

I smiled, his snarky charm impossible to resist. But I nodded at Draven. "I am. And that means I'm worried about you, even though we've only just met."

His mouth pinched, his distrust not fading at my words. But I understood every single thing about him when he hissed, "That's what she said, too, but she *lied*." He bared his teeth, looking like a cornered prey animal. "She said she was my mate, and she'd take care of me, but she forced a bond and made me her *killer*."

My hand flew to my chest, horror like a shooting star

through my emotions. I took another step without meaning to, and then rushed out an apology and moved back again when he stiffened. But I held out my hand so he could see my wrist. "This is real. We have the same mark, remember?"

My shock wore off to reveal a seething core of rage, protectiveness, and—insecurity. Jealousy. This forced mate had made him so suspicious of the mate bond, *any* mate bond.

Did he even want ours?

If he didn't, I wouldn't push him. I'd keep my distance, no matter how badly my instincts urged me closer.

Draven was shaking his dark head, denying our bond even though minutes ago he'd shown me his own mate mark, too lost to nightmares and memory now. I knew what that was like.

"Kaan's right," I said, swallowing my own trauma. "If they come close, we'll tear their pack apart. She won't get anywhere near you. I promise."

I didn't know why I did it, but I held out my hand, my pinky extended, and my bottom lip threatened to wobble when Draven looked at my hand like it was a miracle. His own little finger wrapped around mine—although little was relative—and dark blue eyes boring into my own.

But when he let go, he turned without a word and stalked away.

13

SWEET

Kaan insisted on officially making me a member of the Broken Pack—as they called themselves—so that night I stood in front of the mirror in Bakkhos's bathroom—the door now back on its hinges—and curled my hair with straighteners Bakkhos had stolen from Wild. I'd already put on a dress Kaan had stolen from some poor human's washing line in the nearby village, the soft emerald cotton clinging to my shoulders and chest before flaring at the hips in a flattering skirt.

I felt ... pretty. It wasn't a luxury I'd ever expected to have while on the run from my old pack.

Luneste hadn't spoken to me again, but that wasn't unexpected. Most people went their whole lives never hearing from the goddess, but not only had I spoken to her in a dream place, she'd gifted me her moonlight. It sat in my chest, like a sea of cool mercury alongside the warm glow of my bonds—Bakkhos's being the loudest and brightest. I smiled as amusement cracked through the bond now, and strained my ears for the sound of his high, manic laughter.

He didn't scare me anymore. Neither did Kaan mostly

—no, whenever I looked at him, all I felt was a searing lance of pain at his rejection. But he was a good alpha. The best I'd ever known actually. He hadn't growled anyone into obeying him, hadn't struck anyone who pissed him off, and he'd been true to his word and spoken to Wild. The bastard had given me a wide berth all day, thank the goddess.

I sent a quick prayer up to Luneste, thanking her for guiding me here as I curled the last strand of hair, switching off the hot straighteners and brushing my fingers through the curls until I was happy with how they looked. There was no makeup I could use to cover a blemish on my jaw, no liner I could use to make my eyes pop, but I was happy with the dress. And looking at myself in the mirror, I realised I was nervous—and excited.

I was being made an official member of a new pack. A pack who wouldn't sacrifice me for better crops and fertility. A pack who wouldn't drag me out of my safe space even when I screamed for them to stop. I'd only known Kaan a day, but no way could I picture him doing what my dad had done to me. And no matter how many times he rejected me, he was still my mate—there was still a soul bond there, and he *couldn't* harm me.

I was as safe as I was ever going to get.

Even with Wild in the same house. Even with Draven's demons torturing him, making him liable to snap in warning and fear.

It was the safest I'd felt since my dad and brothers came for me. I didn't know how long the safety would last, especially with Draven's pack circling, but I was going to make the most of it while I had it.

A knock on the bathroom door had me straightening, and I glanced over, smiling when I saw Draven leaning uncomfortably against the doorframe. "Kaan said to come and get you. It's time."

I gave him my brightest smile, intentionally meeting his eyes, doing everything I could to tell him I didn't hold his past against him and I understood him now. "Thank you, Draven."

I paused, realising his dark hair was unbound, falling across the shoulders of his dress shirt. "You look nice. You didn't have to dress up, it's just a ceremony."

"I did." He met my eyes, hesitant but steady. "It's an important night."

"I think so, too. I'm glad I'm part of your pack now."

He nodded, and turned. I almost missed his quiet, "So am I."

"Draven, wait," I called, hurrying into Bakkhos's room after him, physically forcing my arm back down when I began to reach for him.

His shoulders stiffened as he turned, and he didn't readily meet my eyes this time, instead staring at his boots.

"I just wanted to say thank you for telling me what you did earlier. I know it couldn't have been easy; I struggle saying what my family did to me, so I get it. I don't hold any of it against you, and something tells me you don't do any of that anymore."

"No," he replied fiercely, locking eyes with me. "Never."

I nodded, smiling gently. "That says more about you than anything you were made to do." I held out my hand, unwavering. "Walk me downstairs?"

Draven blinked, his throat bobbing. "You're not afraid of me?"

"No," I replied firmly, tilting my head back to look at him when he stepped closer, taking my hand. My toes curled in my stolen shoes when his massive hand wrapped around mine, warm and dry and comforting beyond belief. "Not at all."

His gaze ducked to our joined hands. No—to the crescent moon on my wrist. "It feels different with you. The bond. It's strange, but—" He shook his head, dark hair dancing across his face. "All I feel is affection and comfort. My first bond felt like barbed wire in my chest."

"And our bond doesn't feel like barbed wire?" I asked hesitantly.

There was nothing but raw vulnerability when he peered down at me. "It feels like when you touched me earlier." He held up his other hand, still bandaged. "When you were kind and gentle."

Were softness and kindness really so alien to him? My chest ached, but I put on my biggest smile. "I'm glad it doesn't hurt you," I said, squeezing his hand. "And I don't think I said earlier, with my head still messed up by Wild, and then everything that happened after, but I'm Nixette Tulay. Nix."

Draven mirrored my gesture, squeezing my hand, and my heart turned to sap in my chest. "It's good to meet you, Nix. I'm Draven Rivas."

Slowly, giving him chance to back away at any point, I rolled onto my tiptoes and kissed the arch of his cheekbone before dropping back to the floor. "It's good to meet you too, Draven. Why do you smell like cherry?"

He laughed abruptly. "Do you want one?" Before I could reply, he slipped his hand into his pocket and produced a wrapped sweet. I grinned, letting go of his hand only long enough to unwrap it and pop it in my mouth before I entwined my fingers with his again.

"Always," I replied around the hard candy. "I always want sweets."

Draven laughed, his deep blue eyes twinkling a shade lighter as he watched me, the tiniest smile on his face. "We should go. Kaan will be impatient."

"Lead the way, Draven Rivas," I said, running my thumb over his knuckles, the bandage rasping against my skin. Draven gave me one last smile before leading me downstairs, to the ceremony that would make me part of the Broken Pack forever.

14

CEREMONY

*B*akkhos, Kaan, and Wild were waiting in the field around the cottage, the moon bright overhead. A weight dropped off my shoulders as the moonlight bathed my skin, amplifying the pool of magic inside me until it ebbed with a gentle current.

I was glad to have my magic when my eyes fell on Wild, looking careless and edgy as he leaned against a tree and scowled at the ground. He'd made a scant attempt to dress up, his auburn hair brushed sleek, and he wore dark wash jeans and a charcoal shirt left unbuttoned over his bare, sculpted torso. I glanced away at the dark, mottled bruising and the deeper, older scars all over his chest, ignoring the twist that went through my chest, through my soul, and all the way to the insidious bond that stretched between us.

He didn't deserve my sympathy.

My eyes found Kaan instead, standing in the middle of the clearing watching me, his brown eyes intense as they travelled from my curled hair to my face, and then down my body, to the hint of thigh my dress showed. He glanced suddenly away, his throat bobbing, and a sharp pain twisted my chest. He was attracted to me, but it wasn't enough. He still didn't want me. Like Draven, Kaan wore a smart shirt and trousers, and the attire took him from rugged alpha to dangerous male, cultured and powerful. I shuddered—and growled at myself to stop pining for what I'd never have.

"Ready to be part of the pack for real, Sunshine?" Bakkhos asked, bounding through the long grass to me as Draven and I crossed the clearing to where Kaan stood.

"Definitely," I agreed, banishing all thoughts of my old pack, of Kaan's rejection and Wild's unwanted attention as I grinned at my mate. I was becoming part of a pack that wouldn't kill or sacrifice me, that had promised to shelter me. No matter how today had started, tonight was a good night.

"I didn't even growl at Draven for holding your hand," Bakkhos said, his eyes wide and luminous. "Are you proud of me, Nixie?"

"Very," I agreed, my stomach erupting with butterflies as Bakkhos took my other hand, surrounding me with solidarity and protection.

It felt right having Bakkhos and Draven on either side of me, like we were always meant to be here, side by side.

With them holding my hands, I didn't balk at the full weight of Kaan's stare when he stepped closer, settling his hands on my shoulders. "Ready?"

I nodded, butterflies tumbling through my belly as his thumbs stroked the base of my neck, as if he couldn't help it. "I'm ready."

I'd never been officially made a member of my old pack, I'd just been born into it, but I knew what to expect. I couldn't keep the smile off my face.

"You'll have to let her go," Kaan pointed out, raising an eyebrow at Draven and Bakkhos. Draven squeezed my hand

and stepped back instantly, and I flexed my hand, mourning the loss of his touch. But Bakkhos stubbornly hung on.

"Bakkhos," I laughed, giving my crazed alpha an amused glance. He could dress as smartly as he wanted; there was no concealing his passion or obsession. "You can let go; I'm not going anywhere."

He grumbled, but pressed a kiss to my cheek, breathing me in, and stalked away a few steps.

I had to physically stop myself from biting my lip as I met Kaan's gaze again, the butterflies swarming nervously now.

"You know what to expect, Nix?" he asked, in that low, growly voice that made my breath catch.

"Yes," I replied, and there was no hiding the ache of longing in my voice. Hopefully he'd just think I was wistful for my new pack.

Kaan's brown eyes crinkled with a deep smile. "Then kneel, Nixette."

My next exhale was shaky, and I hoped he couldn't scent the sudden trickle of slick between my thighs as I knelt in the grass before him, my head ducked respectfully. A pack bonding ceremony was so similar to wedding vows that I couldn't stop my heart sprinting, aching in my chest for something I'd never have.

You can have Bakkhos, or any of the others, but not me.

I shook myself. *Focus on the ceremony, on your pack, on your future.* Because I had a future now. My dad and brothers had tried to smother it when they'd ended my life, but my life stretched out in front of me, filled with promise.

It was that thought that made me sit up straighter, my lungs full of forest air and my soul brimming with hope.

"Luneste, Goddess of Wolves, witness the joining of Nixette Tulay to the Broken Pack," Kaan began, his voice deep and clear, filling the clearing beside the cottage. "Nixette, under the light of the moon, do you swear loyalty to the Broken Pack?"

"I do," I breathed, keeping my focus on the future and not the past—not his former words, not my murder, only the bright future, shining teasingly just out of reach.

"Will you defend your packmates above all others?"

I didn't let myself flinch or hesitate, even if packmates included Wild. "I will."

"Will you run with us under the full moon's light?"

"I'd be honoured to," I replied honestly, and felt a pulse of affection through one of my mate bonds. I couldn't tell whose.

"Do you swear never to harm or endanger your packmates?"

"I swear." Rage bubbled up at the thought of my mates hurt, and I had to force a breath in through my nose and out through my mouth to clear the red haze.

"Will you trust your alpha, and obey every command I give you?"

I swallowed, ignoring the way my body heated. "I will," I promised.

Even if it hurt, I would.

There was a smile in Kaan's voice when he said, "Then welcome to the Broken Pack, Nixette." I jumped as a gentle touch ran over my head and through my curls. "You can stand, sweetheart."

I'd done it. I was one of their pack now, a broken wolf, too. I scrambled to my feet and, ignoring the pang in my chest, threw my arms around Kaan's broad shoulders. "Thank you," I murmured so only he could hear. "I'll never forget it and I'll always be grateful."

His hand pressed to the small of my back, holding me close for a second before he let go. I made myself step back.

The adoring look on his face almost undid me. He didn't want me, I reminded myself. He'd been very clear, and deluding myself otherwise would only hurt me more. "We're lucky to have you," he replied finally, his smile quiet and gentle and just for me. At least until Bakkhos let out a loud whoop and grabbed me around the waist, lifting me into the air, and Kaan's small smile bloomed into an amused grin.

I yelped and clung to my crazed mate as he flung me into the sky, never once letting me fall. Elation burst through my chest, and my face hurt from smiling so wide. I was theirs now—officially. I had a pack, a home.

Even if Kaan didn't want me and Wild wanted me too much, it felt good to have a pack—a good pack, worthy of all the things I'd vowed to do. I wouldn't let Draven's old pack threaten us, no matter how dangerous and evil they were. I wouldn't let them take my new pack from me.

15

RIVAL

We'd celebrated a little too hard the night before, so I woke up with a pounding headache, my eyes glued together, and a scratchy rasp in the place of my voice. We'd all passed out in Draven's room of all places, with Bakkhos wrapped around me, Draven snoring at my back, and Kaan splayed like a starfish beside Bakkhos. Wild slept on the bottom of the bed, touching only my ankle, as if to prove he was respecting Kaan's orders. But it felt more like a pointed show than anything genuine. I'd lost track of the amount of lies he'd told last night when he was drunk.

He was a businessman, he'd sailed with pirates, he'd killed an alpha, he'd domesticated a pack of hyenas, he was friends with Elon Musk, he was a talented painter. I stopped believing him after the second lie—he was in love with Bakkhos—and I doubted I'd ever believe a single word that came out his mouth ever again.

But at least he was keeping his distance. For now.

I was the first one awake, so I tried not to jostle them as I squirmed out from under Bakkhos's arm, climbing awkwardly over Draven and praying he didn't wake to me straddling his waist. Successfully free, I gave a silent fist pump and tiptoed out of the room—wincing at the tiny squeak of the door and relieved when they kept breathing deeply—and I padded down the hall to the upstairs bathroom.

Other than curling my hair yesterday, it was the first time I'd had to myself since I got here, and I wanted to take full advantage of it. After I'd seen to my needs, I went quietly downstairs to the kitchen and made myself a strong cup of tea, and then—feeling strangely peaceful—I leant against the window and stared out at the clearing where I'd been made an official pack member.

I hadn't realised how unmoored I'd been, being pack-less, but the stability of belonging to this pack, however broken they were, was like a weight taken from my shoulders.

With caffeine in my system and the sun staining the clearing a beautiful lilac colour, I was even willing to give Wild a second chance to prove he was a decent wolf being. It would make living with him easier if I didn't despise him constantly.

I'd finished my tea and was about to hunt down some breakfast when a shadow caught my eye, moving swiftly through the trees on the far side of the clearing. The hairs on my arms stood on end, and a low growl shook my throat. It was too big to be a rabbit or fox or some other animal who lived in the forest, and I was on full alert, painfully aware of my pack sleeping, vulnerable, upstairs.

I stood there only long enough to be certain the shape was human before I slammed my cup down on the windowsill and took off running upstairs, my snarl growing in volume. I wasn't careful to be quiet this time; I slammed the bedroom door open, and all four of my pack lurched upright. It was Kaan I looked to first, instantly alert and already climbing out of bed.

"There's someone outside," I hissed, my lip pulled back from my teeth and my instincts raging.

Kaan set a hand on my shoulder, meeting my eyes as he pushed past me into the hall. "We'll be fine, Nix," he promised, holding my gaze until my heartbeat steadied and I could take a full breath. But nothing silenced my growl.

"I know," I replied, my heart beating so, so fast. "I'm going to make sure of it."

Wild chuckled under his breath as he squeezed past me, shirtless with his red hair rumpled. "Fearsome little omega, aren't you?"

I met his gold eyes with nothing but violence. "Now's not a good time to be taunting me, Wild," I warned, and he blinked.

"Nix, I want you to stay inside with Draven," Kaan said, heading down the hall as the rest of us rushed after him, Bakkhos dragging on sweatpants and Draven as silent as a grave. "Protect him," Kaan added, meeting my gaze with a stern look as I opened my mouth to argue.

I straightened my back and nodded. "Yes, alpha."

His gaze softened, but as we emerged downstairs and the scent of a wolf—far closer now—hit us, nothing but unyielding wrath filled his gaze. "Wild, go out first. Distract them. Bakkhos, you go left, I'll go right."

Bakkhos's ink-covered face lit up with glee. "My pleasure," he purred.

Wild just laughed under his breath, shaking out his freckled hands as he raced for the door.

"Oh, and Nix?" Kaan added, turning to me just before Wild threw open the door. "Don't be alarmed when you see fur and fangs. The Broken Pack has always been favoured by the goddess; we don't need the moon to shift. And now, neither do you."

I jolted, staring at him as he and Bakkhos hurried out the door after Wild. To face a rival on their own lands. I twisted my hands in front of myself, and prayed they wouldn't return covered in blood.

16

SCOUT

"He was joking, right?" I asked Draven, caught between looking at him for confirmation and watching Kaan, Bakkhos, and Wild stalk out the door into the overgrown clearing.

"No, Nixie," he replied a second before snarls and roars filled the light morning air. "He wasn't."

I stared, a chill of surprise moving through my body as three *wolves* ran into the trees on the other side of the clearing. The man, whoever he was, didn't rush out to fight them; he turned and fled. But I couldn't stop staring at the *wolves*, one sleek and silver, one rangy with reddish fur, and the leader—Kaan—pitch black and twice the size of the others.

"But they're wolves," I breathed, shivering when Draven lightly touched my arm. "How?"

"Kaan told you," he reminded me quietly, his eyes tense and narrowed on the clearing. "Luneste."

I locked eyes with him, processing that fact. "So we're all ... chosen by the goddess?"

"For whatever reason," he agreed, a shadow chasing

across his face. "I understand why she'd choose you, but what makes the rest of us worthy?"

"That," I replied, an ache in my chest. "The fact that you'd even question it is what makes you worthy." I looked at Draven closely, seeing the shadows under his eyes, the tightness around his mouth. "Are you okay?"

His gaze drifted past me, to the trees our packmates had vanished into. "I'm fine," he replied.

He wasn't, but I didn't push him. "You're not alone," I offered instead. "I'm here with you."

"You want to run out after them," he countered, a corner of his mouth twitching up. "I can sense your restlessness."

"What if they're hurt?" I bit my lip, hovering on the threshold of the cottage, my feet itching with the need to run. A bird flitted from tree to tree, barely rustling the branches, but my wolf was so close that I heard its steps.

"They won't be," Draven replied, daring to touch my arm again, the bandage still wrapped around his hands rasping over my skin. "Kaan won't let them be."

I made a sound in my throat. "It's Kaan I'm worried about—and Bakkhos. I couldn't give a shit about Wild. He can rot out there for all I care."

Draven raised an eyebrow, his sapphire eyes inquisitive. "You don't mean that."

I shrugged. "I'm glad you hurt him. I think you were too harsh on him—"

"I don't," Draven cut in, his voice so deep I shuddered.

"But I wasn't sorry to see him hurt."

Mostly.

Only partly.

"He's your mate," Draven replied quietly, a furrow between his brow.

"Not if I don't accept him," I muttered, crossing my arms. "Are you afraid? Because of your old pack?"

Draven straightened, shutters coming down across his expression. "I told you, I'm fine."

I nodded. "Then I'm going out there." I took a deep breath, feeling for the tangle of power in my gut where my fangs and fur lived. "Are you coming?"

True excitement shimmered in Draven's eyes, taking them from deep sapphire to bright cashmere. "After you, Nixie."

I got the impression he liked calling me that, and I flushed. Draven might have been the wolf who'd grabbed me and hauled me into the cottage, but I felt safe with him unlike anyone else. It was a good feeling, and made the tension drop from my shoulders as I walked out into the clearing, dew-stained grass damp on my bare feet and the smell of living things heavy in the air.

All it took was a little tug on that knot of power, and a deep shiver ran over my body, shifting magic wrapping me in its cocoon. There were always a few seconds of darkness and light where I remembered nothing, but then I was tumbling to the ground on four paws, my legs stiff and aching and my back sore. But the expanded senses and the sense of being truly *alive* were more than enough to make up for them.

Coarse fur slid along mine, a powerful caress brushed down my whole side, and a low whine of pleasure formed in my throat, echoed by Draven's soft chuff.

Nix? Didn't I tell you to stay inside the house with Draven?

I jumped, the packbond so new and raw for me that I wasn't used to hearing their voices and feeling their emotions. Kaan was only mildly irritated with me, but absolutely *furious* with the intruder on his property. Bakkhos thrummed with excitement and chaos. Wild ... I didn't want to feel Wild's glee. And Draven, gentle giant that he was, was heavy with apology and nervousness.

I swore to defend my packmates above all others, I replied, my mental voice tentative as I got used to the voices and emotions rushing all around my head. It had been so long since I'd shifted with my pack—healthy wolves shifted every full moon, but malnourished, starving wolves struggled to shift at all. Feeling them so close, all packed inside my mind, was overwhelming.

And yet it felt right—and so damn good. I was with my pack, where I belonged.

You also swore to obey your alpha's command, Kaan replied with a rumble.

I ... I faltered, grass rustling as I padded across the clearing to where I could feel them, deeper in the trees. *That was a command?*

I couldn't hide my confusion, or how he'd thrown me completely off.

Draven brushed against my side, comforting me with touch, and I bumped my snout against him in thanks, blinking at the burst of surprise and warmth through the open packbond.

Yes, Nix, Kaan replied, starting to get irritated with me. I shrank back, braced for pain to spike my head and chest. But ... it didn't? *That was a command, and when I give you one, I expect you to follow it.*

But ... you didn't growl. It didn't hurt.

I felt his reaction—and the others' too. It was instantaneous, a recoil in my head followed by anger and shock, sympathy and violence. I shrank further, creeping through the trees and keeping my eyes open for more intruders.

We'll talk about this at home, sweetheart, Kaan replied, far softer. *Hang back when you reach us, don't come close. Draven —make sure she doesn't get hurt.*

Yes, alpha, Draven replied instantly, purpose pouring through him.

Was that a command, too? I struggled to keep up, Kaan's leadership so wildly different from my father's that it confused the hell out of me. But I'd figure it out; I'd do anything to stay with this new pack, with my alpha who didn't cause pain to get obedience.

Got him, Wild announced. His voice was full of a wicked grin even mentally, and I shuddered, remembering the way he'd looked at me with victory and satisfaction yesterday morning, refusing to let go of me.

Draven rumbled a growl, so surprising that I jolted out of my thoughts and looked at him, his wolf bigger than mine with smoke grey fur and splotches of white across his belly and neck. Like his human form, his eyes were the deepest blue, so deep I could fall into them, and full of pain and fury.

I'm going to kill him, he promised, bumping his head into mine and sending butterflies spinning through my belly.

No, you're not, Kaan said at the same time I laughed and said, *Good.*

Nix, Kaan huffed.

Bakkhos just cackled, wild and crazed.

Don't kill the intruder, Kaan growled at Wild. I could sense their exertion as they ran, and I pushed my own body faster. It felt amazing to run, with trunks and deep green leaves whipping past me in a rush of sound and colour, my paws barely even touching the ground before I flew into my next step. Everything smelled rich and alive and new, not like my old dying lands, and I inhaled greedy breaths of it.

Draven's tongue lolled out of his mouth as he matched

my pace, his happiness spinning through the pack bond and infecting me until my own chest was light.

Flashes of anger, determination, and fierce protectiveness came through the pack bond as the guys reached the enemy on our grounds, and then to my relief, Wild's emotions left the packbond as he shifted back to human, quickly followed by Bakkhos and Kaan.

Thank you for coming with me, I said, now it was just me and Draven.

He bumped my side as we ran, the touch of fur to fur sending deep pleasure through my body. His scent was amplified in this form, a rich earthy scent mixed with the coffee he was always drinking, and I drew it deep into my lungs, calm and safety wrapping me up as we sped through the forest. Draven took the lead now, guiding me through his packlands—our packlands—in a blur of dawn light, vibrant plant life, and natural beauty.

Shit, he hissed, halting deep in the forest and turning to herd me back, to stop me before I saw—before I saw the dead man carved up on the mossy floor, his body in four different pieces, and Wild laughing at the top of his lungs as he rolled in blood pooled on the grass, coating his naked body in glistening red.

17

BLOODBATH

Horror shot through me like a rocket, and I couldn't hide it, rearing back a step on unsteady paws.

It's alright, Draven soothed. *He won't hurt you.*

By his tone, that was because Draven would sooner kill him than let him touch me. And given the vows he'd made to protect our pack, that meant a lot. I took a steadying breath, ignoring the trembling in my body as I dared to lean against Draven's bigger wolf form, taking a moment of comfort before I tugged on my shifting magic.

Blackness and light surged around me as my body shifted, and when I blinked my eyes again, I was slumped against Draven's body, his fur deliciously tantalising on my naked skin. I rubbed against him, loving the sensation, before I caught myself and tugged away with a blush.

Conscious of my nakedness, I climbed to my feet, padding hesitantly across the tree roots and grass until I reached Kaan's side. He stood on the edge of the bloodbath, his big, tattooed arms crossed over his chest and his tan skin bared. I tried not to whimper at every muscle on display, at every cord of strength and every curve of power. I didn't let my eyes drop lower than his stomach, knowing I'd be on my hands and knees on the floor again. I wouldn't make a fool of myself again, no matter what my omega instincts thought of the matter.

"Shouldn't we stop him?" I asked, watching Wild cover himself in blood, laughing like a hyena.

"No, let him get it out of his system," Kaan replied, deep and shiver-inducing. His throat bobbed as he swallowed, and he didn't look at me either. I wrapped my arms around myself, self consciousness making the back of my neck burn. At least until Bakkhos rushed across the path and threw his arms around me, squeezing me so tight my feet lifted off the floor. "He's not really here," Kaan finished, sending a chill down my spine.

Where was Wild then?

I watched the cruel alpha until I was gritting my teeth, his laughter higher and so much worse than Bakkhos'. At least there was an intelligence to Bakkhos's manic cackles. Wild ... maybe Kaan was right; maybe he wasn't really here.

The impulse to comfort him twisted my stomach, but I pushed it off. He didn't deserve it. No matter how heavily worry weighed on my chest.

"Mmm, you feel good pressed against me like this," Bakkhos murmured, his body scorching hot against my back and his erection hard against my backside. His hands only wrapped around my middle, though, instead of wandering.

"Control yourself," Draven muttered, stalking up beside him.

My eyes went right to his cock. I jolted hard, dragging my eyes away, but the damage was done: I was throbbed, slick trickling down my thigh until Bakkhos groaned, pressing his tongue to the vein in my throat. Draven's cock was bigger than Bakkhos's, and so much thicker that I was glad he hadn't been my first. But even my nervousness at taking something that size didn't stop my heartbeat quickening or my pussy clenching harder, more arousal dripping from me.

"Sorry," I rasped, ducking my head.

"You're an omega, Nix," Kaan replied instead of Draven. "You don't have to apologise for being aroused by us; it's what your body was born to do." His hand slid over my shoulder, squeezing, and my toes curled in the grass. I couldn't stop the whine building in my throat, but I trapped the words—*please, alpha*—before they could escape. "You never have to be ashamed," he finished.

I nodded, even as my face burned, and I flinched when Wild's laughter shattered into unhinged giggles. My eyes were drawn to him, to the pronounced curve of his spine as he bent over his knees in the grass, his flame-red hair a mess around his face. Blood splashed his body in crimson smears. He didn't care about the dismembered pieces of the man scattered around him, his face bludgeoned until no features were recognisable.

"What's wrong with him?" I asked, my eyes drifting to Kaan for answers.

The alpha of alphas shook his head. "Some things are not mine to tell. He's reliving something is all I'll say. I can't bring him out of it." The look he gave me was pointed, and I glanced away, glad when Bakkhos's hands began to wander just for a distraction.

But you could, that look said. *As his mate, you could bring him out of it.* But Wild didn't deserve a mate if he was just going to take and demand and hurt, never giving me anything in return. I might have been an omega meant only for sex and breeding, but I had *some* self respect.

"I can smell your need, Sunshine," Bakkhos breathed against the back of my neck, sending a hot shiver down my body. We were out in the open, the bright sun lighting our surroundings—and our bodies—in sharp relief, but it *felt* private, like there was no one around for miles. And my body didn't care one bit that we were in public. "I'm your alpha, your mate. I need to give you what you need," he rasped, breathing faster.

I jumped as his fingers ducked between my thighs and pressed to my clit, but then all I knew was pleasure and relief, my stress instantly dissolving. He was right—my body did need this, and my wolf surged to the surface, so demanding that my embarrassment never formed. I stood between Draven and Kaan, with Wild just ahead, but I didn't stop Bakkhos's fingers as they thrust inside me.

"Fuck," Draven choked out, and I lifted heavy-lidded eyes to find him dragging a hand through his dark hair, his eyes fixed on my chest where ever-fast breaths had my boobs thrusting forward, my nipples hard and swollen. "Nixie," he rasped, but didn't come closer.

My eyes slid shut as Bakkhos's thumb circled my clit, his fingers curving inside me. Wet sounds filled the air, faster and louder with every thrust.

"Oh, goddess," I groaned, digging my fingernails into Bakkhos's other arm as it banded across my middle, holding me up.

"That's it," my crazed alpha murmured in my ear. "Just let go, my beautiful Sunshine. Let me make you feel good."

I rolled my hips, chasing the pleasure he offered, my eyes squeezed shut. Shivers ran up and down my body until all I felt was his touch and the tight coil of pleasure in my lower belly.

Bakkhos's low laugh made my back arch, and I clenched around his fingers. "*Problem*, alpha?"

Kaan just growled, so rich and full that it resonated with every part of me—body and soul—and I shattered. My cry echoed around the treetops as I climaxed, Bakkhos's fingers moving faster until I felt like I was flying.

"Nixette," an unfamiliar voice rasped, and I dragged my eyelids open, breathing hard and fast as Bakkhos's fingers dragged lazily through my wetness now.

My chest jumped when I locked eyes with Wild. He still sat in the middle of the bloody grass, but now he looked completely lost as he stared at me. It was a lie—his hopeless expression, the desperate plea in his eyes. It had to be; all he ever did was lie and trick and deceive.

"Back with us?" Kaan asked, his voice guttural and deep as he stomped through the blood and gore, kneeling before Wild to clasp his shoulder.

Wild nodded jerkily.

"Come here, Wild," Bakkhos said, strangely serious. I jumped when he dragged his fingers through my slick, cupping his palm to catch more, and stroking my hip with his other hand to soothe me as I tensed.

Wild got to his feet, wavering so badly that I thought he'd fall over. But Kaan rose quickly and supported him as Wild took a step, his whole body streaked in blood and violence but his eyes ... those golden eyes were drowning in misery. It looked *real*, but so had everything else he'd shown me.

Bakkhos held his cupped hand out, his arm banded around my middle and his lips pressed to my shoulder. I kept still as Wild approached, looking steadier with every step he took, and I froze completely when he wrapped both hands around Bakkhos's wrist. A broken groan left his throat as he ran his tongue over Bakkhos's palm. Tasting *me* on him.

I stared, not sure what to make of Wild as his breaths came unevenly and he licked and sucked every part of Bakkhos's hand, his eyes shut tight and even his eyelids stained with blood.

There was something desperate in the way he licked, something needy in the way he clutched Bakkhos's wrist, and I didn't recognise this Wild at all. "Thanks," he rasped, finally pulling back and dragging a hand down his face. "I—I needed that."

I frowned deeper. He needed to taste my arousal? Why the hell would he need that? And why did he seem calmer now?

None of this made any damn sense.

"Sorry," he added, darting a glance at me before turning away. I waited for him to smirk and laugh at me for falling for his lie, but he didn't. Wild was ... broken. "I need to be alone," he said to Kaan, stalking away from us.

"Tough shit," Kaan replied, the guttural deepness gone from his voice. "The only thing you're going to do is go home and pack. We all are. You heard what that bastard said before you ripped him apart; it's not just the Magnolia pack we're dealing with." He met Bakkhos's and Draven's eyes and said, almost gently, "They've merged with Zinnia pack. The cottage isn't safe anymore; we need to leave."

18

LEAVING

"Bakkhos," I said gently, watching him move around his room like a cyclone, throwing clothes and possessions into a holdall. His long blond hair was a tangled mess around his head because of how many times he'd raked his fingers through it, his expression tortured, somewhere between anger and fear. "Bakkhos, slow down."

I caught his hands and squeezed both in mine, halting him before he could rush into the bathroom in another whirlwind of anxiety. "Look at me, love."

He paused, more at the name than anything else, his green eyes frantically locking with mine.

"It's going to be okay. Kaan would never let anything bad happen to us."

Bakkhos gently tugged his hands from mine, pressed a long kiss to my temple, and rushed into the bathroom where he gathered bottles of shampoo and stacks of fluffy towels. "You don't know what they're like, Sunshine. Magnolia was bad enough, but now Zinnia are after us—"

He laughed, a low bubble of sound that rose in pitch and frequency until all I wanted was to hug him tight. Zinnia pack—his old pack. The pack who'd caged and tormented him. Who'd sacrificed his sister and—so I'd found out—made a regular habit of abducting humans and sacrificing them, too.

"They're not going to get you, Bakkhos," I swore, my heart aching at his clear panic as he threw more things in the bag. "I promise. I won't let them."

He wasn't just my mate anymore; he was pack, and I'd protect my pack to the death.

His answering snarl was furious and unexpected. "No," he growled, throwing a pile of dirty washing in the bag and spinning to face me. His upper lip curled back from his teeth, twisting his inked face into grotesque anger. "I don't want you anywhere near them. They'll take you, too."

My heart ached, and I reached for him, but Bakkhos was already sweeping the bag onto his shoulder and rushing out of the room. I chewed my lip, watching him, and then huffed at myself, casting a look around the room where we'd first claimed each other. It was decimated, little more than an empty wardrobe and a messy bed, but I'd miss it. I'd never really gotten the chance to settle into life here, but I'd miss this cottage. It was just starting to feel safe.

"Ready, sweetheart?" Kaan asked as I descended the stairs to the bottom floor, watching Wild as he dragged a battered suitcase out of his room and kicked the door shut. I was no longer sure what to make of Wild, so I kept my distance.

"I don't have anything to pack, so..." I gave him a pitiful attempt at a smile.

The scowling expression on his tanned face softened, his lips turning down behind his beard. "We'll stop to get you some clothes while we're on the road." He squeezed my shoulder, and comfort slammed directly into my soul. "I know it must be unsettling for you; you've just got here and now we're leaving."

I shrugged, not really wanting to examine the ache in my chest, already missing the cottage. "It's not me who's in danger. I'm just worried about Bakkhos and Draven."

Kaan's dark eyes crinkled as he smiled, and he rubbed his thumb across my shoulder before he let go, his throat bobbing. "So you're not afraid of us anymore?"

"Not most of you," I replied quietly. For some reason, I didn't want my words to reach Wild as he dragged his suitcase into the living room at the end of the hall.

"Wild won't touch you without your permission again," Kaan promised, jerking his head for me to follow him down the hallway.

"That's a pretty big change of heart from the alpha who said he'd never let me leave that first night. You didn't seem to care about my permission then."

Kaan shook his shaved head. "Do you *want* to leave?"

"No," I huffed.

His smile was wide and genuine. "That's good to hear, sweetheart. Damn good to hear."

Why do you want me to stay so badly? I wanted to shout. *You won't even touch me.* But I reined in the words with a deep breath and just nodded, falling back on old habits of not speaking my mind.

"I would never have forced you to stay," he said seriously, watching me from the corner of his eye as we passed the open kitchen door, the cupboard doors hanging open on empty shelves.

"Yes, you would have," I muttered, wrapping my arms around myself.

Kaan dragged a hand down his beard. "There's something about an omega's scent, your slick especially. It makes good, intelligent men lose their damn minds."

"Oh, so you wanted me *then?*" I breathed, bitter and barbed.

My stomach crashed and I faltered; I couldn't believe I'd actually said that. I increased my speed, hurrying through the front room and out the door before Kaan could reply.

Blood rushed in my ears. I didn't stop until I reached the beaten up car idling in front of the cottage. Bakkhos sat behind the wheel, his need to run palpable. I wanted to give him a big hug and tell him everything would be okay, but I was too nervy after snapping at Kaan to initiate contact. I braced for a growl, for devastating pain, even though part of me knew it would never come.

The boot and back seats were piled high with bags, boxes, and possessions; the cottage had been stripped bare in an hour. I chewed my lip as I spotted the empty passenger seat—clearly left for our alpha—and Wild and Draven crammed into the back seats. "Um," I murmured, hovering by the open doors.

"Sunshine, you sit with Draven," Bakkhos said in a rush, like he couldn't even speak fast enough to satisfy his flight instincts.

Draven's dark head snapped up, locking eyes with me before he stared at the back of Bakkhos's messy head. "She won't want to sit with me, she can share Kaan's seat."

Nope. Hell to the nope.

I dragged air into my lungs, savouring the taste of the outdoors and wondering where we'd end up tonight—and then I gathered all my courage and bolstered myself into the backseat. My palms pricked with sweat as I settled on Draven's lap, but none of the nerves I'd have felt with Kaan, or the dread with Wild, formed with the gentle, giant alpha.

His hands flexed on either side of his legs, and his breath caught, but he didn't say anything. Why wouldn't I want to sit with him? Draven was one of two alphas I was on good terms with.

"How are your hands?" I asked softly, twisting to look at him and appreciating the flecks of brighter blue in his eyes up close.

"Fine," he replied, just as quietly. He curled his hands into fists at my scrutiny, an uncertain look crossing his pale face. "I didn't want to take the bandages off. You went to a lot of trouble."

"Oh," I breathed, surprised by his sweetness. "You can take them off, you know. I just didn't want you to get hurt anymore."

"I—want to keep them on," he murmured, not meeting my gaze, instead watching Kaan lock up the cottage. "Thank you."

I nodded even though I was baffled, and settled against his chest, jumping when Kaan thumped into the front passenger seat.

The slam of the door echoed loudly. He didn't turn to the backseat, not even to assess the structural integrity of the tower of boxes beside Wild. "We've got everything we need. Let's go."

I tried to hide my nervousness, but something in my body language must have changed because Draven's hand settled on my knee, big and warm and comforting.

"Where are we going?" I dared to ask.

Kaan didn't turn to look at me when he answered, "Away from here."

I heard what he didn't say: we had nowhere to go.

19

FEAR

The drone of the radio and the rumbling of the car eventually lulled me to sleep, the journey seeming endless as we put space between us and our enemies. When I woke up, I didn't feel afraid or anxious or like I was on the run from two evil packs—which I was. Fingers ran gently over my scalp, and a warm hand splayed across my thigh as I laid on a solid chest. The scent of blood and coffee teased my tongue as I inhaled, and my soul settled further.

"Sorry for falling asleep on you," I murmured, my voice scratchy.

"Please don't be sorry," Draven replied quietly.

A smile tugged at my lips, and I sighed, snuggling into his chest and letting his scent wrap around me. "I don't want to make you uncomfortable. I think ... you don't like to be touched?" I'd seen him flinch away from physical contact a few times, a growl warning his packmates to back off.

"It's different with you," he said, just as quietly. My eyes rolled back as his fingers slid through my hair, rubbing the back of my neck where a crick had formed. "It's not barbed wire."

Anyone else in the car would have had no idea what he was talking about, but my heart went all mushy and I ached to lean up and kiss him. But I wouldn't push my luck; I was already beyond happy to be here snuggled against him.

"Good," I breathed, pressing my nose to his throat where his scent was thickest, a wave of rightness rolling through me at the rich scent of alpha I instinctively craved. "Because I don't want to budge one bit."

His laugh was like a whisper, but as sweet as honey. "Then you never have to move, Nixie," he promised. "Should I stop touching you?"

"Goddess, no," I groaned. "Not ever."

His laugh was louder this time, deeper in a way that made my pupils dilate and my pussy throb. I lost control of myself for a second, and my tongue darted out to lick his throat.

Draven's breath hitched, his hand tightening on my thigh, and I squirmed, suddenly and painfully aware of the hardness pressing against my ass.

"Sorry," I rasped, forcing myself to pull back a few inches. "I-I didn't mean to."

Draven used his grip on the back of my neck to turn my face to his, and I swallowed at the pleasure and surprise blazing from his blue eyes—and the heat of desire. It felt good to be wanted, but I reminded myself Kaan had looked at me that way, too. It didn't mean Draven wouldn't reject me. I dropped my eyes, chewing my lip, and could do nothing to stop the pain that twisted inside my chest.

"Never apologise," Draven murmured, and tucked me back against his chest. "I'm your alpha; you can touch me whenever you want."

My eyes stung. Did that mean he wanted me—was that what he was saying? I hoped it was so fucking badly. I put my lips to his ear and replied, "I'm your omega, too, Draven. And you can do whatever you want to me."

He answered with a slow, building growl laced with promise and affection, and I melted against him, my eyelids heavy.

"I want to hold you," he said finally, his voice just for me. "I don't want to let go."

"Then don't."

"Kaan," Bakkhos barked, my crazed alpha's voice tight.

I lifted my head off Draven's chest in alarm, the soft gauze of his protection already clearing at Bakkhos' alarm.

Kaan jerked up in his seat, waking with a vicious growl that had me slumping back towards Draven with wide eyes. "What is it?" he demanded.

"There's a car following us," Bakkhos replied, swinging our car around a long stretch of road. There were fields on either side of us, their flowers bright yellow in the late afternoon light, and the road was empty except for us and—I twisted to look at the car—

"*No*," I choked out, instinct making me scramble off Draven's lap, my whole body shaking as I shot to my feet, stooped against the roof, and stared at the car.

"Nix, sit down," Kaan ordered, so firmly that I couldn't ignore it.

I collapsed in the footwell, my arms wrapped around my knees and my breathing out of control. "No," I whispered, shaking so hard my teeth clacked together. "Non*o*no."

I jumped hard when fingers slid through my hair, gripping tight to pull my head back. Pain and a shivery sensation flashed through my body. I breathed raggedly and stared into gold eyes in a sharp, glaring face.

"You're a Broken Pack wolf now, Nixette," Wild said, his teeth bared. "If we have to slaughter everyone in that car to keep you safe, we'll do it. We protect our own. So breathe. No one in that car is going to touch you."

"You're hurting her," Draven growled.

I couldn't look away from Wild, my heart beating crazily and my breathing a mess. But I believed him. He'd mutilated the scout, had torn him limb from limb.

"Was that what happened earlier?" I asked breathlessly, not breaking eye contact. "Is that why you killed the scout like that? Because you protect the pack?"

Wild nodded, his jaw tight. It was the first time he'd touched me since yesterday morning when I'd woken with his mouth on me, I realised. "And I like killing," he added.

"You didn't look like you liked it." I frowned, jumping when he reached for me, pulling me out of the footwell and depositing me on Draven's lap again. Draven's arms wrapped around my middle, squeezing tight.

Wild just shook his flame-red head, turning to look at the car behind us—a dark blue people carrier. My dad's car. "I loved killing him. The blood was another story."

"Why?" I pressed, taking any distraction from the dread twisting up my insides.

"That's none of your business, Lilac," Wild replied with a deadly smirk. I sighed, recognising the return of the familiar, bastard Wild. "The things in my head might scare someone as delicate as you."

I didn't respond to his taunt, just turned to look across Draven's shoulder at my dad's car in time to see it speed up, the headlights flashing as it came dangerously close. Close enough for me to see Dad's bared teeth and the hate in his eyes.

I whimpered.

"Hold on," Bakkhos growled, so deep I didn't recognise his voice for a second.

"Sweetheart, turn around," Kaan said softly from in front of me. "Don't look."

"He's going to get me," I breathed, meeting my new alpha's eyes and searching for safety in the dark depths. "He's going to kill me again."

Four growls filled the car, and my bottom lip quivered. Draven held me closer, his hands splayed across my stomach in broad, comforting touches.

"No," Kaan replied, making sure I met his eyes. "He isn't. He doesn't stand a chance against four alphas."

"And the *alpha of alphas*," Draven added, with a kiss to the spot behind my ear. It was so surprising from him that my terror skipped a beat. "I've got you, my omega, my beauty," he swore. "Nothing's gonna hurt you."

I yelped as our car sped faster, pushing the speed limit as Bakkhos urged us deadly fast down the country road. The fields sped past, a blur of yellow flowers and the blue sky moved dizzyingly fast as we swerved and skidded, Bakkhos laughing like the maniac he was.

I swore I could smell the rubber of our tyres burning, but that could have been my panic. Despite Kaan's words, I couldn't keep my eyes off the window, my father's face twisted with anger and his dark blue eyes narrowed and steely. I'd never been able to reason with him when his eyes were like that. He usually just growled and sent me to my knees, until I pleaded for the crippling sound to stop. It never did stop, and I only cried harder when my chest bound up so tight it hurt, my throat sliced through with the command and my head drumming unbearably.

"Nothing's gonna hurt you," Draven repeated, sliding his hand up and down my back. I wished his reassurance could pierce the bubble of my panic, but Bakkhos's dread was building alongside mine through our vivid bond, both our fear feeding the others until I couldn't stop shaking.

"Let's see him follow us now," Bakkhos laughed, and twisted so suddenly into a turn-off that I screamed. The car tipped so violently to the side, I was terrified it would crash. But with a shudder and a deep, screeching groan, it steadied on four wheels again and Bakkhos sped off, laughing at the top of his lungs. I tried to reach through the mate bond to comfort him, but I was too afraid myself to calm him. The car's engine let out a deep grumble, and Bakkhos and I flinched at the same time, panic feeding panic.

"Shit!" he hissed, slamming his fist into the dashboard, bits smashing off. "Piece of fucking *shit!*"

"Bakkhos!" Kaan growled, so deep that Bakkhos went still, and in the backseat, I froze too, going limp in Draven's arms as my shaking suddenly stopped. "What's the problem?"

Bakkhos laughed lowly. The car answered for him, slowing with a pitiful screech. "That," he snapped, throwing his hand at the hood of the car. "That is the problem. Piece of fucking junk is breaking down."

Kaan didn't panic, he just nodded and took a breath. "Wild, you and me will go out the second the car stops moving. Bakkhos, stay with Nixie, as far away from us as you can. But *don't* stay in the car; if you have to run, run. We'll find you through the pack bond. Draven, the second that bastard gets out of his car, I want you to wreck it."

Draven nodded, his long hair brushing my neck as he kissed my shoulder. "Yes, alpha," he replied, his smooth voice low and serious.

"He's going to kill us all," I breathed, not meaning to say it out loud.

"No," Kaan replied, meeting my gaze and holding it. My eyes fluttered as he offered a purr—rich with protectiveness and promise, and so powerful that I let out a whine, my clothes suddenly scratchy against my skin. I became restless, shifting on Draven's lap and sinking my teeth into my bottom lip at the feel of his erection pressing against my back.

"You might have gone a bit over the top with the purr, alpha," Wild drawled, watching me.

I wanted the cruel alpha with a fierceness that was undeniable, wanted his body pressed to mine, wanted him inside me, and I didn't care that there were still flecks of blood on his neck and hands from earlier. I didn't care that I hated him or that he felt entitled to me.

"I see that, thank you," Kaan bit out, grabbing the door beside him as the car rolled slower. Bakkhos was as tense as a bowstring as he guided us safely down the country road.

"I can see the benefits though," Wild laughed, reaching across to brush his thumb across my bottom lip. I whimpered, wriggling on Draven's lap, and my skin pulled tight over my bones as an unbearable heat built in my chest and neck.

"Don't you fucking touch her," Bakkhos growled, full of dominance. I barely even noticed us crashing into the grassy ditch along the side of the road. I was drugged by that growl, seduced by the power and strength in it. My back arched against Draven's chest, my legs widening without my control.

Oh goddess, I needed them right now. Any of them. *All* of them. I didn't care, I just needed—

"Nix," Kaan said gently, cutting through the haze. Alpha—my alpha. "Can you hear me, sweetheart?"

I nodded, breathing fast as I waited for an order. My

pussy throbbed, slick soaking through my underwear *and* my pants.

"Oh," Draven breathed, nuzzling my neck. "Oh, Nixie."

"I need you to stay with Bakkhos, okay, sweet girl?" Kaan said, maintaining eye contact. "Stay with Bakkhos, and run if he tells you to."

I nodded, my face on fire, and I squirmed against the abrasive feeling of my clothes. I needed to take them off. I reached for the hem of my shirt but Draven's gentle hands caught mine and caressed my knuckles before I could tear the fabric off.

"I'm going to fucking kill this guy," Bakkhos hissed, kicking his door open, "and then I'm going to give my mate what she's desperate for."

Oh goddess yes. Yes, please.

"No," Kaan rumbled, making my eyes roll back. "You're going to stay with her, and protect her. Leave the violence to us." He reached across the front seats and grabbed Bakkhos by his hair. "And if I find you balls deep in omega pussy, I'll fucking kill you. Now is not the time."

"But she's in heat—"

"Later," Kaan growled, and that was that.

I bucked in Draven's hold, my body aching, my pussy aching and desperate—and empty. I'd forgotten what those words meant—but I knew heat, omega, and pussy, and I whined. Why were they denying me? They were my alphas, and I needed them.

"Wild," Kaan ordered. "Now."

I jumped at the sudden rush of movement, staring at the bags and boxes the cruel alpha shoved into the grass as he climbed out, a low snarl curling his lip from his teeth and wiry muscles bunched in his arms. Nownownow, I needed him *now*. I whined, loud and pleading, and his breath caught.

The look he gave me was both pained and simmering. I reached for him, but then he was gone, rushing up the incline to where another car had idled by the roadside. Kaan ran alongside him, my alphas leaving me. Both of them—I needed both of them.

"It's going to be alright, Nixie," Draven, my gentle alpha, promised, pulling my hair off the back of my neck to lay a kiss there. I shuddered with relief. He'd give me what I needed, thank the goddess. "Here," he said, and then I was being passed to another alpha, my first alpha, my— Bakkhos. Names were difficult, and no longer as important as *alpha*. My alpha. I slumped in his arms, barely recognising grass beneath my feet and wind tugging at my hair as I writhed against his hard body. I nuzzled my nose into his neck, groaning as the scent of alpha filled my senses like the best cologne. My mouth watered.

"Sunshine," he choked. "Nixie, *goddess*, you're killing me."

"At least she's not scared anymore," my gentle alpha said, and I wilted as a big hand stroked over my hair and down my back. "Keep her safe, or I'll end you."

A laugh was all that answered him.

I pressed even closer to my crazed alpha to feel the vibrations of his laugh, my nipples aching and so sensitive that I needed his hands on them, or his mouth, but definitely not scratchy cotton. Ugh, why did I ever wear clothes?

"It's alright, my Sunshine," he promised, holding me close. "Everything's going to be alright. Your alphas won't let anything bad happen to you."

I shuddered as his hand slid under my shirt and pressed

to my back, the skin to skin contact *almost* satisfying my devastating need.

"Alpha," I whined, so wrapped up in him that I didn't flinch at the fierce growls behind us, or the harsh words. I didn't even know what they meant. They weren't alpha, cock, knot, or bite, so they didn't matter.

"It's almost over," he promised, trailing his fingers up my arched spine to grip the back of my neck.

My eyes rolled back, euphoria hitting for a reason I couldn't work out and didn't particularly care to. He was my alpha, and he had control of me, and he'd give me what I needed.

"Breathe, Sunshine," he murmured, kissing my temple. I did as he commanded, nuzzling his throat to taste the bite I'd marked on his neck. "They're coming back, everything's alright now."

My pants were stuck to my legs, soaked all the way through, I was as hot as a fire, and nobody was touching me, filling me, or offering the relief I needed more than I needed to breathe. Everything was *not* alright.

"He limped off," someone laughed. "Pitiful bastard."

"And there's no way he's driving anywhere in that car," someone else added—softer, a voice formed of honey. "How is she?"

"Not deaf," the alpha holding me retorted, gripping the back of my neck tighter. I whined, boneless and tense all at once. "Ask her yourself; she can probably put it into words better than me."

"Nixie?" that gentle voice asked, and I went taut all over.

"Alpha," I purred, arching my body and shuddering.

"How are you feeling?"

"Alpha," I repeated breathily, tingles moving across my

body as I sensed *him* approach. The biggest one. The alpha of alphas. "Please."

"Please what, my beauty?" the soft voice asked, and I panted to feel them all close to me.

"Please, alpha—cock, knot, *please.*"

"Let me see her eyes." These words came in the deep rumble of the alpha of alphas. I throbbed as my crazed alpha's possessive hands spun me around, and my mouth fell open on heavy pants as the biggest alpha came close enough to touch me, his eyes dark with lust.

"Fully dilated." He pressed his hand to my forehead and my tongue lolled out of my mouth, aching for something to suck. "And she's burning up."

"She's fully in estrous then," the soft alpha murmured. "What do we do?"

"Give her what she's begging for," a sharper voice replied, and my eyes focused on the tall, redheaded alpha watching me with a dark gaze that promised everything my scorching body needed.

"Alpha," I whined.

His grin grew smug and dangerous, and my body burned for him to touch me.

"Not in a fucking ditch," the alpha of alphas growled, and my knees went weak at the low vibration of sound. It was lucky my crazed alpha was holding me, or I would have slammed into the ground.

But if I fell to the grass, I could wiggle my ass until they surrendered to my need and pounded into me—

"The engine's just overheated," the gentle alpha said, but I had no idea what that meant. "I put some coolant in, we should be good to go in a bit."

"Thank fuck," my crazed alpha groaned, kissing my

neck. "This is killing me. You're killing me, Sunshine, you hear me?"

I turned at the sound of his need, dragging my tongue across the claiming mark on his neck. "Cock."

"Oh, *fuck*," he groaned, holding my hips and writhing against me. But all these clothes were in the way, and I needed to get them off, off—

"Back of the car," the alpha of alphas growled so deep I clenched. "Give her some relief, Bakkhos. We'll find a hotel as soon as we're on the move again," he bit out, sounding as tense as I was.

"Alpha," I said softly, looking at him pleadingly.

"Fuck," he rasped, dragging a hand over his shaved head and not meeting my eyes. "Bakkhos is going to take care of you, sweetheart."

"Alpha?" I asked.

His shoulders slumped. "I'd only hurt you, sweet girl. Bakkhos, get her in the fucking car."

A knot of pain tightened my belly at his rejection, but my crazed alpha swept me into his arms and the feeling of his hands on the backs of my legs, so close to where I needed him, had the pain scattering.

20

HEAT

"Fuck, Sunshine, your pants are drenched," my crazed alpha—what was his name?—growled. He laid me on the backseat of the car, kicking bags into the grass outside to make room.

My clothes made a gross sound as he peeled them off me, but I didn't care one bit because he was finally giving me what I needed: my skin bared and his hands on me.

"My poor omega," he murmured, throwing my sweatpants out the open door. I lifted my head, my eyes wide at the growls that tore through the air, and I watched my soft alpha and the cruel smirking one fight over my jeans. But I didn't see who won because my crazed alpha ran his thumb over my soaked underwear, and my head fell back to the cushioned seat. A deep groan tore up my throat.

"I never would have made you wait so long," he said, sliding his body along mine to brush kisses to the bite on my neck. A chill trembled down my body and my pussy spasmed hard, aching for more. "But I can't ignore an order from my alpha."

"Alpha," I gasped, seizing on that word.

"Yes, my Sunshine, I'm your alpha," he promised, swirling his tongue over his bite as he tugged my underwear off. I sank my teeth into my bottom lip when his fingers glided through my wetness, two thrusting inside my pussy while his thumb found my clit.

My back arched off the seat, and I knew I was making a mess of the leather but I didn't care at all.

"I'll always give you what you need, my omega," my alpha swore, dragging his lips from my throat to capture my mouth in a bruising kiss. I clenched around his fingers, broken gasps in the back of my throat as his tongue devoured mine, adding another delicious layer of sensation as he mirrored his thumb's steady caress on my swollen nerves. "My omega," he growled, his moss green eyes flashing with possessiveness.

I whined, on the edge of bliss.

His fingers curled inside me, and I was gone, my cries so loud there was no doubt the alphas outside the car heard. I shook with deep shudders as my pussy squeezed his fingers tight. It wasn't as fulfilling as a cock, and *nothing* compared to his knot, but relief slackened my muscles until I slumped into the backseat, my eyes fluttering shut.

"Alright," a deep, rumbling growl commanded. "Everyone inside."

"Can I lick the seat?" a raspy voice replied.

"*Only* the seat," the alpha of alphas answered.

"Come here, my Sunshine," my crazed alpha murmured. I didn't resist when he pulled me up and settled me against his chest, only cracking my eyes open when someone stacked boxes and bags beside us. On the other seat ... I trapped my bottom lip between my teeth as the hollow-faced, red-haired alpha dragged his tongue desperately across the leather, sucking up every bit of my arousal and cum. His eyes glowed the most beautiful shade of gold as he locked eyes with me, bent over the seat from outside, his tongue extended to catch a drop of slick as it rolled towards him.

My inner walls clenched hard, and I whimpered, more arousal gushing from me and soaking into my crazed alpha's pants.

"That's enough," the alpha of alphas said firmly. "You're just getting her worked up again."

"I could give her some relief, too," he replied as he climbed into the car and slammed the door. His fingers tiptoed across my thigh, and I shuddered, goosebumps covering my body from head to toe.

"That's up to her," the alpha of alphas snapped. "But not here. Draven, get on your phone, find us a hotel."

"Yes, alpha," my soft alpha replied, and I sighed, watching his profile as he sat in the passenger seat. His voice soothed me.

I was reaching for him before I realised I'd moved, my fingers trailing gently through his dark ponytail. He jumped, twisting around, but his confrontational expression melted into affection when we locked eyes. "I like when you talk," I breathed, getting lost in his dark blue gaze.

Beside me, the cruel alpha laughed softly. "Wow, she can talk again. Must have been some orgasm, Bakkhos. I'm impressed."

"Shut your mouth, or I'll rip your throat out."

"You could try."

I let their words flow over me, washing against my skin like warm water, and lost myself in my soft, honey-sweet alpha.

"You do?" he asked shyly. He didn't look at my body even

though I was half naked, didn't look at the slick pooling between my legs even as I widened them on instinct.

I nodded. "I like everything about you. Please talk more."

The softest, sweetest smile curved his scarred face, and I ached, running my fingertips over the silver cuts. "Beautiful," I breathed, wishing I could kiss them, but I couldn't reach from the backseat.

"Would you like me to tell you a story?" he asked, caressing my cheek with a knuckle.

I nodded, leaning into the touch. My eyes went heavy lidded. "Please, alpha."

"Draven," he corrected softly, his eyes like deep blue velvet.

"Please, alpha Draven," I murmured.

His laugh was as rich as chocolate, and it moved through me like a shiver. "Alright, my beauty," he said, and began a story about birds and fire, castles and kings.

I fell asleep to the rhythmic murmur of his voice, wrapped up in my crazed alpha's arms, with my sharp alpha's hand nestled against my thigh, and my soft alpha's words lulling me into decadent safety.

21

BURNING

Burning heat woke me, and I whimpered, twisting into a cramped ball as sweat prickled my skin. A soft mattress hugged my back, but the covers pulled up to my shoulders were stifling and scratchy. "Off," I rasped, pushing at the sheet and gritting my teeth at the slide of material over too-sensitive skin.

"Nix," a welcome voice rumbled, and I sighed, my eyes fluttering open to find the alpha of alphas. He sat in a chair in the corner of an unfamiliar room decorated in shades of gold and blue. "Tell me what you need, sweetheart."

I met Kaan's eyes and swallowed, my chest rising and falling quickly as his dark eyes travelled down my naked body, making my inner walls clench and drip, eager to receive his cock. The others weren't here, and the wrongness of that made my skin crawl with discomfort.

"The sheets are all wrong," I rasped, kicking the covers off the end of the bed and gazing around the room. The bed was massive, bigger than any I'd seen before, and a large window filled the wall to my right, curtains thrown open to show a twinkling sky of stars and high rise buildings. "I want the window open; I'm hot."

"Alright, sweetheart," Kaan agreed easily, pushing out of the chair to heave the window open. I sagged as sounds of lazy traffic crept in and cool, nighttime air brushed my bare skin, such a relief that I groaned. Kaan cursed softly under his breath, but his voice was normal when he asked, "What's wrong with the sheets, Nix?"

"Scratchy," I replied, testing the pillowcase and much happier for the smooth glide over my cheek. "The pillow's nice, though."

"Silk, then," Kaan mused. "I'll find better sheets for you, sweetheart. Do you want to nest?"

I went taut and alert, my breath catching as I nodded. I did. I really, *really* did, and I didn't know why, but that didn't matter right now. "Please, alpha," I begged.

"What else do you need, sweet girl?" he asked, his dark eyes full of so much warmth that my belly squirmed and my face went redder. His bearded face was calm, soft with care as he watched me. "There's water here for you; I need you to drink it all, okay?"

I nodded, eager to make him happy, and gulped down the water when he twisted the cap off and put the bottle in my hands. I watched him lean against the windowsill and punch something into his phone, and I swallowed the last of the water so it sat cool in my belly.

"Draven's going to get you the right sheets and some nesting materials," he said, not looking up.

"Where are my alphas?" I asked, shuddering as my temperature rose again, need blinding me to anything but the alpha by the window. Why was he *over there* when he should have been covering my body with his, pressing me into the mattress with his strength, claiming every inch of me. My breath quickened, and a shudder took over my body until I was trembling, grasping the wrong sheets in tight fists.

"In the bar downstairs, trying not to overwhelm you with too many alphas at once. And Draven's gone shopping for you now, but he'll be back soon."

I whined, wishing he'd meet my eyes.

"Please," I whispered when he remained focused on his phone, denying me what I needed so badly I couldn't breathe.

"Are you hungry, sweetheart?" he asked, crossing the room to where a few bags had been piled. "What do you want to eat?"

My mouth filled with saliva, heat moving down my neck and chest, pooling there in a blush. I panted, sweat sticking my hair to my head as the alpha of alphas unzipped the bag and produced a punnet of strawberries.

"No," I complained, my voice breathy and high. "I don't *want* food, I want—"

But there was still enough Nixette left in me to halt my tongue, not *quite* drowned out by an omega's need. Embarrassment stopped me from finishing the sentence.

A muscle feathered in Kaan's cheek, just above his beard, and my tongue itched, desperate to feel that twitch against it. I needed to be straddling his lap, wrapped up in his arms, his leather and whiskey scent overwhelming my senses.

"Can you be good and sit still for me?" he asked, and finally met my eyes. A jolt went through my whole body, followed by a shudder of pleasure.

"Yes," I whispered, my heart racing as he approached the bed and perched on the edge beside me, so close I could reach out and touch him, run my tongue over the spot on his neck where I would bite and claim him—

No. I could sit still. I *would* sit still for him.

I dragged in a breath through my nose and trembled harder, but I stayed where I was.

"That's my sweet girl," he praised, and lifted one of the strawberries to my mouth. I didn't need a command to close my lips around the fruit, biting down and groaning at the sweetness that burst across my tongue. When I was finished, I sucked the juice from his fingers and moaned deep in my throat at the taste mixing with his skin.

"Nixette," he warned, and I inhaled jaggedly, forcing myself to release his fingers. "Good," he rumbled, and I sighed as his lips curved into a smile, crinkling his beard as he fed me another strawberry.

It was just enough to hold back the cramping need, but nowhere near enough to satisfy me, keeping me right on the edge. I lost track of how many berries I ate, lost in a dizzying blur of fingers and juice and murmurs. I jumped when the door opened, and then sagged in relief as my alphas walked in, followed by the sharp, red-haired one who made my blood boil in the best of ways. Worst of ways? I couldn't remember anymore.

"Sunshine," my crazed alpha said, his green eyes manic and urgency carved into his tattoo-covered face. He went over to the window and pushed it further open, then opened the second, giving me a soft look. "How are you feeling?"

"Alpha," I greeted, smiling at him, my heart pounding faster. The alpha of alphas wouldn't give me what I needed so badly my stomach cramped, but this alpha was perfect. I needed more than his fingers this time, needed his cock, his—

I still couldn't admit it, even to myself, but I knew the omega would win this battle, knew the heat and need and desperation would eat away at that tiny bit of my mind left until I was mindless and pleading for everything.

The sharp alpha snorted, watching me with desire. "Completely lost to her heat again, then? So much for you taking pity on her, Kaan."

The alpha of alphas snarled a soft warning. "Don't make me rethink this. You're only here because she might exhaust Bakkhos, and I'm not leaving her unsatisfied."

I whined. *Wrong.* He left me unsatisfied every moment he didn't touch me.

"Sure about that, alpha?" the redhead laughed, prowling across the room.

But he was shoved aside by my tall, dark-haired giant. Pleasant shivers broke across my body, and my toes curled as he beat even my crazed alpha to the bed. I sighed as his fingers stroked down my lilac hair.

"I've brought what you asked for, Nixie."

My half-mast eyes widened as I peered up at him, breathless with hope. "Cock, alpha?"

He laughed softly, and hesitated a second before his lips pressed to the space between my eyebrows. "No, my beauty."

My shoulders dropped, tears stinging my eyes as hormones raged, but I went still as a pile of fabric was placed in my lap. It felt *so good* against my skin that my eyes rolled back, and I spread out on the bed, moaning as I covered myself with cool, perfect fabrics. It felt like water and kisses against my skin.

"I'm glad you like them, Nixie," he murmured, stroking my calf before moving back.

My crazed, inked alpha laughed as I rolled in the new

fabrics, luxuriating in the blissful feeling of them against my skin. "Build a nest, Sunshine. I'll join you in it."

I caught my breath, excited as I scrambled onto my knees and began arranging the pillows, plus all my new sheets, into a nest. The door opened and shut, footsteps leaving the room, but I didn't look up. I adjusted the sheets until they were *right*, moving the pillows until something clicked in my chest, and I sagged in relief. It was good, but ... not quite. It was missing something, missing scents.

I dragged a breath into my lungs, and followed the scents I needed, climbing off the bed and surprised when my legs were unsteady under me.

"I've got you, Sunshine," a raspy voice promised, and arms supported my back as I rummaged through the bags in the corner. I pulled out a black long-sleeved shirt that smelled of coffee and blood, and a T-shirt permeated with the whiskey and pine tree scent that made my mouth water. With my alpha's arms around me, I stumbled back to the nest and placed them delicately against the sheets and pillows.

Almost—almost right.

I turned, and met the heated gold eyes of the sharp alpha who watched my every move. I couldn't help but shudder at the predatory gaze even as I walked willingly closer. "I want this," I breathed, and tugged at the shirt he was wearing. He didn't hesitate, and quickly pulled off his leather jacket so he could give me the soft green cotton. I rubbed my face against it, and smiled as his hand swept down my hip in a proprietary caress.

"Knew you wanted me, Lilac," he purred.

If I hadn't been so far gone, I'd have told him to shut up, but I just turned my back on him and placed my prize in the nest. I'd barely turned to my beloved crazed alpha before he was stripping and putting his clothes in my hands.

"Thank you, alpha," I murmured, leaning up to kiss the bite on his throat. He shuddered hard as I pulled away from him to put the final touch to my nest, sighing at the rightness of it. It was *perfect*, and a weight fell off my shoulders as I stretched out on my back in the center of the nest, my legs falling open as I met his mossy green eyes.

"Can I come into your nest, Sunshine?" he asked, his eyes trailing over every part of my body with darkness and need.

A cool rush of tingles moved down my body, excitement and anticipation coming to a head, and I nodded fast, holding his gaze. "Please, alpha."

"You don't need to beg, my omega," he said gently, climbing into the nest and making my eyes roll back as his naked body covered mine, cool against my heated skin. "I'll give you everything you need."

"And I'll give you even more," a smug voice added. I looked up, a rush of sensation sweeping down my spine as the sharp alpha prowled closer. "Invite me into your nest, little omega."

My pussy throbbed, slick pouring between my legs. Two alphas—yes. There was only one word in my head as my body set on fire with need. Yes.

"Please," I whined, breathing fast as I held his cocky gaze.

"Please, what?" he coaxed, walking closer until his knees met the mattress, his arms crossed over his slim chest.

My breath caught as he slowly unfastened his belt, the metallic *clink* making my body tense all over. I gripped my crazed alpha harder, pressing him closer to me as the other, sharper male made sure I was watching when he dragged down the zip on his jeans torturously slowly.

"Please come in my nest," I managed to gasp out, arching my body against my crazed alpha, the skin to skin contact making my eyes heavy lidded.

"Is *this* what you want, little omega?"

I wrapped my thighs around my inked alpha as the other taunted me, stepping out of his jeans and pumping his cock in his freckled hand. My mouth watered; it was so thick, so veiny. I nodded fast, unable to drag my eyes from it.

The chest pressed to mine vibrated with harsh words. "Don't be an asshole, Wild. Just get in the fucking nest."

My sharp alpha laughed, and finally climbed into my nest, the satisfied smirk on his lips making me *ache*. "Just making sure she's begging for us."

"She already is, you're just being a dick."

I gasped, lifting my head in interest. "Alpha?"

"It's alright, Sunshine, I know," he murmured, kissing my shoulder. "I know what you need."

I tensed with anticipation as his hand trailed between us, sliding through the puddle of wetness between my legs and finding my aching clit.

"Yessss," I exhaled, my head falling back to the pillow of my nest as all my attention centered on that point of contact.

"You moan so prettily when you're like this, little omega," the sharp alpha laughed. "Shame you're not so sweet when you're not high on estrus."

"You shut your fucking mouth, Wild," my crazed alpha snarled, pressing harder on my clit and sending explosions through my needy body. "She's fucking perfect all the time. *All the time*," he repeated, growling. He kissed my neck, my collarbone, and trailed affection down my chest until he reached my breasts. When he sucked my nipple into his mouth, I shattered into a million pieces, so desperate that my orgasm came without warning.

I'd never felt relief this sharp.

I sighed, melting into the soft fabrics of my nest when my whole body went loose and relaxed. But it wasn't like in the car where the orgasm cleared the haze; now I'd seen their cocks, it only grew until I needed more, faster, harder.

"Please," I whined, squirming under the solid press of his body. "Alpha, cock, please—"

My back arched as my crazed alpha removed his fingers and slid his cock inside me in one smooth, devastating thrust.

I cried out, wordless and euphoric, as he smoothed hair out of my face and kissed me sweetly, filling me in long, slow thrusts. Divine relief made me boneless. Finally, this was what I needed so badly. Every cell in my body lit up, every nerve sparking with pleasure, and I held my alpha tight as his hips rolled in measured, beautiful movements.

"Mine," he growled, and electric sparks shot through my pussy as his tongue swirled over the bite on my throat. His voice filled my head, echoing the claim with our bond, and I flashed into his sight, seeing my needy, rapturous face in *his* vision before it snapped back. "My Sunshine."

"My alpha," I gasped, clinging to him as he adjusted his hips, settling deeper inside me and making my eyes roll back. His pleasure amplified mine through the bond until I couldn't breathe. "Please, please—"

"Please, what, Sunshine?" he asked in a strained voice, scattering kisses across my throat.

A low laugh made me jump, and I remembered the sharp alpha all at once. I peered out from under my crazed alpha to see him kneeling beside us, his cock in his hand and his stare fixed on the place where my alpha filled me.

"She has your cock, and I know she can beg for your knot. I heard her that first night," he added, smirking at me. "I know what you want, little omega."

"What?" my crazed alpha snapped even as he drove into me, slow and deep.

"Say it," the cruel alpha growled, so fierce and sudden that my inner muscles locked tight around the cock driving into me, and slick poured out of me.

"Please, please, please," I cried.

"Please, *what?*" he demanded, his growl so deep and forceful that I arched, clinging to my crazed alpha. I couldn't breathe, couldn't think—and then he growled louder, and it tore the answer from me.

"I need your cum!" My eyes blew wide, any last vestige of embarrassment scattering as his growl deepened. "Please alpha, I need it, I need it—"

"Shh, Sunshine." Lips pressed to my cheek, reassuring and sweet.

"Don't knot her," the harsh alpha laughed. "She wants it in her mouth."

My crazed alpha groaned, and the sound drove me wild until I was squirming, clutching so tight I left bruises all down his back.

"No!" I cried as I was suddenly empty, throbbing around nothing. Tears of frustration built in my eyes.

But then a wicked laugh made me jump, and my pussy was stretching around a bigger cock. My eyes slammed shut as it pushed deeper, so thick that it pressed on every blissful spot, erasing everything else. "*That's* it," a cruel voice hissed. "You stretch around me. Feel good, little omega?"

I whimpered, opening my eyes as a gentle hand cupped my cheek, turning my face. My mouth widened automatically as the scent of alpha cock hit my senses, and I sucked greedily as my crazed alpha pushed into my mouth. A ragged sigh of relief loosening my chest when he growled and spilled nectar across my tongue.

"Told you that was what she needed," my sharp alpha laughed, though his voice was tight. "She's purring."

Their words didn't matter, didn't even compute in my mind, but their voices didn't stop me sucking every drop of cum from the cock in my mouth, or moaning as the alpha roughly driving into my heat reached up and to clasp my throat.

"Bite," I gasped when the cock left my mouth, my inked alpha stroking hair back off my face.

"No," my sharp alpha replied, as hard as iron.

I whined, arching my back and pressing my throat into his hand. "*Bite.*"

"*I said,*" he growled, so deep that my eyes dilated fully, heat and tingles washing down my chest. "*No.*"

"You can trust her, Wild," my other alpha said gently.

"Fuck off, Bakkhos." The thrusts turned rougher, driving pleasure into me so sharply and suddenly that I screamed, coming so hard the room blacked out around me.

"She'll be good to you if you're good to her," my crazed alpha said, still in that gentle voice that was so unlike him. "I promise, Wild."

"She's not biting me," my sharp alpha snapped. He groaned as I throbbed around his cock, whining for his bite, his knot. "I don't care how nice she is, or how good her cunt feels. Holy fuck," he grunted as I squeezed around him one last time before going limp and sated—for now.

His thumb stroked over my lazy pulse, and it felt good enough that I stopped whining for his bite. A deep purr settled in my chest.

"Let her sleep, Wild," my crazed alpha said, and snuggled up against me in my nest. My sharp alpha rolled beside me with a rough curse, still hard.

I clutched the arm around my waist and draped my hand across the chest of my sharp alpha as sleep wrapped around me.

But I knew the heat hadn't broken, and was far from ending. How long would it take for this haze of need and desperation to end?

22

PRIMAL

I woke up to the pleasant feeling of hands stroking down my back and across my thighs, gentle, sweeping touches that made me feel cared for and cherished. I snuggled into the hard body beside me, a smile curving my lips as I inhaled his scent—and jolted awake. It wasn't the wildfires of Bakkhos's scent, but rich, syrupy sweetness. And the second Wild realised I was awake, the caresses stopped; the stroking fingers left my body. Left me feeling cold.

"About time you woke up, Lilac," he said in a tight voice. "You've been dead to the world for a few hours. And we haven't even knotted you yet."

At the suggestion, my body went from pleasant warmth to scalding heat, and I bit my lip, blinking my eyes open to meet Wild's carnal stare. His irises were dark gold with hunger, his sharp face tight with want and ... discomfort. Because I'd caught him in a moment of tenderness?

I turned onto my side, nestling into his body and silently reassuring him that it was okay to be soft, to let his guard down. But instead of more light touches, he just laughed cruelly. "Don't tell me you think we're close now, Lilac," he sneered.

I flinched back at the stab of hurt.

Stupid—so stupid. Because for a second I *had*. I'd thought we'd shared something, that his cruelty would have softened for me.

"Did you think I cared about you?" he laughed, the sound like a whip across my soul. I shoved at his shoulder, wanting him out of my nest, wanting Bakkhos here to temper his harshness. "I'll never say no to sweet omega cunt when it's offered, but I'm not your boyfriend, Lilac."

"Bastard." My face heated with equal fury and tears, and I bared my teeth, a growl deeper than any sound I'd made before in the back of my throat. My instincts rose suddenly enough to crush me. Any reason and intelligence I had was replaced by primal, animal rage. "Out," I growled.

Wild ignored my snapping teeth and cupped my face, red hair tumbling across his forehead as he leaned closer. I vibrated with fury as his breath fanned across my face, smelling of—me. My arousal, my slick. A cold shiver moved through my body and the primal thing in control of me right now liked that. A lot. "You don't want me out, little omega. You want me *in*—you want me buried to the knot inside your desperate, throbbing hole. You want me fucking you until you're screaming, until your eyes roll back and you lose your mind to pleasure."

I shook harder, pushing at his shoulders, failing to put space between us.

"I'm not sweet like Bakkhos," he went on, his smile kicking up one side of his mouth and baring a sharp canine. My body flashed hot, and I couldn't trap the whine that surged up my throat, wanting his teeth on my neck. I *hated* him, couldn't stand to be in the same space as him, yet I wanted him to bite me, to *claim* me. It made no sense, but sense wasn't important right now.

I writhed in the nest, slick rolling down the inside of my thigh and a squirmy sensation in my gut. I needed him so badly. Hated him so much.

"I'm not dependable like Kaan or loving like Draven," he went on, his hand sliding down my face to my neck. Not squeezing, just holding me there, taunting me against the place he'd never bite. "But I think you like your pleasure with a bit of pain, don't you, little omega? I might be cruel and unfeeling, but you're desperate for me. Look at you grinding against me; look at your dilated eyes. You're already halfway gone."

I panted, unable to speak anymore.

"I fucking love your heat," he laughed, and grabbed my hips, flipping me onto my hands and knees. A full-body shiver made me tremble at the position. Oh fuck yes, this was what I needed, what I'd been waiting for ever since my body filled with demanding heat—the weight of a body against my back, pushing me into the nest, the animal submission and dominance, the *rutting*. "I hope it never ends. I want this sweet cunt for the rest of my damn life."

I shouted, my mouth falling open when he drove inside me, his tip narrow but shaft so thick that I panted, struggling to stretch around him even drenched in slick.

Wild laughed again, deep and guttural. "This is how I like you—struggling to process the blend of pain and pleasure, not sure if you hate it or if you need more." He ground his hips against my ass, dragging a shriek from my lips at how full I was. "But we both know you'll always need more. You're my little omega, aren't you?"

His words washed over me, meaningless compared to the stretch and fullness, the relief of no longer being empty.

I throbbed, my inner muscles clasping his cock tight, and I curled my fingers into the luxurious fabrics of my nest, tensed muscles relaxing all down my naked body when the scent of whiskey and leather hit my senses. My boobs met silk as I flattened to my nest, rubbing my face all over the shirt and covering myself in the delicious scent, barely hearing the sharp alpha's derisive laugh as he pulled my ass back to meet his hips.

The hand left my throat, and I let out a small sound of complaint, startled into silence when it cracked down on my backside. Heat and stinging pain flashed through my ass, and I tightened around his length.

"Say it," he growled, his voice so deep and demanding as he slid forcefully out of me and slammed back in, sending me across the nest.

Another slap to my other cheek and the flash of sensation sent me head-first into a blinding orgasm. I cried out, my body locking as waves of devastating pleasure wrung me out, crumbling my last brain cell into dust and leaving me at the whim and mercy of the heat. And the alpha brutally using me.

He laughed as I shuddered and twitched, my inner walls squeezing his cock as he stilled inside me, keeping me so full that I couldn't breathe. A hand slipped under my hips and found my clit, and it was too much. It was going to break me.

Shrieking, I squirmed, overwhelmed and trapped between pleasure and sharp sensation. I shook my head, trying to get away from the heartless alpha even as my pussy spasmed again.

"No, you don't," he growled, and the growl reduced me to a puddle of desperate aching. He growled away my squirming need to escape, until I was writhing my hips back against him, trying to take him deeper, begging for more. "I'm not done with you yet, Lilac," he warned, and circled my clit as he fucked me again, taking no mercy on me and ignoring my begging pleas. "I get to do whatever I want to you, remember? You're just a desperate omega who needs alpha cock, a knot, and my cum. Aren't you?"

"Knot," I whimpered.

He laughed, his voice strained now as his hips slammed into my stinging backside harder. "That's right, little omega. Knot. You're going to take it like a good girl, aren't you? You're going to clutch me as I swell inside you, and you're going to come so hard and so many times that it's fucking heaven for me. And you're going to stay tied to me, full of my cum, while I make you come again."

My eyes rolled back at his words, even if I could only make out one in five, and I wriggled my hips against his cruel body, shaking all over. Desperate for what he offered —what he threatened. I jumped when he circled harder on my clit, a sharp stab going through my nerves, but he growled again, and I shuddered, relaxing into the sensation.

"What do you want, Lilac?" he demanded, leaning his whole body over mine and pushing me into my nest. My sensitive nipples brushed silk, another layer of sensation that made goosebumps and shivers move through me.

"Bite," I gasped.

"No," he growled, and my breath caught at the fury and ferocity in the sound, my pussy clenching around his cock as he fucked harder, wilder.

I whined, tilting my head back, baring my throat. "Please."

"I swear to the goddess, Nixette, you're testing my patience. Try again."

I frowned at the shaky tone of his voice, but the alpha

rested his hips against my backside, nestled deep and teasing my entrance with the feeling of his swelling knot. I gasped, shaking so hard his arm slid around my hips to hold me in place. "Knot," I whispered.

"Good girl," he praised, and held me still as he thrust, coating himself in my slick before he pushed so deep I lost control of myself, screaming and crying and pleading. I stretched impossibly around his knot, so much thicker than Bakkhos's that I thought I would tear—and then it was nestled inside me, and my alpha was groaning low in his throat. It was a sound of such profound relief that even I sagged into the nest.

The knot pressed on every nerve, every sensitive spot, every stimulating place inside me that my toes curled tight, my body locked. I collapsed into an endless orgasm, throbbing with every grunt and groan my alpha made in my ear, his arm wrapped around my stomach as he ground his knot deeper inside me. A string of sounds came from me, babbling words with no meaning, and pleasure built higher, so good and so obliterating that it unmade me.

"Oh, *fuck*," my alpha hissed, and pressure built inside me as his cock swelled and throbbed, massaging my overwrought pussy with every spasm of his orgasm, with every rush of cum that filled me.

"Yesss, Lilac," he breathed, expelling a long breath and sagging against my back. The weight of him pressing me into the nest was delicious, and his relief trickled through our bond until I let out an answering sigh and relaxed into the sheets.

If I hadn't been so aware of the knot stretching me, locked with the threat and promise of yet more destructive pleasure, I would have drifted to sleep. Instead, I laid there in a daze, so satisfied that I'd never experienced this before. I'd never dreamed I'd get it from my sharp, cruel alpha.

"Goddess bless omega heats," he laughed softly, nudging my shoulder with his nose, so close to a caress that my soul cried out, aching for more. "Bakkhos, bring that wand from my bag—the red bag over there."

I jerked in surprise, twisting my face to peer above my nest, not expecting to find my crazed mate dewy from the shower, his dirty blond hair slicked back from his face, and every inch of obsessively inked skin on display. I throbbed around the knot filling me, drawing a tight moan from my sharp alpha. He'd been ... watching us. As the alpha taunted and tortured me, he'd stood and watched. And judging by the engorged cock hanging between his thighs, he'd touched himself, too.

"This one?" my beloved, crazed alpha asked, unzipping a red bag and pulling out—oh no. No, no, no. I knew what that was, and I was too sensitive for a vibrator, let alone one with a bulb that big. No, I *couldn't*.

"Yes, you can," my sharp alpha growled, low and menacing. He nipped my ear, making me jump. "And you will."

I hadn't said that out loud. I hadn't. He'd heard me. *I hate you*, I thought.

"But you love this big cock, don't you, Omega?" he replied, laughing. "You love the way I fill you up, and you love the way your pussy's stretched so tight around my knot, keeping you full of the alpha cum you love so much."

My tongue fell out of my mouth and the heat descended once more, stealing any sense I'd begun to regain.

"That's it," he praised. "Just a cock-drunk omega. You're so pretty like this," he added, brushing hair off the side of my face. "You'd do anything I told you to, wouldn't you?"

"Wild, don't taunt her," my crazed alpha huffed.

"I'm just giving her what she craves," the sharp alpha replied cockily. "Yeah, that's the right one. Plug it in over there."

My sharp alpha gripped my hips and pulled me up with him as he settled against the side of the nest. A strangled sound tore up my throat, and my breathing broke into shattered shards as sensations exploded inside my pussy, the knot stimulating every devilish spot near my entrance.

"No," I whimpered when Bakkhos crawled into the nest and knelt beside us.

"You need more, Sunshine," he said gently, brushing sweaty hair from my face and leaning close to press a gentle kiss to my lips. Desperate for affection, I clutched at his shoulders, running my tongue along his bottom lip with a pleading whine in the back of my throat.

He answered my plea with a deep, thorough kiss that fed my soul, and kissed me long after I sighed in relief, sucking my bottom lip, nipping with his teeth until I was limp and needy and fulfilled.

"Your heat's not broken yet," he said gently, kissing the spot between my eyebrows. "You're not satisfied yet, are you, my Sunshine?"

I watched him with wide, pleading eyes, my chest rising with fast breaths as we shared air. "I want to be," I whispered.

His next kiss landed on my forehead, and he slid gentle fingers across my scalp and down my hair, turning me into a sighing, dreamy doll.

"Huh," my sharp alpha said, readjusting me against his body until I laid comfortably with my back to his chest, my thighs wide and his knot stretching me wider. My eyes flew back open at the reminder of their plan, and I grabbed Bakkhos's arm in a silent plea as he moved away. I was too late to stop him settling on his front between my sharp alpha's legs, my pussy stretched and exposed for him. "A little softness and she turns to putty," he remarked. "Wish I'd known that when she was fighting for my bite."

"She wants you to claim her, Wild," my crazed alpha said with reproach on his inked face. "She's your mate—your fated mate. Trust her."

"Give me the wand," the bastard snapped back, "and keep your shitty opinions to yourself."

"It'll be different this time."

My sharp alpha growled so viciously that I produced so much slick, it forced past the knot and dripped onto my nest. I went taut at the scent of mixed slick and alpha cum, the blinding need of the heat striking so forcefully that I slumped against his chest, panting fast.

He laughed when I jumped at the sudden, loud buzzing, but I melted at the slow circles he stroked across my stomach, my eyes fluttering shut. "Damn, it works," he murmured. "Fucking life hack."

"Stop being cruel," my crazed alpha snarled, and I slitted my eyes open as hands ran over my inner thighs, smearing my slick across his fingers. My gaze turned hooded when he licked his hands clean and groaned with desperate need, burying his face in my pussy and licking around the place where I was knotted. "She's the best thing to happen to us, and you know it. She doesn't deserve you being an arsehole. Fuck, Sunshine," he groaned in the same breath, digging his hands into my thighs and pressing his whole face against my pussy. "You taste so good."

"Oh," I gasped, not minding the loud buzzing as the smooth head of the vibrator caressed my legs, my belly, and then up the valley between my breasts. It felt ... strange, different. Impossible to describe. But good.

I sank my teeth into my bottom lip as the vibrator found my breast, teasing my nipple at the same moment Bakkhos's tongue slicked from my stretched pussy to my ass, circling my tight hole. I clenched hard around the knot and cock filling me, and my sharp alpha let out a strangled groan.

"Holy..." he panted. "Fuck..."

His hand left my stomach to drag through his hair, and I turned to look at him, finding his eyes wide and strained, his face flushed red. I smiled, liking him looking as undone as he'd made me. "No one warned me it would be this intense," he grunted. "The grip she has on me ... shit, I could come again."

My crazed alpha laughed, his tongue vibrating against my tight entrance before it swirled up to my pussy, and I couldn't see what he did, but my sharp alpha grabbed my waist, holding me tightly as deep, guttural sounds tore from his throat and his cock jolted inside me once, and then twice, filling me with heat and cum.

I sighed, a satisfied smile on my face. This was exactly what I needed, what the heat demanded. Complete obliteration of both me *and* my mates.

"Wha..." my sharp—or rather dazed—alpha asked, and I grinned as my crazed alpha gave me a wicked, conspiratorial look as he took the vibrator from slack fingers.

"I think it's time for payback, isn't it, my beautiful Sunshine?" he asked, his green eyes glowing with adoration and mischief.

I bit my lip, knowing what he planned, knowing it would feel so damned intense, but also knowing we could completely ruin my cruel, heartless alpha. So I released my lip from my teeth and nodded, my eyes sparkling back at him. "Yes, alpha."

My sharp alpha was still too dazed to process what was

happening, but he growled at the first squeeze of my pussy as my beloved, inked alpha slid the wand through my wetness to tease my aching clit. I gasped at the shot of stimulation, my eyes locked with beautiful, adoring green. I couldn't look away, didn't *want* to even as my other alpha gripped my hip hard enough to press fingertip-shaped bruises into my skin.

"No, *fuck*," he rasped as the vibrator slid through my pussy again, nudging my clit and making me clench hard. "Oh, goddess," he whined, holding onto me like I was a life raft in a storm. "Bakkhos, stop. You're not the fucking dom."

"I am now," my crazed alpha replied with a deadly grin, and ducked his head to circle my ass with his tongue as he pressed the vibrating bulb to my clit—and turned up the vibrations until I screamed, my back arching. My sharp alpha's freckled arms trapped me against him, both of us roaring in torture and rapture. "It's nice to change things up, don't you think? Keeps things fresh and exciting."

"I'm going to—" my cruel alpha panted, dragging his lips down my neck, "Rail your ass—so hard—you bleed."

"Awww," my crazed alpha replied with big, sparkly eyes locked on me. "You promise?"

My sharp alpha just groaned, breathing hard and fast.

I laughed along with my beloved, crazed alpha, never once looking away from him even as I panted and writhed, getting closer to climax. It could have made me furious and territorial that they were familiar with each other's bodies, but the feeling never formed; instead, I loved that I was right here, in the middle of them. Where I belonged.

"Yes," my cruel alpha hissed, his hips jerking. I couldn't tell if he was responding to my thoughts or hissing because Bakkhos's tongue had travelled from my ass and—ohhhh—licked his heavy balls. I smirked, but then his knot swelled and I choked on a cry, my head thrown back against his shoulder.

"I can't get enough of your taste," my crazed alpha groaned, devouring my pussy now, removing the vibrator so he could wrap his lips around my clit—and move the wand down to the knot, pressing so the vibrations travelled deep.

A deafening roar sounded in my ears, and then my cruel alpha was coming for a third time, jerking fast and frantically inside me and dragging me over the edge with him. I came so hard I cried, tears stabbing my eyes and deep spasms tightening my inner walls. It hit me like a tidal wave, making my ass throb, too.

It was a neverending wash of pleasure, pain, and satisfaction, and when it faded, I was so sated and exhausted, I couldn't move.

"No more," my sharp alpha rasped. "Bakkhos, please. I can't take it, and neither can she."

"That'll teach you to torture my beautiful Sunshine, won't it?" my crazed alpha crowed, unapologetically smug as he pressed a kiss to my hip and switched off the torture device.

"Trying to—fucking kill me," my sharp alpha grunted.

I laughed, my eyes heavy lidded as Bakkhos laid out beside us, not caring about the body fluids soaked into the sheets. "I love you," I said, stroking my hand over his tattooed shoulder. I meant it, completely. "Not just because of the heat. Because of you."

Bakkhos's throat bobbed, his eyes squeezing shut as emotion cut into his face. "You know I love you, Sunshine. It's pretty obvious, I'm not hiding anything of what I feel."

"I don't love either of you bastards," Wild muttered, squeezing my hip. "In fact, I've decided I hate you. You especially, Bakkhos." But in a moment of weakness, he wrapped both arms around my middle and hugged me close—until he remembered himself and dropped his arms like he'd been burned.

But I heard his thoughts drifting through my mind, and knew his harshness was a shield. *Fuck, I wish I hated you. I can't be broken again.*

I turned as much as I could and stretched up to press my lips to Wild's neck, realising I'd got more of my brain function back. More than I'd had since my heat had first struck. "You're safe with me, Wild," I murmured, just for him. "It's me that's not safe with you, remember."

"Don't be nice to me," he said through gritted teeth.

"Why?" I breathed.

He didn't answer—aloud.

Because it makes it impossible to push you away.

But he did push me away; the second his knot shrank enough to withdraw, he pulled out of me and scrambled out of my nest, throwing on clothes and not even bothering to clean himself of our combined fluids before he marched for the door.

"He'll come around," Bakkhos promised, snuggling up to me.

But I wasn't sure. Wild really had been broken, and he refused to let me close. Which was fine; I had bigger things to worry about.

"What happened with my dad?" I asked, scrubbing my eyes, the clarity like waking from a heavy sleep. The heat wasn't over, but it was sleeping, content to stay in the background for now. "Is he gone?"

Bakkhos winced, and stroked the bond mark on my neck. "It'll be better coming from Kaan. I'll go get him."

He climbed out of the nest before I could stop him, leaving me cold and afraid in my dirty nest.

23

ANSWERS

I covered myself in a white silk sheet as the door opened again, Kaan's heavy tread easily recognisable.

"What's going on?" I asked the second he came into sight—and frowned when he staggered to a stop, the door slamming hard behind him as his nostrils flared. His eyes went pitch black, and his barrel chest expanded on a sharp breath as a growl filled the hotel room—a sound of primal, carnal need.

I whimpered. The heat threatened to send all my thoughts scattering again.

"What happened with my dad?" I demanded before I forgot to be worried at all.

Kaan sighed and dragged a hand down his face, stalking over to the chair in the corner with a slump in his shoulders.

"The scout Wild tore to shreds managed to get a message out to his pack before we took him down," he muttered, rubbing a hand down his beard and looking at a spot on the wall instead of at me.

My heart battered my ribcage; dread of being caught and dragged back to my old pack—or killed before I could try to fight back—gave me palpitations. "What message?"

"Where to find the Broken Pack for starters," Kaan replied, anger twisting his voice. "He told them he scented an omega, and it turns out your father has allied with Magnolia and Zinnia packs, or whatever they're calling their combined pack, so he heard the message."

I covered my mouth with shaking hands, any arousal turned to chilling ice. "My pack have two other packs helping them look for me? They're going to find me. They'll kill me again—"

A vicious snarl made my words catch in my throat, and I shook, pressing my knees to my chest under the sheet. "Your *old* pack, Nix. You're not theirs anymore. And no way in *hell* are they going to hurt you." He met my panicked stare, and the eye contact made my heart cinch tight, my bottom lip weak. "You're one of us now," he said, and I swore I felt a phantom rush of protectiveness in my chest. "You're a broken omega for us broken alphas. And we protect our own."

His hands curled into fists, and I ached to crawl out of my nest and take refuge in his big arms. "I don't give a shit what your dad says, you're ours."

"What does he say?" I breathed, not liking the sound of that at all.

Kaan shook his shaved head, a muscle feathering in his cheek. "He thinks he's owed Luneste's power, that you stole it from him and the pack. It was supposed to make the lands fertile, he claims, but instead..."

I blinked. "Instead, *what?*" I could guess, but I almost didn't want to know.

"Instead it amplified your own fertility, Nix."

I swallowed hard, thinking of the fluids covering the nest I sat in, leaking down my thighs. "Oh, goddess," I whimpered.

"Alright, that's it," Kaan muttered, and shoved out of his chair. "Make room for me, sweetheart, I'm coming into your nest. I won't claim you, but I can tell how terrified you are, and nothing in this world is going to stop me holding you."

My bottom lip finally gave way as tears stung my eyes, and I moved so Kaan could settle beside me, not seeming to care about the dampness of the sheets.

"He's not going to get you," he promised, holding my gaze. His voice vibrated so much deeper this close. "Come here, Nix."

Falling into his arms was the most natural thing in the world, and my tears finally overflowed. They slid like scalding water down my cheeks as Kaan's arms wrapped around me, solid and strong and so big they covered every part of my back. I screwed my eyes shut and breathed his whiskey scent as every bit of tension fell from my body.

"What if he finds us again?" I whispered. "What if my brothers do? And the other packs, too?"

"Then we'll do to them what Wild did to the scout," Kaan replied gently, his words moving through his chest to mine. I laid my head on his shoulder, drugged on his comfort. "We'll tear them to pieces before they can even lay a finger on you."

"But my dad—"

"Ran off with his tail between his legs, injured and bleeding," he interrupted, his hand flexing on my spine. "We won't be seeing him for a while. Sleep, Nix, I've got you."

I wanted to argue, but the comfort of being so close to

him—feeling him breathe against me, with his scent surrounding me—was an irresistible lure. When Kaan started a soft purr that promised safety, I let it wrap around me and comfort my soul.

I could almost pretend he wanted me.

24

DRAVEN

I'd slept deep and dreamless, but by the time the sun rose and woke me, I was so tense and squirmy with arousal that I could barely stand it. Kaan had wrapped himself around me, chest to chest, with my nose against the spot on his neck that called me to bite. His scent was thickest there, tempting me with alpha pheromones, and I could do nothing to control my body's reaction as I blinked awake, slick pooled between my thighs.

But *fuck*, it had felt so good to sleep beside him, his strong arms keeping me safe, his heat wrapped all around me, and his low, comforting purr rumbling even as he slept—answering a subconscious need to offer me protection and care.

I tried to shift slowly, carefully, but he still woke up, his purr turning to a long, sleepy groan that did things to my insides. I wanted to writhe against him and wake him properly, the way I craved to—with my tongue caressing the ridge on his thick shaft, finding every spot that made him tense and grunt until he was spilling in my mouth. I had to force myself away from his tempting body; I dragged a shaky breath into my lungs and rolled aside.

"Morning, sweet girl," he said, scratchy and endearing. Great, now my needy pussy *and* my soft heart wanted him.

"Morning," I breathed, trying not to inhale too much of his scent in case I lost the fight with my instincts. He didn't want me; I'd only hurt myself. And I might have *been* desperate, but I didn't want to *look* it. Or make a fool of myself with my new alpha, especially given he was a good, considerate, fair alpha, and I was so grateful to be in his pack.

"Not one for morning cuddles, sweetheart?" he asked, a corner of his mouth curved beneath his beard.

I muffled my groan, but it still rumbled the back of my throat quietly. All these terms of endearment were going to wreck me. "If I cuddle you, I won't be able to control myself," I whispered, my face burning. "And I won't—I won't do anything you don't want. I know we're just alpha and pack, nothing more."

The look he gave me was almost pained, and I didn't understand it one bit. If he wanted me, why push me away? I held very still as he lifted his hand, a knuckle trailing down my cheek. "I appreciate it, sweet girl."

My eyes slid shut, and a tremble started in my hands. I wanted him so badly it hurt.

"I'll go see if the others are up," he said, still in that soft, sleep-scratchy voice that made me want to melt into him. My eyes flew open as soft lips pressed to my cheek, followed by the rasp of a beard that almost made my eyes roll back. Oh, I wanted to feel that *everywhere*. My hand shot out of its own accord, wrapping around his wrist as he made to leave the nest, a whine filling my throat. "Nix," Kaan said sadly, rejection in his eyes.

A flash of pain burned through my heart. I dropped my hand, forcing a smile. "I know, sorry."

I tried not to cry as he left the nest, but hormones and chemicals whirled around inside me, making my eyes sting and my pussy clench all at once in a confusing blur of emotion. I groaned, frustrated at this damn heat.

"You'll be alright, Nix," Kaan promised, fastening his shoes and grabbing a jacket I hadn't even noticed him remove the night before. I was sad to see his big arms disappear, sad to see black canvas hide beautiful inked moons and twisting, thorny vines. I wanted to run my tongue up their winding path from his wrists to his shoulders, and a pleading sound tumbled out before I could stop it.

"Fuck, Nix," Kaan breathed, running a hand over his head. "I wish I could, sweet girl, I really do."

The rejection was like hot poison in my belly. It shocked me out of the haze of need, and I sank into my nest, turning so I couldn't see Kaan and get distracted by wanting him again. He didn't want me. Would *never* want me.

I held in my emotions until the door softly shut and his footsteps marched down the hall outside, and then they came tumbling out, adding tears to the mix of fluids soaked into the sheets and pillows of my nest.

I'd be fine. I'd survive this. I had to—what other options did I have? I'd rather hurt every minute of every day than walk away from this pack. I ... I belonged here. I really, properly belonged in a way I hadn't expected to after how my first pack treated me. Kaan would never stab a knife in my heart; he'd gut anyone who even tried to.

Even if he'd never want me as his mate.

I curled into a ball and held myself, running through all my memories of Bakkhos's sweet kisses and obsessive love, Draven's soft smiles and tentative affection, and even Wild's ruthless need. I was wanted; I held tight to that fact until the door snicked open again.

I knew him by the quiet, measured footsteps—like a shadow stalking the sun—and tension fell from my shoulders in relief.

"Nixie?" Draven murmured. "I brought you something to eat."

I found the cleanest sheet and wrapped it around my body, climbing out of the nest and flushing as his dark blue eyes ran over my face, my shoulders, and the shape of me through the sheet. As if I was a beautiful work of art and not an over-sexed hot mess. "Hi," I said, feeling shy as he stared at me.

"Hi," he replied, his voice huskier than it had been a minute ago. He blinked, and cleared his throat, bringing a tray over to the desk by the window. I watched with interest as he laid several things on its dinged wooden surface—a bowl of cereal, a plate of fruit, french pastries, a full cooked breakfast, a glass of orange juice, a bottle of water, a mug of coffee, and a cup of tea.

I laughed, my cheeks aching from how wide I was smiling. "You brought everything I could possibly want."

Draven's gaze settled on me as I came up beside him, soft and calm in a way that made me feel ... free. Free to be myself, awkward and imperfect and needy as I was. "*Almost* everything," he disagreed, and dug around in the pocket of his cargo pants with reddened hands until he produced a bar of Cadbury's Dairy Milk. My eyes flew wide, and I had *no idea* how the sound I let out was so high pitched; I bounced on my toes and reached for the chocolate, butterflies taking flight in my belly. "Alright," he said in that soft, honey-smooth voice of his as he handed it over. "*Now* that's everything you could want."

He watched with a look of fond indulgence as I ripped the purple wrapper and placed a chunk into my mouth, groaning as it dissolved on my tongue. Fucking heaven.

Draven laughed as I put the bar on the desk and threw my arms around him, hugging him tight.

"Thank you," I breathed, only self conscious now I'd thrown myself at him. But his arms wound around me before I could let go, hands splaying against my back, and I melted like the chocolate had melted on my tongue.

"You're welcome, Nixie. Do you want breakfast, too?"

"I suppose I *should* be a grown up and have more than chocolate for breakfast, shouldn't I?" I pretended to pout, resting my head on his chest and feeling something inside me settle, like he'd been what I needed for so long.

"If all you want is chocolate, I'll get you seven more bars," he promised, his soft voice like a caress.

"What do *you* want, Draven?" I asked just as quietly, and tilted my head back to peer up at him, my heart drumming fast.

His expression softened even further. "What I want isn't important, Nixie."

I shook my head, winding my arms around his middle and hugging him tight. "You're wrong. And how do you know we don't want the same thing?"

He laughed, glancing over the top of my head—not difficult given I didn't even come up to his shoulder. "I'm a killer, Nixie. I've hurt people—a lot of people. I'm not a good man. There's blood on my hands, and it will never wash off."

"Oh," I whispered, my heart breaking as I realised that was why he washed his hands so often. He was trying to get the blood off. I glanced at his red hands. Had he made himself bleed already this morning, and simply healed so nobody could see the damage? "Oh, Draven," I breathed.

"Bad men wouldn't torture themselves over it; bad men wouldn't care who they hurt. Trust me, I know bad men, and you're not one of them."

"Maybe not anymore," he replied, his throat bobbing. "But I was once, and there's no forgetting that. And I'll become that again to keep you safe."

I'd been holding myself back, keeping my touches to appropriate, platonic places, but I surged onto my tiptoes at those words, grasping the back of his neck and bringing his face down to mine. I kissed him slowly, willing him to feel how much I cared for him.

"I don't care who you killed," I said against his lips, my thighs starting to burn from how far up I had to lean to kiss my gentle giant. "None of that was your choice, Draven, and it doesn't make me like you any less. You're mine," I whispered, my stomach cramping in anticipation of his rejection —but Draven just grabbed handfuls of my backside, kissing me deeper and so passionately that my head spun.

"I'm not scared of your darkness," I said between kisses, gasping for breath. For such a quiet, reserved man, he could kiss damn well. I was panting, slick rolling down my thigh and onto his dark jeans. "It matches my own."

I gasped when he ducked and caught me under my thighs, lifting me up against him so he could kiss me deeper, harder, until I was clutching at his shoulders, desperate and aching.

A whine built in my chest, the haze of need descending again as Draven sucked on my tongue. The groans of pleasure in the back of his throat made me even more frantic. When he dragged his mouth from mine, looking deep into my eyes, still questioning that I wanted him, I rolled up against his chest and pressed a lingering kiss to the scar on his jaw, and then traced every silver slash and cut, tracing my way up his cheek until I reached his temple.

"You're mine," I breathed, emotion catching in my chest, squeezing my heart. "All mine."

"Yours," he agreed, fastening his lips to my throat, kissing every inch of skin. "Goddess, Nixie. Is this real?"

I rolled my hips against the bulge in his jeans, trusting him to not let me fall as I made sure to rub my needy pussy over every millimeter of hard, aching cock. "It's real, Draven. I promise." I held his gaze when he lifted his head to look at me, and pulled the silk sheet away from me, pressing my naked body against his clothed strength. "And I'm all yours. I want—" A bolt of shyness struck, and my cheeks burned as I finished, "I want you so much."

His hands flexed on my bare backside, the feeling of skin to skin making my chest hitch and my pussy soak his jeans. The heat was eating any bit of sense and intelligence I'd gained, and I didn't care one little bit. I just needed him, I just needed Draven all to myself.

"Fuck, Nixie," he growled. My whole body went electric at the growl, so soft compared to Kaan's but powerful and deep. I felt it in every part of me, felt it *inside* me. "You really want me—broken and scarred and bloodstained?"

"So, so badly," I confirmed, wriggling against him, trying to get the hands on my ass to move closer to my core. "Do you want me?"

"More than anything I've ever wanted before," he rasped, setting my bare ass on the desk beside my breakfast so he could strip out of his shirt, baring a taut, defined chest and stomach. His scars continued down to his abs and, and there in the middle of his chest, bigger than mine, was a crescent moon and star—the mark that made him mine. I wanted to taste it, and saliva pooled in my mouth. "I want you more than freedom," he said softly, and set himself between my spread thighs, ducking his head for a deeper, longer kiss that reduced me to a puddle of senseless need.

"Here," he said, moving back and ignoring my pout. "Drink this, my beauty. You need to hydrate with all the slick you're producing."

I watched his every move through hooded eyes, the controlled power in his motions making me even hotter. Everything he did was calculated and precise, every action careful and determined. "Do you like my slick, alpha?" I purred, throaty and rough.

"I love it, Nixie," he replied honestly, and set a bottle of water to my lips. I drank it all, never taking my eyes off my tall, scarred, beautiful alpha. He was a contradiction of hardness and softness, strength and vulnerability, and he drew me like a moth to a flame. "Good," he praised when I swallowed the last drop. I strained towards him, aching deep inside, but he kept his distance. "Now some food. What do you want to eat?"

"You," I moaned.

His mouth kicked up into a smile, deep blue eyes crinkling. "From the tray, my beauty."

"Alpha," I whined.

I melted with a sigh, turning my face into his hand when he touched my cheek.

"How about a pastry?" He watched my expression for something, but I just stared at him, pleading silently. "Open wide, Nixie," he said, lifting a croissant from the tray.

I widened my thighs instantly, slick rolling down my pussy and pooling on the table.

He laughed, a deep huff of sound that made me wetter. "You're so cute," he murmured, and pulled me in for a deep, loving kiss. "Open your mouth, I meant."

I obeyed without thought, and ate the pieces of pastry he placed on my tongue, sucking on his fingers whenever I could catch them. I made sure to swirl my tongue so he let out choked, groaning sounds. I loved those sounds, and wanted so many more.

"I-I brought you something," he said, his throat bobbing when I'd finished the croissant plus a pain au chocolat. "A gift. Is that okay?"

I sat upright, staring at him in surprise, a warm, fizzy feeling in my belly. "My alpha brought me a gift?" I asked, husky and low.

His nervous expression turned to satisfaction, and only briefly dipped to my open legs, to the mess I was making of the countertop with every glance, touch, and word he gave me. "Your alpha did," he agreed.

"Is it more chocolate?" I asked eagerly, wondering if I could lick the melted sweet off his fingers, already missing having them in my mouth.

"No, my beauty," he laughed, squeezing my knee with one hand—delicious and calloused and so, so good.

He reached into his pocket with his other hand. "I know you're deep in your heat now," he said gently, "and all you want is to be satisfied, but I didn't want you to be scared when your heat ends. And I..." He ran a hand over his head and tugged at his dark ponytail. "I know what it's like to be running from someone who wants to hurt you. I wanted to give you something so you'd always know you're strong enough to fight your demons."

I blinked, more at his sweet, caring tone than his words —I only understood half of them.

"So this is for you," he finished, and opened the soft jewellery pouch in his hand, taking out a strand of silver. "It's a bracelet."

A strip of gleaming, curved silver connected to a length of chain on either side, and there were words punched into its shiny surface. He'd brought me a gift. My alpha.

"What does it say?" I asked, holding out my wrist for him to put it on me, mostly to feel his fingers rasping over my skin. He didn't disappoint, and my eyes slid shut at the touch on my sensitive skin.

"Day by day," he answered, pressing a kiss to the inside of my wrist once he'd fastened the clasp, "I will not break."

"Alpha?" I asked, drowsy with the feeling of his fingers on my skin.

"Yes, my beauty?" He laid another kiss on my wrist and stood, but he didn't let go of me, stroking my fast pulse.

I swallowed, a shadow of fear darkening my mood. But his slow caresses made me brave, so I reached up to push my lilac hair off my shoulder and tilted my neck. "Bite?" I whispered.

His breath caught, and my soft alpha's hand trailed up my arm to my shoulder and back down my side to my hip, until I was purring. "You want to be bonded to me? Fully?"

I nodded, capturing his gaze when he gave me another of those questioning glances. "I want. *Please.*"

"Shh, beauty," he murmured, wrapping his arms around me and ducking his head to meet my gaze. He was so damned tall, and for some reason that made me squirmy and even more aroused. "There's nothing I wouldn't give you. If you want my bite, it's yours."

I held his stare, pleading, arching my neck.

"Come here," he murmured, pulling me close and lifting me from the desk. A shiver ran down my spine, and a sense of rightness locked in my chest as he kicked off his shoes and carried me to my nest, laying me down in the soft fabrics. He even went back for the sheet I'd dropped and passed it to me, like it was the most important thing. I didn't know how he'd sensed that I wanted it back in the nest, but I gave him my brightest smile and spread the silk across the wall of my nest, fluffing until it was perfect again.

"Can I sit there, my beauty?" my alpha asked in a soft, honey-smooth voice. I nodded fast, my need rising to a fever pitch and a tight cramp in my gut as I ached to have him closer. I watched like a hawk as my soft alpha settled against the edge of the nest, stretching his legs out in front of him, and when he held out a hand in invitation, I fell over myself to straddle his lap. A sigh fell from my lips when his arm settled across my back and everything felt *right*.

My alpha traced the bumps of my spine, pressing a kiss to my neck, above my crazed alpha's bite. "Here?" he asked, guttural and raw.

"*Please*," I breathed, closing my eyes as anticipation made me breathless.

"Nixie?" He kissed my neck again, his breathing as ragged as mine. "I think I love you."

I opened my mouth to reply, but all that came out was a moan as he bit deep, sparks and emotions erupting to life inside my chest. I felt like my chest would explode as the bond expanded, sharpened, and filled with colour and life.

He felt everything so deeply that my head spun, my body aching as it tried to contain the enormity of his devotion and awe. He really did love me; I felt it, clear and true, like a gleaming river.

"Wow," I breathed, wincing slightly as he withdrew his teeth, and then I moaned as his tongue lapped over the punctures, soothing the sting. Turning me molten with desperation. "*Alpha*."

"I know, my beauty," he soothed, stroking my back as he licked my bite. "I can feel how badly you need me now." His voice was soft and on the edge of a laugh, as if he couldn't believe what he was feeling. "I'm sorry I didn't sate your need earlier," he breathed, kissing the column of my throat now and making me hot and squirmy. "I'll never deny you again."

He clutched me close, my chest to his, my head on his shoulder, and something rippled through the bond, like a shadow across water. "Alpha?"

He blew out a breath, tracing my spine with gentle fingertips. "Sorry, Nixie, I didn't mean to be gloomy. I just ... can't believe how good it feels, how *right*. It doesn't hurt at all."

I had just enough presence of mind left to realise he was thinking about the alpha who'd forced him into a mate bond. The bond he'd described as barbed wire, as if it had cut him inside until he bled and scarred. A deep, guttural growl built in my chest and curled my upper lip, and I held my alpha tighter, ready to rip out the throat of anyone who tried to hurt him. I growled louder, until the sound filled the whole room, just *daring* anyone to touch him.

I startled at the kiss placed on my throat, as if he wanted to feel the vibrations against his lips. Kisses travelled down to my collarbone, and then to my chest where the growl rattled powerfully, lingering on the ugly scar there.

"I know I'm safe with you," he said, soothing me. "I can feel that, Nixie. And you're safe with me. Can you feel it?"

I nodded, but I didn't stop growling. "Mine."

He laughed, his deep blue eyes twinkling, no longer bloodshot like when I'd first seen them. "Yours, my beauty." His hands flattened to my back and pressed me to him, my breasts against carved muscle and my growl vibrating through both of us. "Of course I'm yours; who else could love a beast like me?" He kissed my cheekbone, smiling. "No one would dare. But you're not afraid of anything, are you, Nixie? My brave Nixie."

I loved the sound of my name in his mouth. I wanted to taste it, so I kissed him, my growl tapering off as the hands roaming my skin distracted me.

"Here," he said between kisses, and I loved the throaty quality of his usually smooth voice. "Get me wet and ready for you, beauty."

I shuddered as he squeezed my hip, adjusting our positioning so his cock pressed to my pussy. I wasted no time obeying his instruction, sliding my wetness along his shaft, gasping every time he brushed my clit.

"It makes no sense that this is real," he laughed, sinking a hand into my long hair and dragging me to his mouth for a deep, sucking kiss. Slick drenched both of us as I rubbed my pussy up and down his dick, my body so tight with need.

"My brave, beautiful Nixie." He met my eyes, cashmere blue so dark with need and desperation—and a hint of wickedness. "Take me. Take me deep, and don't stop until we're both ruined."

25

PLEAS

I pressed my hand to the mate mark on my soft alpha's chest, and caught his lips in a deep, claiming kiss. I swore we both held our breath as I lined his curved, veiny cock up with my entrance, and I exhaled hard when the tip thrust inside.

"Oh—fuck," he gasped, one hand buried in my hair, sending delicious sparks across my scalp, while the other gripped my waist. I rolled my hips, taking him deeper every time.

"Nixie, *fuck*," he swore, a delicious growl deepening his voice until I throbbed around the inches already filling me. I watched his face obsessively, rapt as blue eyes rolled back and his throat bobbed in a hard swallow. His neck proved irresistible; I ducked my head to run my tongue along his adam's apple, and my eyes fluttered when his growl soared, louder, harsher.

Yess. I wanted my alpha to lose control, to let go of everything except this—except us.

I was so wet that my pussy eagerly took him deeper, sensitive flesh clinging to him as I settled with my ass against my alpha's hips. My eyes blew wide at the feeling of his tip pressing insistently on the front wall of my pussy.

"Oh," I gasped, the muscles in my legs starting to shake. Was that ... my G-spot? I was going to lose my damn mind. Even the insatiable omega in me was stunned.

"Just," my alpha choked out, wrapping an arm around me, so tense I was worried about him. "Just stay there, my beauty. I want to feel you. *Shit.*"

I laughed softly, unable to help throbbing around him as I settled with him fully inside, filling me so much it was hard to process the sensations. Thinking was a long, lost memory I waved goodbye to.

"I could stay like this forever," he rasped, nudging my chin up to suck on his bite on my throat.

I whimpered.

"You have no idea how good this feels," he groaned, his voice muffled by my neck, his tongue lapping at the bite as if I tasted amazing. "Everything that happened to me, everything in my past, it was all worth it to be here, feeling you grip me tight, knowing you feel the same about me. Knowing this means something."

I dug my fingernails into his shoulders, trapped between satisfied and desperate. "Alpha," I whined.

He dragged a hand through his hair, ripping out the band tying it back, and I rumbled a pleased purr as silken dark hair fell around his shoulders, brushing my knuckles. "This is gonna kill me," he laughed, but he gripped my hip, guiding me up his length and back down again.

It was all the encouragement I needed, and I grasped his scarred shoulders, loving the flex of muscle there as he held my waist with both hands, his palms so big they swallowed my hips with delicious heat and pressure. I was already losing my mind before I sank down on him again and again and again. My alpha's eyes were deep and adoring, scanning every part of me as if he couldn't decide what to focus on—my flushed face, my strained expression, my bouncing boobs, or my pussy swallowing his cock with every fast, needy thrust.

The bond in my chest filled with so much emotion I expected it to spill out in a burst of light. Adoration, need, and ecstasy mixed up with relief, disbelief, and possessiveness, a storm filling my soul—his storm.

"Yours," I promised, sliding my hands down his chest, obsessed with the pale crescent moon and star on his chest and the silver scars covering him. I curved over him, the smack of skin against skin echoing through the nest as I rode faster, running my tongue over his scars, tasting the salt of his skin. "Alpha," I whined, wanting more, wanting him to take control.

Knowing exactly what I was desperate for, my alpha's hands tightened on my hips and he growled, so sudden and deep that I slumped against his chest, my eyes fluttering with pleasure so intense that I hugged him so tight.

"Goddess," he choked out, grabbing a fistful of my ass as he growled in a strangled voice.

The curve to his shaft was rapidly undoing me, and I writhed, right on the edge of overstimulated but still wanting more. I dropped a hand to my pussy and frantically circled my clit, my body tensed all over.

"Come with me," my alpha begged, choked and tight and still growling for me. "Nixie, please—"

I clasped him close and slammed my hips up and down on him, achy and taut and pleading. Words tripped off my tongue with no meaning. My alpha knocked my hand aside and replaced my fingers with his, strumming my swollen clit and throwing me over the edge into a shaking orgasm.

"Alpha!" I shouted, throbbing sporadically when he thrust deeper, stretching me around his knot. My eyes rolled back. There was *nothing* as satisfying to an omega as being full of their alpha's knot, the swollen bulb pressing on every nerve, and dragging one orgasm into two and three and four.

I choked on a whine, grabbing my alpha's wrist in a bruising hold as he kept massaging my clit.

"Nixie, please," he begged, breathless and gasping. His pupils were as wide as mine must have been, a red flush creeping up his jaw to his cheeks when I locked eyes with him. "Please don't stop, it feels too good."

I shook my head, but I wasn't sure if I was promising not to stop or pleading for mercy.

My back arched when he resumed stimulating my clit, his knot pulsing and swelling inside me. His eyes rolled back, and sheer bliss filled the bond, infectious and demanding. I cried out as he coaxed a second orgasm from me, groaning in rapture as my pussy milked his cock and knot, prolonging his orgasm.

His deep, strangled groan was so hot that I clenched around his knot again, dragging more of those choked sounds from his strained throat until he was panting like me, gripping my ass so hard he'd leave marks behind. "I don't want this—" he rasped, "to ever end."

I pressed my head to his shoulder, my tongue on his throat. "Bite, alpha?"

"Oh holy fuck yes," he replied in a rush, grinding his knot deeper inside me, the two of us locked together.

My gums ached as my teeth sharpened, and a sense of blissful relief washed over me when I sank my teeth into his neck, claiming him for all to see. With the mark on his chest and my bite on his neck, no one could ever take him from me. He was *mine*.

His broken whine was loud in my ears, strangled by his gasp when I spasmed around him, pleasure feeding pleasure, amplified through our tether until my head swam and all I knew was he was my alpha and I could never let go of him.

"Nixie," he grunted, frantically tugging at my hair to bring my mouth to his. His lips demanded and devoured, and I sank both my hands into his long hair, holding him tight as I slicked my tongue over his, nipping his lower lip and earning a shudder from my soft alpha. "One more," he pleaded against my mouth, his eyes heavy lidded and drowsy. "Please, my beauty, let me feel you come one more time."

My inner muscles clenched at the thought, and even though my clit was sensitive, I nodded, wanting to give him everything.

"Alpha," I gasped as his thumb moved over my engorged nerves, slowly and patiently despite the sharp edge of need in his deep blue eyes. "*My* alpha."

I held him bruisingly tight, leaning closer to taste the pale slashes of his scars, like I'd wanted to since I met him. My inner muscles tightening with every brush of his fingers against slick flesh, I laid kisses on his temple, his cheek, his jaw, and his bobbing throat. I swore he held me tighter with every kiss, his breathing uneven and his pace increasing on my clit until my breathing was every bit as wrecked as his.

"Alpha," I choked out, the only word I knew as my body tensed and my toes locked tight. I slammed my mouth on my alpha's in a wild kiss as my climax tore through me.

"Nixie," he growled into my mouth, wrapping his arm tight around me until I was trapped against his chest, exactly where I wanted to be. The spasms pulsed harder through my pussy at his deep voice. "Nix—"

He shuddered harder, wrapping both arms around me and holding me desperately as he ground his knot deeper, breathless gasps—his and mine—filling the air as aftershocks gripped me hard. I whined at the sensation of him spilling in me again.

"Goddess, Nixie," my alpha breathed when I went limp in his arms, my eyes drifting shut. "That was..." He laughed, kissing his bite on my throat. "Unbelievable."

I just snuggled deeper into him, our scents thick in the air—a comforting blend that tugged me towards a nap. It was bright outside the windows, and sun streamed into the hotel room, but I was exhausted and more than ready to sleep wrapped up in my alpha.

Tightening his arms around me, he slid down until he lay on his back, holding the back of my head to his chest as if he knew exactly what I needed. Maybe that was part of our mate bond.

"Sleep, my beauty," he murmured. "I'm not going anywhere."

With his arms around me, I fell swiftly asleep, nightmares of my father hunting us kept at bay by his purr.

26

BOMBSHELL

I floated through unconsciousness like a lantern sent into the sky, aimless and free. It was the best I'd felt in so long, and I knew it was because of my bonds to Draven and Bakkhos, because my alpha and my pack made me feel safe.

But like a lantern, I eventually landed, and I knew I wasn't alone.

"You listened to me," Luneste said, in that ageless voice of whispers and lullabies. She closed the distance between us as I blinked at our surroundings—a forest of ivory trees, with leaves the colour of paper and grass the colour of snow. "You found the Broken Pack and the alpha of alphas."

I nodded, blinking at her glowing face. She was youthful and wise all at once, her features like carved marble, like a sculpture that should be in a museum where thousands of people could admire her each day.

The look she gave me was fond, her mercury eyes crinkled and warm despite the cold radiating from her. The pool of moonlight in my belly reacted, surging like a wave, and I shuddered. It felt like I'd swallowed ice water. "Stay with them, and you'll be safe."

Her smile deepened, and I jumped as her cool hand pressed to my abdomen. "And so will this seed of life."

"What?" I asked, scratchy and raw. One half of me recoiled so hard my breathing cut off, while the rest of me wanted to cry with happiness. I couldn't have a baby—I couldn't. My dad wanted me dead, and my old pack would hunt me, and kill me for real this time. I wasn't safe. And worse: what if I was as bad a parent as my dad had been these few years? What if I'd lost my mum too young to be a good one myself? I wasn't ready.

But I *wanted* to be ready. I wanted the happily ever after with a protective pack, two loving mates, and a raucous pup running around our packlands. It was what I'd always known I was meant for as an omega—for sex, for breeding, for pups. But I *couldn't* want it.

Not now.

"Tough," Luneste said, both harsh and wry. "Life waits for no one. But I can promise your pregnancy will be successful."

I bit my lip so hard I bled, panic spiralling through me.

"Your old pack are close; you need to move before they catch you. But there's a place for you," she added, cold seeping into my jaw as she cupped my face until I met her silver eyes. "Where only my chosen children can find you, and where you'll never be threatened."

Hope made my chest hurt. I wanted to believe there was a place like that, but I didn't believe in fairytale endings. Those were just for books.

"Be brave, daughter," Luneste ordered, her voice like iron. "Hope won't kill you—it will save you."

I dragged a cold breath into my lungs and nodded. I could hardly refuse *the goddess*, could I? "Okay. I'll try."

Cold lips pressed to my forehead, and she stepped back. "You already know how to find it. It's there, in your mind."

And it was. I shuddered, and not just because of the cold. This was impossible to believe, but Luneste had only steered me right so far. I stared as her walking stick manifested, and she took steady steps away from me.

"Wait!" I called out, taking a frantic step.

But the goddess was already gone, leaving me to reel from everything she'd told me.

There was a secret packlands where we'd be safe.

But Dad and my brothers had almost caught up to us.

And I was pregnant.

Fuck.

27

AFTER

I wasn't surprised to wake up and find my heat had broken. Its purpose had been served, after all. And thanks to Luneste's magic in my blood, making me extra fertile, there was life growing inside me.

I felt sick—and not because of morning sickness.

I made a face at the wet squelch of the sheets as I rolled over—and found I was alone in the nest. Alone, covered in slick and cum, and panicking. I wanted Draven and Bakkhos and Kaan, but I'd have settled for Wild right now. At least his bullshit would have distracted me.

Ugh, I couldn't believe I'd slept with him. And enthusiastically—desperately. He'd knotted me, for goddess's sake. And even with my estrus over, it didn't stop wetness pooling between my thighs at the memory. At least it wasn't a deluge of slick rolling down my thigh. But I was still *covered* in the stuff—the evidence of my mindless need.

"Ick," I hissed as I sat up and crawled out of the nest, wrinkling my nose as wet sheets pressed against my bare skin. The scents were still comforting, and always would be, but with my brain function returned, the rest of it was gross.

We should probably tip the hotel when we left; we'd definitely ruined the mattress.

I left a trail of wet footprints on the carpet as I padded to the bathroom, pausing to grab a dry pastry from the breakfast tray Draven had brought this morning—yesterday morning? How long had I slept? I swore it looked like early morning outside the window. But he must have knotted me all through the afternoon...

"Fuck," I swore viciously. Another day lost. How long had we been here, in a haze of sweat, sex, and scents?

The pastry scraped my dry throat, stale and unappetising, but I chased it with half a dozen strawberries and the glass of orange juice. Nothing stopped a pleasant warmth spreading through me at how thoughtful Draven had been. Had he given me a gift, or had I dreamt that in my estrus haze?

No, there on my wrist was the curved silver band, engraved with his meaningful words. My heart softened as I set down the empty glass and ran my finger over the words stamped on the bracelet. I'd never been given a gift by a man before, not even by someone I was dating. It made me feel ... special.

And still covered in sticky fluids.

Ugh. I let my hand fall back to my side and trudged into the bathroom, starting the shower while I emptied my bladder. Not that there was much to empty; any water I'd drank had gone right to creating slick for my alphas to fill and knot me.

I shuddered at the flashes of memory, my skin tightening, heating.

"Enough," I growled. "You've had enough sex for a year, Nixie, think of something else."

But damn, it was hard.

Just like my alphas' cocks had been hard.

"Goddess *dammit.*"

I stepped into the water when it was scalding—and then panicked like crazy when I remembered I was pregnant, scrambling to turn it to a balmy warmth. Wasn't hot water bad for pregnancies? Or was that hot baths? I didn't know, and my panic sharpened, shooting through the hotel roof. What was I going to do? Dad was going to find us, and even if he didn't kill me, what would he *do* with me? What would he do with the baby growing inside me? The pack had been desperate for pups—would they take my baby from me?

A growl rushed up my throat in warning, even though there was no one there to hear it. I might have been terrified to be a mum, and completely clueless where to begin, but no way in *hell* was anyone taking them from me.

I didn't stop growling the whole time I showered, but by the time I stepped out and found a towel, I felt better. Calmer for being cleaner, and more myself for the time to think without alphas all around me. I was less like the mindless omega who lived only for alphas bearing down on her, grinding her into the nest as pleasure detonated inside her.

The one good thing about being pregnant was I wouldn't have to deal with another estrus for nine months.

Wrapped in a towel that barely hit my thigh, I stood in the middle of the bedroom and frowned from the nest to the bags stacked in the corner. I'd have to borrow someone's clothes. Bakkhos' or Wild's, maybe. Wild was probably the closest to my size.

As I rifled through their things, I searched my chest, too, trying to figure out how I was feeling—beyond being terrified to be a mum. My body should have hurt after the pounding it had taken, but except for a few bruises and my bites, I was fine. Better than fine; an achy tightness that had always been with me had eased, finally satisfied, and I felt light, unburdened. Which was a lie, of course. My old pack was coming for me, I wasn't safe, and I wasn't too sure what to do with the fact that I was mated to two wolves now, and there were two others who refused to bond with me.

Their rejection hurt, like a jagged tooth I couldn't help but prod with my tongue. But having Bakkhos and Draven ... I should have been overwhelmed and unsure about the newness of those bonds. Yet they slotted into my chest like missing puzzle pieces. I glanced at the crescent moon on my wrist, and thought of the ones on Draven's chest and Bakkhos's thigh. I'd never expected to be given a fated mate, let alone two. Well, four—but I couldn't think about that. I knew exactly how I felt about Kaan not bonding me and Wild refusing my bite. Heartache and relief in equal measure. Longing so extreme it sat like a weight on my soul.

My thoughts kept circling back to Luneste's warning about my dad finding us, so I pulled on a pair of Bakkhos's sweatpants and one of Wild's tight T-shirts. On a whim, I stole a black hoodie from Draven's bag, and wrapped myself up in the fabric. I didn't care that it dwarfed me; it smelled of coffee and copper and made me feel better. Made me feel brave.

I glanced at the bracelet on my wrist for strength, and took a step to leave the room in search of my alphas when I spotted the phone Draven had left behind, maybe for emergencies, maybe carelessly. Either way, I grabbed it and scrolled through his contacts until I found Kaan's name. I didn't hesitate before calling, more than a little reluctant to leave the room alone. What if Dad was lurking around the hallways, waiting for me to emerge?

"Nix?" Kaan asked, answering on the second ring. Draven had definitely left the phone for emergencies.

"Where are you all? Can we leave? I had a dream—Luneste says my dad's going to find us soon."

"I'm coming," he promised, and the line clicked dead.

I dropped my hand, not sure if I should be relieved or even more nervous.

He hadn't said if we would leave, or if we'd stay and fight my dad head on.

I knew if that happened, we wouldn't be as lucky as we were last time. Someone would get hurt.

28

COLD

I wound the car window down until wind tugged strands of lilac hair from my ponytail, trying to subtly clear my scent from the car in case the alphas smelled my secret. Kaan hadn't taken any convincing to leave the hotel, thankfully, but he didn't believe there was a paradise waiting for us out there, where Luneste's children would be safe. He'd agreed to follow the directions the goddess had left in my head, but only because we had nowhere better to go.

As for my pregnancy ... I was too cowardly to tell them. What if it changed things? What if Draven and Bakkhos didn't want me anymore? I swallowed the knot in my throat, tilting my face into the wind and sucking down the biting air.

I'd definitely slept through yesterday, and fucked the previous week away, but I refused to lose any more days. I needed to be lucid and aware so I could stay safe, and always one step ahead of Dad and my brothers.

"Hungry, Nixie?" Bakkhos asked, leaning around in the passenger seat to look at me as the motorway blurred past outside. I scrounged up a smile for him, and nodded. I'd been hungry all morning, even with the fruit and pastry I'd eaten. "Kaan, can we stop somewhere? I'm starving."

"You're always starving," Kaan muttered. He'd been tense ever since my warning, and now his hands clenched around the steering wheel until his knuckles turned white.

Draven, always the quiet, calming influence, proposed, "We could stock up on food, and then drive for the rest of the day."

Kaan grunted. I wasn't sure if it was in agreement or argument until he turned off the motorway toward the next service station. I bit my lip, anxious to leave the relative safety of the car, but I'd be glad for the fresh air to hide my scent.

How none of them had realised it yet, I didn't know, but I was lucky. Not just because I was scared of the future, but because wolves were stiflingly protective when their mates were pregnant. I wanted to be safe, but not shut up in a room and left there while my pack guarded the door like I'd seen wolves do in my old pack. Back when they could actually conceive, when I was much younger.

"Right," Kaan growled, turning off the engine when we'd pulled into a parking space in front of a McDonalds, Subway, and a little shop. "Everyone stick together. No arguments about what we're going to eat; we go in, we order, and we get out again."

His no-nonsense voice sent a chill down my spine, but I lifted my hand like I was in class and said, "Um. I need the bathroom. Am I allowed?"

Kaan sighed, less in exasperation and more in ... disappointment. "Of course you do, Nix, I'm sorry sweetheart. You three go order food, get something nutritious not just junk food. I'll take Nix to the bathroom."

"I don't need to be guarded," I offered, but Kaan was already getting out of the car and ignoring my complaint. Right then.

"Just let him do his overprotective routine," Wild said with a snort. "He'll never leave you alone; it's better to let him get on with it."

I jerked my head in a nod, not speaking to that bastard.

"I can hear you," Kaan said from outside, and then slammed the door shut.

"It'll be fine, Nixie," Draven promised as I climbed out, dragging air into my lungs and glad I'd borrowed—well, stolen—his hoodie when the cold slashed at my hands and face. The rest stop wasn't huge, but it still felt massive and unknowable. Was my dad hiding somewhere, watching us? Was he already one step ahead of us?

"Don't be dramatic," Wild huffed, rolling his eyes. "He's far behind us, and you know it."

I crossed my arms over my chest and ignored him, ignored his ability to hear my damn thoughts, and I stalked around the car to Kaan's side. He raised an eyebrow at my surly expression, but I didn't offer an explanation. "You really don't have to wait outside," I said instead. "I'll be fine by myself."

"Humour an overprotective alpha," he replied, his gaze gentling even as he scoured the car park around us, zeroing in on everyone who went in and out of the shops.

"Oh, fine," I huffed. "But just so you know, I think you're being ridiculous."

Kaan laughed loud enough to draw the eyes of people eating outside McDonalds on wooden benches, and I bit my lip at the attention even as part of me went all soft at Kaan's laugh. "Good to know, sweetheart. I've made a note of your opinion."

I slanted a look at him. Was he joking with me? I wasn't sure until his brown eyes glittered, and then I huffed, knocking my shoulder into his.

"Here, take this," Kaan said, leaning across me to hand three twenties to Draven. "Don't let those two shits go too crazy."

"I'll try," Draven replied with a quiet laugh, his blue eyes trailing across my face before he followed Bakkhos and Wild towards McDonalds.

"This is embarrassing," I complained as Kaan and I set off towards the separate toilet block, heat creeping up my face.

"No, this is being part of Broken Pack. We protect our own, and that means guarding you when you're vulnerable. Even in the bathroom."

I gave him a look that told him he was mad, only belatedly realising I should have been nervous to give an alpha such a sassy look. But Kaan only smirked and swept a magnanimous hand towards the aqua blue door. I pushed it open and turned on the threshold to say, "Thank you. For protecting me. Even when you're being ridiculous."

"You're welcome, Nix," he replied, ignoring my remark. His deep brown eyes were soft with fondness as I shut the door, forcefully reminding myself he wasn't mine, no matter what my instincts said. He was my alpha. Just my alpha.

Inside, the bathrooms were clean and surprisingly sweet smelling, with fake flowers between each sink. It was a nice treat to not wince at the state of the toilets. Even sheltered by my old pack, I'd seen some gross bathrooms.

When my bladder was lighter, I avoided my reflection in the mirror, knowing I'd find bloodshot eyes and deep shadows carved by stress, and I took my time using the hand wash and lotions. Had we stepped into an alternate dimension? Was I actually in a department store? At least I could reassure myself that my dad would never come to a place like this—not a ladies bathroom, and definitely not a service station where a packet of crisps probably cost one pound fifty.

I wasn't at all surprised to find Kaan's eyes fixed on the door when I pushed it open. He'd probably strained his ears for the sounds of my movements, and I didn't want to think about that any further. Kaan took protection to a whole new level, but it felt good to have an alpha who cared what happened to me.

"I survived the bathroom," I announced wryly, delighted with the flash of amusement that crossed his face.

"I'm relieved to hear it," he replied, a grin splitting his beard and crinkling his eyes. "Ready to eat and get back on the road, sweetheart?"

"Definitely," I replied.

It was only because my gaze shifted towards the McDonalds where the others had disappeared that I spotted the movement to our left. I didn't recognise the scruffy haired man in the black jacket, but his movements were too fast, too purposeful.

"Kaan!" I warned, but too late.

The man jumped forward, and light bounced off a knife in his hand.

I stopped breathing, throwing myself at my alpha, frantic to protect him, *my mate*, but Kaan was already spinning away. His big hand wrapped around the throat of the attacker, and his other hand went to his hair. I flinched at the loud crack his neck made when Kaan snapped it, and I froze, struggling to process everything that had happened in a split second.

"Out of the way, sweet girl," Kaan said gently, nudging

me away from the door as he looped his arm around the attacker's waist and made it look like he was drunk, not dead, as he guided him into the men's bathroom, and let him thump to the floor.

"Time to go," Kaan said, his voice like iron even though his hand was gentle on my upper arm, guiding me away from the bathroom block and towards our car.

"Cameras, Kaan," I breathed, my mind whirling like a tornado, too fast, too fast. "There'll be CCTV."

"Wild can handle them when we're on the road." He squeezed my arm, leading me across the tarmac and ignoring a Fiat 500 that thought to pick a fight with him. The car braked before we ever stopped, and I knew we were causing a scene, that people were noticing and we needed to be smarter, needed to blend in.

"People are watching us," I hissed. "What do you think they're going to think when a dead guy's found? They're going to remember us."

Kaan stopped dead in the middle of an empty parking space and turned to me, his pupils swallowing the brown ring around them.

I swallowed, and dread tightened my chest, but I didn't hesitate. I drew my hand back and slapped his cheek, shouting loud enough for everyone to hear, "I knew you fucked my best friend. I *saw* the way you looked at her."

Kaan's eyes had turned dark at the slap, but now they glowed from within. "Clever Nixie," he breathed, only for me. Louder, he said, "You're seeing things, Carrie. I'd never touch your best friend."

My heart beat so fast, panic and exhilaration mixing together, and I jumped at the low, unhealthy growl of a car as it collapsed into a parking spot. "Then who?" I cried, throwing my hands out at my sides, noticing that people were studiously glancing away from us even as they kept listening. They bought it, then. Thank the goddess. "I know you're sleeping around, Darren!" I threw out the first name I thought of.

Kaan's eyes were simmering now, deep and endless. "We'll talk about this at home," he growled, thankfully not unleashing his alpha growl as he towed me across the car park again.

"You're welcome," I panted.

"You're brilliant," he replied, stroking my arm with his thumb.

I could finally breathe again when we reached the car. The others weren't back yet, but I prayed they'd be done soon.

When Kaan reached out to put the key in the lock, his jacket lifted, and I made a horrified sound at the red spilling down his side, soaking his white shirt. "Kaan, fuck, you're hurt."

"It's fine, sweetheart," he replied, motioning me inside the car. "I've had worse, I'll heal."

But I couldn't stop staring at the blood soaking his side. Everything inside me went cold—frozen. A rumbling growl poured from my throat, and my breaths came fast. "He hurt you," I said around my growl.

"Nixette," Kaan said carefully, stepping closer but keeping an eye on everyone else in the car park. "Get inside the car, sweetheart. I'm going to be fine."

But my wrath would not be soothed, and my power couldn't be contained. It built until there was no space left in my body for more moon-cold magic. And then it exploded from me in a powerful wave. I was distantly aware of CCTV cameras turning to cracking ice, of the body of our attacker shattering into shards that would melt to nothing, of my chill moving through the minds of everyone watching us and freezing their memories. All I could do was stare at the blood running from my mate, at the wound that had been dealt to him while I watched helplessly. I hadn't even known.

Holy fuck...

My head snapped up, my glare moving from Kaan's injury to Wild as the cruel, redheaded alpha jogged across the road, his golden eyes wide and fixed on me. Kaan used my distraction to bundle me into the open passenger seat and slam the door shut, and I seethed, cool magic sloshing inside me, seeking a way out.

"What the hell happened?" Wild demanded, throwing himself in the back seat.

It took me a moment to realise he was talking to me, that Kaan was still outside, gesturing at Bakkhos and Draven to hurry up. "Someone attacked us," I answered coldly. "Kaan killed them. But he got hurt. He's bleeding."

"And that made you do ... this?"

"Yes."

I jumped as Draven and Bakkhos climbed in the car, instantly bombarding me with questions—what happened, was I okay, why was I so cold—but my eyes glued to Kaan as he got into the driver's seat beside me.

"Tell me you got enough food for the whole day," he muttered, slamming his door and putting on his seat belt. I watched blood soak through the grey canvas and I vibrated, my rage reaching a higher pitch.

"We did," Draven confirmed, but quietly. "Do you want to eat something, Nixie?"

"No."

I stared at the blood even as we drove away, even as

miles blurred past the window. "Stop," I said finally, pouring an omega growl into the word.

"Nix" Kaan replied with a wince. "We're on the motorway."

"Stop," I snarled, my lips pulling back from my teeth.

"She said stop," Bakkhos snapped, adding his own growl to mine. "Pull the fuck over."

"Fine," Kaan bit out. "But we need to keep moving." He slid a look my way—but I held it and refused to back down. "There, we've stopped."

"First aid kit," I ground out, and Kaan dragged a hand down his beard.

"I told you I'm fine, Nixette."

"Here, Nixie," Draven offered gently, leaning across the seats to place a green box in my hands. My anger started to settle as I sorted through the kit, removing antiseptic wipes, bandages, gauze, and a needle and thread. Their eyes burned my cold skin as they watched, but I focused on my task, using a wipe to sanitize my hands before I opened another and reached for Kaan's shirt, ignoring his growl of surprise and pain as I lifted it and began to clean his cut. It wasn't deep thankfully, he wouldn't even need stitches. But the sight of blood running down his skin had me shaking again, whatever calm my task had given me shattered by rage that he'd been hurt.

Kaan sat in silence, letting me clean the slash on his side and press sticky gauze to the site, my fingers tingling wherever I touched him. Satisfied that he was cared for, I sat back, and my throat bobbed with a swallow.

"I should have warned you sooner," I rasped, tracing the inked skin around the gauze pad. Pressure built behind my eyes.

"It would have been far worse if you hadn't warned me

at all," Kaan replied, brushing a vein in my wrist and shocking me with the touch.

So wound up with protective rage and fear and the need to protect him, I was tilting my head before I knew it, offering my neck for his bite. *Please*. He was already my mate in the ways that counted, he already took care of me and anticipated my needs and kept me safe, but if I had his bite, his cock, his knot…

"No, Nix," he breathed, and something broke in me as he gently guided my head down, covering my throat with my hair. I dragged my fingers from his ribs, dropping them in my lap. My face red hot, I put everything back inside the first aid kit just for something to do with my hands.

He'd spoken softly, but he might as well have shouted at me.

No, Nix.

I felt sick, felt truly broken for the first time since I'd joined the Broken Pack.

A tense, suffocating atmosphere settled over the car, and none of us spoke to break it. I rolled the window down and curled up with my knees to my chest, turned away from Kaan, the alpha who would never want me.

Ever.

29

WRONG

The second hotel wasn't as nice as the first, but it was clean and it would do. They also didn't have more than one room to spare, so we were all crammed into one family room, sharing a double bed and a pull-out sofa bed. Me, sharing a bedroom with Kaan. It was killing me. Maybe literally. Everything I ate came straight back up, even water wouldn't settle in my stomach for long, and I'd been laid in bed for four hours now, boiling hot and unable to sleep.

I rolled out from under Bakkhos's arm, blinking when I found Draven awake, watching me.

"Something's wrong," he murmured, lifting a hand to my face.

The feeling of his fingers tracing my jaw was the only good thing to happen all day, and I sighed, sinking into the sensation. But heat grew inside me, not like my estrus but like I had a temperature, and I couldn't stay still even for Draven's touches.

I eventually fell asleep some time around dawn, but I knew my sleep hadn't been restful when I woke up and found myself drenched in sweat, my back aching. And a curve where my stomach had been flat yesterday.

"Oh, no," I breathed, pressing my hand to my mouth as I stared at that little bump, just starting to grasp what it meant to be blessed with Luneste's enhanced fertility.

My mates were no longer in bed with me, but huddled together with Kaan and Wild by the small window. They all jolted at the sound of my voice, and Bakkhos rushed across the dingy grey carpet to sit on the bed, catching my hand to press obsessive kisses to my knuckles. "How do you feel, Sunshine?"

"Like shit," I rasped, earning laughter from Wild, the one person I didn't want it from.

"Like pregnant shit?" the bastard clarified, a smirk on his sharp face. He looked frustratingly good in a tight hunter green T-shirt, with dark jeans low on his hips. I wanted to kick him in the nuts.

"I could kill you," I replied with a scowl, my temperature shooting higher and sweat rolling down my back, sticking my clothes to me even more. "The rest of the pack would probably forgive me for it. Thank me for it, even," I added.

Wild whistled, crossing his arms across his chest as he leaned into the window, sunlight framing his red hair and making it look like fire. "Damn, the baby's made you feisty."

"Wild, knock it off," Kaan sighed, dragging a hand down his bearded face. "It's too early for your nonsense."

Wild just shrugged, still smirking.

I wanted to scratch the smirk off his face, and I was sorely tempted to do just that. But that would require effort, and I was too hot and exhausted for that. Plus, I was going to throw up. "Move," I mumbled, pushing Bakkhos as gently as I could, trying not to be unkind as I lurched out of bed and into the en-suite bathroom, the only saving grace of the shitty hotel room.

Bile hit the toilet, and I groaned, feeling wretched.

"She shouldn't react like this to a pregnancy," I heard Draven murmur. "Kaan, I'm worried."

"I know," Kaan replied, just as quietly.

"I can hear you bastards," I growled, wiping my face and flushing when I was sure my stomach wouldn't revolt again. Cold tap water was a relief to my heated skin when I threw it on my face, swilling out the taste of vomit from my mouth while I was at the sink.

"Try to eat something, Nixie," Draven said, approaching cautiously. Tears burned my eyes, and despite the heat rolling off my body—and knowing I'd only make it worse—I fitted my body to his and wrapped my arms around his waist, silently asking forgiveness.

"I don't want to eat," I admitted. "I feel ... really bad."

"This isn't normal," Wild commented. When Bakkhos growled, he sneered. "Come on, I'm not the only one thinking it. Omega's are born for babies, it's what they do. They don't even get morning sickness, let alone what's got her sweating and not sleeping."

I glanced up at Draven, falling into his cashmere blue eyes. "Will you love me even if I kill him?"

"Even then, my beauty," he confirmed with a little smile of wickedness, pressing a kiss to my cheek and letting me go, as if he knew I was close to overheating. "Open the windows," he said to no one in particular. "She needs air and cold."

Bakkhos fell over himself to follow Draven's guidance, throwing the windows open to let in a trickle of relief in the form of fresh air.

"Come here, Nix," Kaan said, calm and even. I swallowed, not daring to meet his eyes, but I approached slowly—and suppressed a flinch as he caught my chin, tilting my face up. "Tell me exactly what you're feeling."

"Sick," I replied, wetting my bottom lip. "Too hot, and … and I'm so tired. I just want to sleep, but my body wouldn't let me last night. And I'm hungry," I confessed at a whisper. "But I know I'll just be sick."

"Water," he said, throwing a cool command at Wild. His eyes gentled as they settled on me again, but that only made me feel worse, and a headache pounded between my eyes. "Drink slowly, sips at a time. If that's all you can manage this morning, that's alright. We'll go at your pace. Alright, sweet girl?"

At the name, my stomach cramped hard, and I twisted back to the bathroom just in time to vomit up more acid.

Something was very, very wrong with me. And I wasn't sure it was the pregnancy.

30

BATHING

Four days and two hotels later, it was just as bad. Worse, maybe. Every night I tossed and turned, drenched in sweat despite all the windows thrown open—for me *and* to soothe Bakkhos's fear of being trapped. Every morning, I woke so weak I could barely walk to the bathroom to be sick. I'd managed to keep down sips of water and tiny, nibbling pieces of biscuits, toast, and chips—things that tasted of practically nothing. Headaches came and went, specific enough that I began to realise just why I felt so wretched, and why I was so weak that my moonlight had receded far from my reach.

"This is ridiculous," I muttered, sharp and careless as I staggered across the carpet of yet another hotel room, newly checked in. This one had dark blue carpet and white walls with framed pieces of art, but I no longer cared what they looked like.

I staggered because Luneste's fertility magic ran rampant in my body, taking an ordinary omega pregnancy and turning the dial up to crazy-fucking-fast. I could no longer see my feet; my stomach was huge and heavy, pulling mercilessly on muscles I didn't even know I had in my back. Why did TV make pregnant bellies seem perfectly round? Mine was a wonky oval that changed whenever the life growing inside me shifted, and my skin wasn't glowing; it was red and flushed and covered in sweat. But maybe that was my 'sickness.'

Pressure built behind my eyes as I moved haltingly across the room, aiming for the bathroom in the corner. I was losing control of everything, especially my own body, and I'd never felt so helpless. I wanted a hug; I wanted everyone to stay far away from me. I wanted a whole feast; I never wanted to eat again. Most importantly, I needed to pee. My bladder had been screaming at me since the lobby downstairs, and the lift up to the room had been a very dangerous journey. That was another thing I'd lost control of; my bladder had a life of its own now, and it lived to make mine hell.

I threw the bathroom door open and then slammed it shut behind me even harder, sinking onto the toilet with a growl of annoyance at nothing in particular. It was always rough after I'd sat in the passenger seat with Kaan driving, my awareness of him at an all-time high and his rejection loud in my thoughts.

No, Nix.

I flinched even now, sinking my face into my hands.

You've got to get over him, an unwelcome voice intruded in my thoughts. He kept doing it, shoving his way into my mind.

Go fuck yourself, Wild, I snarled.

His answer was simply a laugh. The more I snarled and insulted, the more he liked it.

I pulled at my greasy lilac hair, as if I needed more

discomfort to add to my aches and my cramping, nauseated stomach.

My head shot up as the bathroom door creaked open, and I bared my teeth when Wild stalked in, already smirking at my snarl. He looked annoyingly good like always, in black jeans, a tight vest, and his signature tan leather jacket. His short red hair was artfully rumpled; I'd watched him style it for twenty whole minutes this morning.

Need cramped my stomach at the sight of him, but I didn't have the damn energy. *Or the inclination*, I reminded myself. I hated him. Everything about him.

Especially the way he watched me and saw my discomfort every damn day.

"Stop whining about Kaan," he said cruelly, turning on the taps in the bath and putting in the plug. "And get in the bath. You'll feel better when you're clean."

"How would *you* know?" I demanded, my face burning as I stood and pulled up my leggings. But he'd fucked and knotted me; he'd already seen everything I tried to hide.

His mouth flicked up on one side, his smirk even more infuriating than his sneer. "Your growl's big, little omega, but you've got no strength to fight me like this. So take off your clothes and get in the fucking bath."

I glared, making sure he knew how much I loathed him, but I didn't struggle when he grew impatient and pulled my oversized top over my head, and then tugged my leggings and underwear down. Lust throbbed between my legs, but I didn't have the energy for that, either.

"In," he commanded, as bossy as Kaan.

I huffed, but I grabbed his shoulder for stability and stepped into the quarter-full bath, scowling as he lowered me carefully into the tub.

And why was he being so considerate, so damn caring?

Because he was convinced it was *his* baby growing inside me. He wasn't taking care of *me*, but his heir. Bastard.

"Would you just relax for two fucking seconds?" he muttered, hovering by the bath as it filled and I seethed, my ever-fluctuating mood currently stuck on burning rage.

I cast a murderous glare in his direction, not lessening the heat of my anger even as I watched him strip off his shirt and jacket and unbuckle his belt. "If you think I'm fucking you, you're severely overestimating how much I like you. I don't want you anywhere near me."

"Cute," Wild replied, sliding his jeans down his legs. "And need I remind you that you lost your mind coming on my cock, and you never liked me *then?* Why would liking me come into it now?"

"If you come anywhere near me, I'll drown you," I warned, my teeth bared.

Wild ignored the threat and stepped into the bath, scooting me forward so he could sit behind me with his legs framing my body. As if to prove he wasn't going to ravage me, he kept his underwear on.

Vibrating with rage, I crossed my arms over my chest—bigger and heavier than it had been four days ago, and always fucking tender—and seethed as his hands settled on my shoulders.

"You'd have killed me already if you were serious," he said, putting pressure on the aching spots at the top of my spine where I carried all my tension.

"I'm just biding my time," I fired back, but tension slid from my shoulders as his hands travelled across them, finding my aches and massaging until they soothed. "Waiting for the right moment."

"Sure," he agreed, and I hated that I could hear the smirk in his voice even though I couldn't see him.

He pushed my hair over my shoulder and massaged lower, taking his time soothing my pains, finding each spot unerringly. "I look forward to your murder attempt. I'm sure it'll be adorable."

I snarled.

But then his hands reached the base of my spine where it hurt the worst, and my breath hitched at the stab of pain, quickly dissolving into a groan as he tenderly soothed my strained muscles. I stopped threatening him and bit my lip as the aches that had been punishing me all day were, one by one, calmed to mere niggles.

I hated him so much.

"No, you don't," he laughed, reaching over my shoulder to shut off the tap before the bath overflowed. "You want to, but you don't. You can't—I'm your mate."

"Funny how mate and hate rhyme," I replied, softer than I'd been all day. As if he'd soothed my irritability along with my aching muscles.

"Clever, Lilac," he murmured. I growled halfheartedly in warning as he gripped my shoulders, leaning me back against his chest. For a second it felt like I would fall beneath the water and choke, but even though I loathed him, I knew he'd never let me.

"I still can't stand you," I muttered as I relaxed against him, sighing at the feel of him wrapped all around me, especially as his arms settled above and below my bump.

"I'd expect nothing less," he replied, his lips brushing my shoulder.

I said nothing as his fingers caressed random patterns across my stomach, closing my eyes as it soothed me. I knew he was tracing the stretch marks striped like tiger's markings across my engorged middle.

She's growing too fucking fast, his voice slid through my

mind courtesy of the bond between us. *She's too weak to handle a pregnancy like this.*

"Thanks for the vote of confidence," I huffed.

"Hungry, little omega?" he asked, as if I hadn't acknowledged his thoughts.

"Starving," I replied honestly, gifting him one truth in return for the massage and calm he'd gifted me. "But I won't be able to eat much."

"Bakkhos and Draven have gone for food, they won't be long."

I didn't ask about Kaan. I'd just end up being sick—it got worse every single day. "Fine," I sighed, resting my head on his shoulder as he caressed my middle, the only thing he cared about.

"The only thing I won't ever hurt," he corrected. "There's a difference."

I didn't open my eyes, but my mouth pressed into a thin line. "You hurt the things you care about?"

He didn't answer for a long time. But finally he said, "Yes."

"That's fucked up, Wild."

I'd been right when I saw him slaughter the scout in the forest. He really was the most broken of us all.

But if I kept ignoring the taint on my soul, I might just end up more broken than even Wild.

31

NOTHING

I don't know when I fell asleep, but I recognised the calm, motherly feeling of Luneste long before she materialised in the white forest in front of me, dressed in a long dress with her icy hair flowing to her waist. She didn't embrace me this time, and she didn't smile—no this was the cold face of the moon.

"*Tell him,*" she commanded, holding my gaze until I wanted to glance away. Tears stabbed my eyeballs, but they remained fixed to her, as if she forbade me to turn my face away. "If you don't, you will die. The babe will live, but you will *die.*"

I stumbled back a step, a hand on my chest. She wasn't exaggerating; as a goddess, she knew the future.

"It won't change anything," I whispered. Misery clogged my throat, made my soul shrivel and weaken. As it had been doing for weeks.

"*Tell* him," Luneste repeated, stern in a way I'd never seen her before.

"What's the point?" I sighed, heartsick to my stomach. "He doesn't *want* me."

"Kaan's rejection is withering your soul. Your weakness is because of *him*."

I knew. I'd figured it out days ago, but I knew exactly what he'd say if I opened myself up again, if I begged him to want me.

The same thing he'd already said so many times.

No, Nix.

"He'll never accept the bond," I told her, choking on the truth. "He'll never want me."

"Foolish daughter," Luneste sighed, irritation and pity mingling in her dark gaze. "Tell him."

"I'll be fine," I rasped. Lied.

What was the point of telling him I was matesick? What would it change? Nothing. Absolutely nothing could make Kaan want me. Not even this. Not even dying.

32

AMBUSH

Because they found us every time we were on the road, I refused to leave our current hotel even when my pack blurred around the room, throwing things into holdalls and boxes, all but Bakkhos ignoring my latest temper tantrum.

"We have to leave, my Sunshine," he said gently, sitting beside me on the bed to wrap his arms around my middle, his hand splayed across my bump. "We need to keep moving, outrace them, remember?"

"Can't you just kill my dad and brothers and be done with it?" I huffed, throwing long lilac hair off my face, boiling hot and annoyed, *and* hungry and tired. All the windows were thrown open, mostly because Bakkhos felt better without them shut, but my temperature refused to drop.

"The second he shows his face, we will," Draven promised in a quiet, deadly voice. "Here, Nixie," he added, handing me a box of crackers—one of the few things I could eat. I devoured them as fast as humanly possible, and gave him a pleading glance for more.

My soft alpha bowed over me to press a kiss to my forehead, sweetly brushing crumbs from the corner of my mouth with raw, red hands. I *hated* that his worry for me made his stress and compulsions worse. "We need to stop for supplies when we're on the road. I'll get you more crackers then."

I stared up at him and my throat went tight, my face hot and tingly with tears. "I love you so much."

Draven cupped my face, and came back for another kiss, this time to my lips. "I love you too, my beauty. And I know you don't like it, but we do have to move hotels."

I grumbled, my brow coming down low over my eyes. In times like these I wished crossing my arms had the same impact as before I was pregnant.

"Nix." Kaan's growl of command made my pussy wet and my soul flinch all at once. I was so desperate for his affection, for his acceptance. "We're leaving now. Do you want Draven to carry you, or can you walk?"

"I can walk," I muttered, scowling at the carpet—green this time. I wondered what colour the next hotel room would be, wondered if we'd ever find the promised safe place Luneste was guiding us to. I was starting to think the paradise was as unlikely as Kaan ever accepting me as his mate. Yet I kept leading us towards it, taking us across the country, hotel by hotel.

With a grunt, I heaved myself off the bed and onto my aching feet, avoiding Kaan's stare as Bakkhos wrapped an arm around my waist to support me as I aimed for the door.

Maybe if I hadn't argued, hadn't slowed us down, we might have escaped. We might have fled to another hotel and outraced my old pack.

We spilled onto the car park behind the hotel, little more than a square of concrete dotted with cars and stripes of paint to denote each spot. I gagged at the scent of rubbish, courtesy of the huge industrial bins the hotel stored back here, and covered my nose with the sleeve of my stolen hoodie—Draven's still—as I aimed for blue car that had become both familiar and hated this past week.

"Nix!" Kaan growled, so deep and sudden that my knees would have hit the tarmac if Bakkhos hadn't tightened his hold on me. "Get her back!"

I whipped my head around, panicked at my alpha's tone, but shadows rushing closer drew my attention, and a gasp tore up my throat as they coalesced into shapes I recognised. There was Owen, my dad's best friend, and Oliver, his son, and there creeping around the side of our car was Dale, the man who'd whittled my first toy, who'd handed over the ropes to tie me down.

"They've found me," I rasped, my body shaking all over. "It's my old pack—they've come to kill me."

"Like *hell*," Wild snarled, and threw himself at the nearest man before he could come any closer. Silver flashed in Wild's hand, and I glimpsed a knuckle duster with silver spikes before it slit Owen's throat end to end.

Blood erupted like a fountain, drenching Wild as he slashed through more parts of Owen, a dizzyingly fast blur of gore and violence.

With blood running down his face, neck, and hands, Wild grinned like a fearsome creature, laughing as Oliver roared in grief and threw himself at Wild to avenge his father.

I took a step forward, desperate to help him even though I was massive and slow and aching in a dozen places. But Bakkhos's arms were an iron cage I couldn't escape, and Kaan and Draven jumped forward to fight alongside Wild, transforming into wolves before their feet touched the concrete.

"Let me go," I breathed, sickness clawing at my stomach, bile in my throat. "*Please*, Bakkhos, I can't—"

I can't just stand here and watch them get hurt.

"No chance, Sunshine," he replied, his voice dropping into a growl that made my breath catch and my eyes sting. There was so much protectiveness in his voice that it made me weak. "We're not putting you in danger, no fucking way." He turned me around and caught my face in his hands. I shook hard at the sound of violence behind me, unable to tell who was winning. "Stay behind me. Stay safe."

I shook my head fast, but Bakkhos kissed a tear from my cheek and pushed me behind him, crowding me back against the wall of the hotel. I couldn't see around him, couldn't tell if the sudden growl of pain came from Kaan or one of my old pack, if the whine was Draven's or Dale's.

The laugh, low and warm, was definitely's Dale's, but I didn't recognise the cruelty in his voice when he said, "I know you. You're that troublemaking little shit from Marlowe Pack. Last I heard they'd given you to Auden Woods to break. Rather you than me, kid," he laughed. "The stories they tell about that man would make a serial killer shudder."

Wild laughed, even louder and harsher than Dale. "Oh *trust me*, Mincemeat, the stories are tame compared to what that man was really like."

"Who the fuck do you think you're calling Mincemeat?" Dale demanded, growling. But he was no alpha, and his growl was weak in human form—nothing like the full, resonant growls of *my* alphas.

"Did he really keep you lads in a cellar and invite all his sick buddies around to make your holes bleed?"

I staggered back into the wall, pressing my hand to my mouth as Dale's words struck my soul like a whip.

No, he couldn't have, Wild couldn't have been through that.

No.

"For days at a time," Wild replied with a crackling laugh. "Why? You looking for me to recreate it with you as the entertainment? I'm sure we can make that happen, Mincemeat."

Kaan's deep, throaty growl had me sagging, my stomach bound up in knots, and all my aches and irritations melting into bone deep terror as Wild laughed louder, Kaan growled deeper, and Draven—I couldn't hear Draven.

"Let me out," I said in a small, choked voice. What that man, Auden Woods, had done to Wild...

No wonder he was broken and cruel and full of lies.

"No, Sunshine," Bakkhos replied, so unlike my crazed alpha when he was this serious. "I can't."

"Then *help* him," I pleaded, pressing a hand to my throat as if I could stop the bile clawing up it. Not because of the pregnancy, but what that monster had done to Wild, *my* Wild.

He *was* mine, no matter how much I loathed him, or how much he taunted me. Bite or no bite, he was my mate, and I knew once the horror had worn off, lethal fury was going to burn in my blood at what he'd suffered.

"*Please*, Bakkhos, I'll stay here. I won't fight." If I even *could* fight with a body that looked—and very much felt—seven months pregnant. "I promise I'll stay back, just please. Help him."

"Sunshine..." Bakkhos turned halfway, keeping an eye on the fight even as he cupped my face to brush another stray tear from my cheek.

"He needs you more than I do," I rasped, looking past him to see Wild grappling with Dale, the dark-haired, bearded man from my old pack superior in height and strength. Wild was ruthless and fast, but he was also limping. He danced awkwardly out of the path of Dale's knife, not resting his full weight on his right foot. "*Go*," I pleaded.

"Fuck," Bakkhos growled, torn with indecision until Dale slammed his bigger body into Wild's and sent him skidding across the tarmac. Friction burned his jeans to threads and scraped his thighs until they were red and raw.

Through our bond, I heard a sound—not a word, but a whimper.

It's okay, I promised. *You're going to be okay.*

Empty, useless words, but they were all I had. I needed my moonlight, needed Luneste's cool power to fill my veins, but I was too weak to summon even a drop of it.

My eyes flitted to the enormous black wolf tackling one of my pack to the ground, and my eyes stung harder. Maybe if I'd taken Luneste's advice and told him why I was so weak, I might have had my magic now.

But I was useless, and we were all going to get hurt. Or worse.

More and more of my old pack spilled out of the side streets around the car pack. Kaan's huge jaws crunched down on legs and broke their bones, but they kept fighting, refusing to leave us alone.

Draven—where was Draven? I scanned the car park, searching for shadows beneath cars to show he was hiding, scouring the rooftops, praying for a glimpse of my gentle giant.

But I couldn't find him.

"Don't move, okay?" Bakkhos pleaded, his green eyes big and desperate. "Stay right here, Nixie."

I nodded, but movement drew my attention back to Dale and Wild just as my ex-pack member brought his foot down on the Wild's knee so viciously that I heard the crunch from several feet away.

"No!" I screamed, taking a step before I froze, remembering the fragile life relying on me to keep them safe.

Goddess fucking dammit. I *had* to stay back.

Bakkhos launched himself into the fray with a growl so low it rattled the hotel windows behind me. He raced across the tarmac as Dale grabbed Wild's ankles and began towing him across the car park. As if he'd been told to take hostages. Leverage.

To get me to go back to my old pack, no doubt.

I wouldn't. I refused to. But if it meant keeping them safe...

I didn't know what I'd do. Or rather I did, and I wanted to pretend their cruel plan wouldn't work.

I wrapped my arms around myself as Bakkhos transformed into a vicious, snarling silver wolf, mottled with darker markings, and glared murder from deep green eyes as he chased after Dale. The dark haired, bearded man had managed to drag Wild across the car park and out of sight. Hidden behind a white transit van, I could only guess at what was happening to him, and my stomach twisted with more sickness.

I couldn't lose them. Any of them. I struggled to breathe just at the thought of it. I wanted to run into action and unleash my own wolf, but a shift could cause a miscarriage this late in a pregnancy, and that thought made me even sicker.

I took another step, my heart in my throat as three men surrounded Kaan's huge, bristling form, a knife in each of their hands. The whole pack must have been here, all the men at least. Which meant my dad and brothers had to be here, too.

As if my thoughts had conjured him, brutal hands closed around my upper arms and my feet fell from under me as I was hauled backwards.

"You," Conn seethed, "are supposed to be dead."

"Sorry to be an inconvenience," I snarled, bucking against his ruthless hold as he pulled me away from the hotel, away from my pack.

No. *Please*, no.

"Don't talk back, Nixette, omegas should be quiet."

I sneered, drawing some of Wild's sharpness into myself. "What would you know about omegas, Conn? I'm the only one you've ever met."

Conn laughed, and my throat burned at the familiar sound. He wasn't familiar anymore, wasn't safe. He'd *killed* me. If it wasn't for Luneste, I'd have stayed dead.

But there was no erasing years of memories, and they pelted me like rocks.

"That's where you're wrong, Nixette," he sneered, and I froze long enough for him to drag me out of the car park.

What the hell did that mean? Where had his alpha found an omega? And was she safe, or were they going to sacrifice her like they'd sacrificed me?

Lilac, a weak voice cut through my mind.

Wild? I breathed, relief hitting me deep even just hearing his mental voice. *Wild, they've got me.*

I know, he said, strained. *Hold on, little omega. Just hold on.*

But Wild's kneecap was shattered, and I knew there was little hope of him racing to my rescue. My bottom lip wobbled, but I flattened my mouth and threw my head back into Conn's face as he hauled me around the side of the hotel.

I couldn't let him get me into a car. If he did, I had no doubt I'd be taken right back to the sacrificial stone. They'd probably cut my baby out of me first, but goddess knew what they'd do with them.

True, frozen rage poured through my veins, and I growled full and deep, struggling harder. But I was still too weak to call any magic, and throwing up most of my meals definitely didn't help. Neither did my sleepless nights and the damaged bond between me and Kaan.

Still, I refused to go quietly. The omega who would have obeyed them without complaint had died that night on the rock, and the new me refused to go down without a fight.

"You're a coward, Conn," I hissed, kicking at his ankles even as I threatened to overbalance, dizziness rippling through my mind. I should have eaten something more than crackers before we left. Should have done a lot of things differently.

But none of that was going to help me now. Nothing would.

Because as Conn dragged me around the front of the hotel, *there* was the blue car, with Sander and Dad leaning against the bonnet, waiting for him to deliver me to them.

"No," I rasped, struggling harder, but getting weaker with every kick and fist I slammed into my oldest brother. And none of it had a single bit of impact. "I won't let you kill me again," I snarled, my teeth bared and my eyes wide, the whites no doubt showing my panic. "You're not my pack anymore."

"Enough," Dad growled. "This has gone on long enough, Nixette. You know your duty to your pack."

I met his eyes, the same dark blue as mine and even though I was sweating and dizzy and weak, I nodded. "You're right. I do. *Luneste*," I called, my voice ringing loudly, drawing the eyes of a businessman striding out of the hotel lobby. "If you can hear me, help me access my power, just this once. It's the last thing I'll ask. And I'll ... I'll tell Kaan."

"What's she talking about?" Sander demanded, running a hand through his long, sandy hair and throwing an uneasy look at Dad. "She can't actually talk to the goddess can she?"

"No," Dad scoffed, his grizzled face unamused. "She's just desperate."

"Don't touch me," I snarled as Dad came closer, his hands outstretched. Conn's grip was already lightening, handing me over, but I didn't make it easy for them. I'd stop fighting when I finally passed out. And I would; I felt unconsciousness creeping up like a predator in the dark.

Even knowing they would successfully manhandle me into the car, I kicked my feet hard, slamming my soft slippers into my brothers and swearing when they slid off my aching feet. I jammed my elbows into anything fleshy I could reach, and bared my teeth at hands that came too close, bending as much as I could—about two millimeters thanks to my belly—to rake my sharp teeth across fingers and knuckles.

"Fuck," Conn spat, shoving me into Dad so hard I almost toppled over. Terror darker than my fear at being taken cut through me at the thought of falling, the impact surely enough to harm my baby. But Dad's unforgiving hands closed around my shoulders. My relief was short lived when he grabbed my throat and squeezed.

I gasped uselessly for breath. Black spots crowded in at the edges of my vision, blurring the road in front of us, and the car that Sander had crawled into and started up.

It was happening again. I was being dragged away from my safe place, taken to my death.

"Luneste," I croaked, darkness stealing my vision of Dad's victorious expression, "will punish—you all."

Dad just laughed. "She might have given you her magic, but that doesn't mean she's coming to your rescue, Nixette. Do you know how rare it is to get one audience with Luneste. She won't grant you two."

She'd given me three, but I didn't have enough air to tell him that. Panic clawed up my throat, and I pushed at the hand squeezing my throat, my lungs desperate for air. The sounds of traffic on the road distorted and stretched into one blur of noise, even Dad's voice merging with the roar.

"Let me go," I whispered, but I couldn't hear my own voice over the noise. My fighting got weaker and weaker as he hauled me towards the car door Conn held open, the expression on my brother's face disapproving and dark, glimpsed between waves of darkness and disorientation. "I'm not your pack," I choked out as Dad pushed my head down, sending me sprawling across the back seat. "You can't do this."

All I heard of their replies was a rumble of nonsense sounds, like shouts through water, but the door slam was loud and clear. Dad grabbed my arm, pulling me upright and sitting me on the backseat like I was a doll he could place how and where he liked.

Anger seethed in my gut, but instead of hot fire, it formed cool, icy moonlight. My breath hitched, and I realised I could *breathe* again, his hand wasn't around my throat, so I gulped down air. I didn't care that it tasted of unwashed car and stale food wrappers, a smell that had once been exciting, that had meant I was going on an adventure outside our packlands.

Now the smell meant my death. Would they even drive

back to Tulay packlands, or just slit my throat somewhere on the side of the road?

Magic and fury roiled in my stomach, and I held tight to it even as I shook with fear, letting its chill send goosebumps up my arms and down my legs. My throat throbbed where Dad had choked me, and my arms pulsed with quick-forming bruises where Conn had manhandled me. I wished the bruises were from Bakkhos holding me too tightly or Wild's cruel affection; I wished Draven were here to wrap me in his comforting embrace and Kaan could growl my dad into submission.

No matter how strong Han Tulay thought he was, he was *nothing* compared to the alpha of alphas.

But I didn't have my pack here with me; all I had was myself, and the magic forming a pool of frozen moonlight in my belly, just behind my baby. Luneste had heard me, had given me more power, and ... and that meant I had to tell Kaan he was killing me.

If I survived this, which was a big *if*.

The car rumbled beneath us, the engine growling as Conn swore at a van that pulled out in front of us, and the cool moonlight in my gut doubled, tripled, and swelled even further.

"I'm not going with you," I croaked, every word hurting my sore throat.

I clenched my hands into fists and let all my fury and fear erupt. A sea of icy, furious power answered my wrath, crashing out of me. Shimmering and ruthless, the magic rushed past the seats, past Conn and Sander, and found the engine and fuel tank, turning both to ice. I shattered them with a thought, the same mindless way I'd shattered the CCTV at the service station.

Pain stabbed between my brows, but I panted, sweat dripping into my eyes as I kept hold of my power.

The car ground to a loud halt barely two paces from the hotel, and my heartbeat slowed, my breathing evened out. Refreshing coolness filled my body, soothing the aches on my throat and arms, and easing my chest until I could breathe fully again.

I felt ... powerful. Fragile and faint, but limitless.

"Piece of shit!" Conn growled, slamming his hands into the stained leather steering wheel.

"You'll displease Luneste if you keep talking like that," I said coldly, ice spreading through my whole body. I swore it cradled my baby gently, too, as light and cold rose to fill every part of me.

"What's she doing?" Sander demanded, throwing me an uneasy stare. "This is *her*. I told you we should have left her alone."

I gave him a cruel smile I borrowed from Wild and watched his face blanch.

"She stole our magic!" Dad exploded, his face twisted in anger. "That power is ours!"

"No," I replied, turning to face him and letting him read every bit of loathing in my face. "I didn't. Luneste *gave* it to me. She never would have chosen you. You're pathetic." It had taken me so long to see it. I'd always known he was ruthless and willing to do anything for the pack—even if what he did made absolutely no sense—but now I saw his desperation, the way he clutched at straws to maintain the appearance of an alpha in control. His control had been crumbling for years, ever since he refused to ask for help when our packlands began dying. It wasn't caution that stopped him approaching our neighbouring packs—it was pride. Cowardice.

Even if it would crush his pride and admit fault as an alpha, Kaan would never let us suffer just to save face. *Never.*

Dad's hand connected with my face, and my head snapped back, pain cracking through my skull. A sharp cry tearing up my throat, I threw my hands up to ward off more hits, my breathing all but non-existent as dizziness raged. But I couldn't cower, couldn't let him beat me into submission, no matter how much it hurt—and would hurt more.

If I didn't fight back, I'd be dead. Or maybe ... maybe fighting back would be the thing that sealed my fate.

"You don't deserve the title of alpha," I growled, looking him dead in the eyes and ignoring the part of me that wanted to flinch away from his furious stare, from the wrath of an alpha. I knew he was going to growl me into submission, and I knew it would hurt—it always did.

Dad grabbed my hair and dragged me upright, fury darkening his eyes to black. I gasped as pain split my scalp, so bad that tears streamed down my cheeks. But I dragged in a jagged, pitiful attempt at breathing, and refused to give up.

The Nixette I was now wouldn't back down. Not ever.

Pushing at his shoulder, trying to force him back, I braced for the growl that would make me scream, make me break—but something heavy and big landed on the roof of the car with a huge bang.

The ceiling dented with a horrible shriek, and I flinched, accidentally yanking hairs from my scalp. Whatever was on the roof was massive, and dangerous, and—judging by the powerful, thunderous growls—*furious*.

My heart skipped a beat. More enemies, or pack?

Please be my pack.

"Fuck this," Sander spat. He couldn't get his car door open fast enough. I didn't see where he ran, or if he got away; I was focused on the roof as claws tore it open, metal wailing as it was prised apart.

"Drive!" Dad yelled at Conn, full of the growl that was meant for me.

Conn whimpered and bent over himself in the driver's seat, making pitiful sounds of pain as he tried to obey. But the car wouldn't start, and now a deep grey wolf poked its head through the gap and locked deep blue eyes with me.

"Draven," I breathed, a sob catching in my throat.

He gave me strength, gave me the power I needed to—to do what had to be done. I knew it as clearly as I knew Luneste's paradise was waiting for us.

The pool of freezing moonlight inside me swelled with a phantom current, and I cupped inner hands in its waters, pulling on the power until my whole body shook with chills. The car swerved and blurred—not because of Conn's driving, but sudden dizziness that struck without warning or mercy. I whimpered, hating the black moments between blurry patches of vision.

When I couldn't bear holding the moonlight anymore, I let the icy power erupt from me in a fatal wave. Bright white light bleached the car, blinding Conn and Dad in milliseconds, and the cruel cold reached past their skin, past muscle and bone, and froze their organs to stillness.

I slammed a hand into the seat in front of me as I wavered forward, so dizzy that the car swirled like a fairground teacup. My eyes burned with tears—both from grief and relief—as Luneste's magic brushed against me, encouraging me to make the final blow.

My heart cracked down the middle, and I was going to be sick at what I had to do, but that didn't stop me panting through my dizziness and releasing a final sea of frozen moonlight.

I slumped against the seat back in front of me, holding myself up with numb hands to watch through teary eyes as silver light covered them from head to toe. It turned them to ice statues like Kaan's attacker at the service station.

I hadn't been there to watch *him* shatter, but I couldn't look away now as the moonlight faded to silvery softness and Conn exploded into shards of ice in the front seat, my father collapsing beside me.

I was a killer. A heartless murderer. It didn't make a difference that they'd killed me first and this was revenge.

I was a killer.

Draven rumbled a soft, inquisitive sound, but I couldn't reply. Dizziness rushed for me like a wolf after prey, and I slumped against the rough weave of the back seat as the price for Luneste's help exacted itself and dragged me firmly into a healing sleep.

My dad and brothers wouldn't hunt us anymore, couldn't threaten my baby anymore—Sander didn't have the guts to come for us alone—but Magnolia and Zinnia packs still shadowed our every move, wanting revenge for Kaan rescuing Draven and Bakkhos.

I didn't know what would happen with the pregnancy either, and I was terrified to tell Kaan that *he* was what made me weak. But as unconsciousness wrapped me in its comforting embrace, I almost felt ... peace.

33

RUIN
KAAN

*B*lood soaked into my black fur, slicking it to my sides as I raced around the side of the hotel. Terror filled every single part of me at the realisation that Nixette was gone. They'd *taken* her. They'd tricked us, and we'd fucking fallen for it. What kind of alpha did it make me? She'd been abducted when I was supposed to be watching her. She'd never forgive me, and even if she did, I'd never forgive myself.

Where the hell is she? Bakkhos demanded, panic making his voice sharp in my head. *Where is she?*

We'll find her, I promised.

I wouldn't let her down, and I wouldn't fail Luneste that way, either.

You've already failed me, a cold female voice replied. Inside my head, not in the pack bond. I jumped, my hackles rising.

Draven and Bakkhos ran ahead, and Wild sat in the hotel lobby with a shattered kneecap, but I froze, canting my head to one said as that unfamiliar feminine voice echoed around my skull. It couldn't be Luneste. No way. The goddess might have blessed us with the ability to shift whenever we chose, but we'd never heard her voice.

What difference will it make if you save her from her treacherous family? that cool voice demanded, and I shuddered hard.

Luneste—it had to be. And she was *furious* with me. I held my breath, waiting for a ray of moonlight to strike me down.

Goddess? I asked meekly.

Will you save her from her father, only to watch her waste away in front of you? Will you continue to let her die, Kaan?

No, I swore. *Never.*

Her answer was a sound halfway between a growl and a laugh. *Do you know why she suffers, why she's weak and dying, alpha of alphas?*

I trembled, her wrath and power blinding me to the path around me, to the trees rustling and the cars zooming down the street not far away. *No, goddess.*

I'd looked up every illness and sickness, had tried every remedy I could find, but nothing cured her. I watched her slip away from us more every day, and it killed me.

You, Luneste seethed. *You are the reason she weakens. You are the reason her body isn't strong enough for her pregnancy. You are the reason she can't eat, sleep, and the reason she won't survive.*

I staggered back a step, my paws failing me. Luneste's anger made it impossible to breathe. Or was that what she suggested—that I'd failed Nixette so badly that she was *dying?*

How? I rasped, shaking from head to tail. Had she been poisoned while I wasn't paying attention? Had one of our attackers harmed her while I was distracted?

I jumped back with a bark when the goddess manifested

in front of me. Looming and unforgiving, she stood over me in physical form, her white hair flowing to the waist of her black dress and her face so beautiful it hurt to look at her. The goddess's expression was full of so much shame that I couldn't bear to meet her eyes.

"You *rejected* her," she hissed, so much power in her voice that I whined and backed up three steps. "Every time you pushed her away, every time you said no, every time you told her you didn't want her, it corrupted your bond until it sat frayed and poisonous inside her. So I ask you, Kaan, what difference will it make if you save her from her family if you're only going to keep rejecting her—keep killing her?"

I lowered to the ground on my belly, showing her submission. *I won't. I promise.*

Fuck. Never. *Never* again would I push Nix away. I'd been trying to keep her safe, for fuck's sake, and instead—

I was killing her.

A broken howl built in my throat.

"No one ever said you had to love her, alpha of alphas." I flinched as footsteps sounded, and Luneste towered over my quivering wolf form. "But keep rejecting her, and you kill her."

A tight knot formed in my throat. I couldn't speak, couldn't even think.

"Make the right choice, Kaan," Luneste murmured, stopping directly in front of me. I shook hard as fingers moved gently over my fur, a mother's forgiveness. "And trust yourself. You are not your father."

If I were in human form, my eyes would have stung and overflowed with tears of shame, gratitude, and awe.

My father—who'd killed my mother with his dominance and alpha power. Who'd literally growled her to death in a fit of rage while I was forced to watch, paralysed by his dominance on the kitchen floor. My father, who'd been an ordinary alpha, not the alpha of alphas.

He'd *killed* my mum with his dominance, but I was far more powerful. Far more dangerous.

I couldn't allow myself to get close to Nixette.

I lifted my head to tell Luneste that, but she'd vanished as quickly as she'd appeared. Leaving me with an impossible choice.

Reject Nix and sentence her to a cruel death. Or accept her like every broken part of me ached to do, and risk killing her in a single moment of weakness.

I looked at the pale crescent and star marking on my shoulder, visible even in wolf form, and didn't know what to do.

THANK you for picking up The Omega's Wolves - I hope you loved Nixie and her men! There's more steam, magic, and romance in book two, The Omega's Mates, which is out now!

You can let me know you love the series by leaving a review of this book.

Thanks for the support you've shown Nixie so far—it means the world to know you love her and her broken alphas as much as I do <3

Leigh

NEED MORE?

For more steamy, psycho goodness, check out the following books I highly recommend for Broken Alphas fans!

Killer Crescent: Rebels and Psychos 1. Complete twisted paranormal RH duet with psycho wolves, obsessive vampires, a cruel male witch, fated mates, a rejected mate, and LOTS of steam.
books2read.com/killercrescent

Crazed Candy: Killers and Kings 1. Twisted, dark romance with demon criminals, a demon hunter/serial killer heroine, fucked up men, fated mates, and of course steam.
books2read.com/crazedcandy

Guardian: Alpha Knights MC 1. Dark omegaverse motorcycle club MF romance with fated mates, growling, knotting, hot biker alphas, and a HEA in each book.
books2read.com/alphaknights1

And something tells me you might enjoy my complete Blacktower series, which has a badass heroine, devoted and slightly obsessive fated mates, hot AF scenes, MM, and a seriously fucked up guy called Ravenmaster you'll accidentally fall in love (or lust) with. Read the complete series in the box set Shadowfire Mates:
books2read.com/shadowfiremates

If you want more from the Broken Alphas world, let me know! I'd love to give some of the side characters in this series their own story.

THANK YOU FOR READING!

To stay updated with what I'm working on next, come join me in my Paranormal Den on Facebook, or sign up to my fortnightly newsletter! (Links on the next pages, so keep reading, loves.)

If this is your first Leigh Kelsey book, I have lots more books for you to sink your teeth into, and three completed series. I've got vampires, wolves, shifters, angels, and demons - and of course plenty of growly alpha males with tragic backstories.

Reviews make the world go 'round - or at least they do in my world. If you loved this book and you can spare a minute, please leave a review on Amazon or wherever else you like to review. Even the smallest, one-line review has an impact, and helps me reach new readers like you awesome people.

Thank you to everyone who's already reviewed. Your words mean I can keep writing the books you love!

LEIGH KELSEY
REVERSE HAREM ROMANCE AUTHOR

COMING APRIL 24TH 2022: GUARDIAN

These hot bikers are called Knights for a reason. Get in their way and meet your maker.

Guardian

As the sergeant-at-arms of the Alpha Knights MC, it's my job to protect the omegas we save from the twisted men who abuse them. It's a bloody, violent job, but I'm damn good at it.

I've never been tempted by any of the broken women we rescue until Vienna lands in my lap. She's more damaged than the others, but with a spark of fire that calls to me. I know from the second she locks eyes with me, she's my mate.

And I'd walk through hell to keep her safe.

Vienna

I know exactly what alphas are. Vicious, heartless, and deaf to my pleas to stop. The bruises on my body are a testament to their cruelty.

But why do the Knights kill my abuser? And why is Guardian gentle and caring? The badass, tattooed biker looks at me like I'm more than what's between my legs. Like I'm precious. Like I'm his.

The warmth in my chest tells me we're bonded, but can I be brave enough to let him in when all alphas do is hurt me?

Alpha Knights motorcycle club is a dark romantic suspense series *perfect for lovers of protective men, fierce damsels, fated mates, and romance that's equal parts sweetness and heat. These bikers will fight for their club and their women, and they're not afraid to get their hands dirty to keep their families safe.*

PREORDER NOW

DARK PARANORMAL RH STAND-ALONE!

After a hundred year sleep, my curse has been lifted by seven sinful demons.

The bad news is my rescue comes with a price: obey them. All seven of them. And give them a child.

There's King, the notorious criminal with a dark, dominant heart.

Fallon, the gentle giant who makes me feel safe.

Steel, the snarky smartass who makes me laugh.

Huxley, who's deadly serious about my protection.

Luca, the man I should never underestimate.

Max, whose gentle affection makes me feel treasured.

And Vega: more beast than man, with fangs, claws, and horns to match.

These seven demons are irresistible, devoted to my pleasure, and I know there has to be a catch. But for now I'm going to enjoy every second of my freedom and pray the devil doesn't catch up to me.

READ FREE IN KINDLE UNLIMITED

COMPLETE TWISTED PARANORMAL RH SERIES

If a secret wolf society thinks they can take me down, they've got another thing coming. There's a reason they call me Graves.

It's not my fault I'm a psychopath. What else would happen to someone who witnessed her sister's murder? Without magic in my arsenal like the rest of my family, I have to rely on other methods: sharp knives, stealth, and killer instincts. And hey, killing pays the bills.

READ FREE IN KINDLE UNLIMITED

JOIN MY READER GROUP!

To get news about upcoming releases before anywhere else, and early access to my books, come join my Leigh Kelsey's Paranormal Den group over on Facebook!

THREE FREEBIES FOR YOU

Join my newsletter for 3 exclusive freebies!

Fancy some freebies? I'll send you three when you join my newsletter! I promise never to spam you, and I rarely send more frequently than once a fortnight so you won't be overloaded with emails.

Join here: http://bit.ly/LeighKelseyNL

ABOUT THE AUTHOR

Leigh Kelsey is the author of sweet and steamy books for anyone with a soft spot for steely women and the tortured men who love them. No matter what stories she's writing – vampires or shifters or rebels – they all share a common thread of romance, heart, and action. She is the author of the Lili Kazana series, the Vampire Game series, the Moonlight Inn series, and the Second Breath Academy series. Leigh also writes new adult and young adult books under the name Saruuh Kelsey.

FIND THESE OTHER BOOKS BY LEIGH KELSEY!

All solo books free on Kindle Unlimited*

99c Preorders

The Goblin's Bride (99c Enemies to Lovers Fantasy Romance)

Bargain Box Sets

Spells and Shifter Mates (Paranormal RH Leigh Kelsey series starters)

Fae of the Saintlands series

(Enemies To Lovers RH Romance)

Heir of Ruin

Heart of Thorns

Kiss of Iron

Touch of Darkness (Mid 2022)

Broken Alphas series

(Complete Rejected Mates Dark Paranormal RH)

The Omega's Wolves

The Omega's Mates

Alpha Knights MC series

(Dark Omegaverse Biker MF)

Guardian (April 24th 2022)

Killers and Kings series

(Twisted Paranormal Demon RH)
Crazed Candy (Coming 2022)

Rebels and Psychos Duet
(Complete Twisted Paranormal RH Romance)
Killer Crescent
Blood Wolf

Shadowfire Mates/Blacktower Prison series
(Complete Dragon Shifter Romance series)
Complete Series Box Set
Start with Prison of Embers

Lili Kazana series
(Complete RH Angel/Demon Romance series)
Complete Series Box Set
Start with Cast From Heaven

Vampire Game series
(Complete RH Vampire Romance series)
Complete Series Box Set
Start with Vampire Game

Moonlight Inn series
(Complete Wolf Shifter RH series)
Complete Series Box Set
Start with Mated

Second Breath Academy series
(Complete Paranormal Academy RH series)

How To Raise The Dead

How To Kill A Shadow

How To Banish Evil

Starcrossed Alien Mates

Dead Space (RH Sci-Fi Stand-Alone)

Dark Stars (RH Alien Bikers)

Dying Stars (RH Alien Bikers) (Coming 2022)

Stand Alone Stories

Sinful Beauty (RH Demon Romance Stand-Alone)

Moonlight Inn series returning soon!

Printed in Great Britain
by Amazon